The Ways We Connected

Kitti Pierce

This book is dedicated to my family in room 1313.
I am grateful for everything that all of them have
done for me. Thank you to Ms. Dyche and to my
workshop group for helping me to produce my first
book. It is by no means perfect, but it was created
in the space that I call home.

His
Last Painting

Monty

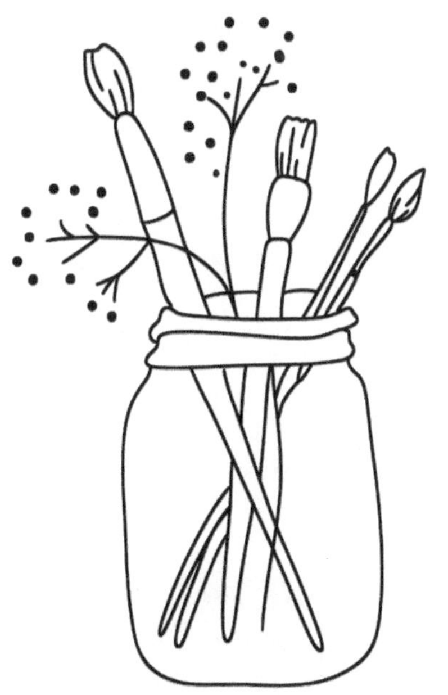

His Last Painting (Monty)

October 7th, 2022

I wondered what she would say if I told her how beautiful I thought she looked.

The sun broke through the art room windows, reflecting off the stained glass projects from AP art, painting rainbows across the floor and the face of the girl who sat at the easel in the center of the room. She had paint smears scattered from the tips up to her elbows, despite the relatively clean workspace she sat in the center of. Her hair was brown and dripped down her shoulders like dark chocolate.

She painted with her fingers, running them across the canvas in fast and delicate movements, almost as if she was dancing with the colors she laid out in front of her. Her apron had stars and hearts messily scribbled across its pocket. There was a name written along the top edge; I didn't know how to pronounce it. The writing was sloppy, letters overlapping and the lines of the stars and hearts shaky.

She ran her fingers along the edge of the canvas,

almost as if she was trying to figure out where the painting ended and space around her began. I watched in awe at the girl in front of me. The color fell from the canvas, brightening the world around her with rivers of blue and gold. She made everything around her look brighter, and at that moment, I couldn't help but smile at this girl in the art room.

She hummed under her breath, tilting her head from side to side. She didn't seem to notice me standing there in the doorway. After, she took a brush and used it to cover both of her thumbs in black paint, putting her thumbprints in the corner of the canvas in the shape of a heart. She pulled her apron over her head, folding it over her arm. I felt a hand on my shoulder.

I jerked my head back to see Mr. Collymore staring down at me. He shook his head and covered his mouth with his finger, gesturing for me to be quiet. I watched in silence as my art teacher walked past me into the art room, giving a very gentle knock on the door. The girl at the easel whipped her head around to where Mr. Collymore and I stood.

She seemed to stare for a moment, her eyes wandering the room and the air around him and me, her gaze never quite falling onto our faces.

"Sonali," *So that's how you pronounce her name.* "I have to close up now," Mr. Collymore said, walking over to where she stood. "This is a great piece. What does it mean?"

I looked at the canvas, layers of different shades of gray covering the entire thing in swirls similar to that of Van Gogh's work. Two streaks of metallic gold paint across the entire canvas.

" I'm sure the two streaks of gold over the gray have got to mean something special."

"I'm not quite sure if I'm being honest," She sighed, running a hand through her hair. "It was just how

I was feeling," She shrugged and stood up, walking over the hooks along the back wall. She held out her hand as she took a step forward, running her hand over the last couple until her hand found the last one, hanging her apron on it. "I'll start cleaning up."

"Monty, did you need something?" Mr. Collymore turned to me from his desk, calling me into the room.

"Oh," I pulled my eyes away from Sonali, who had begun cleaning up, and walked over to Mr. Collymore. "I just finished up studying with Noah and Leo, and I remembered that I left my lunch box in here this morning. I wanted to come see if I could get it."

"You're lucky I stayed after school today to help out Sonali. Usually, I leave school as soon as the bell rings along with the rest of you." He chuckled. "Go grab it," He said, nodding over to where I usually sat. "Sonali, do you need any help cleaning up?"

I watched her as she walked between her easel and the counter by the sink, carrying over palettes, brushes, and cups of paint water. "Nope, I've got it," she said. She turned on the sink and ran the palettes underneath it, using her hands to scrape at the dried paint that remained.

I went over and grabbed my lunch box, finding it hard to take my eyes away from Sonali as I walked toward the door.

"It's a coincidence that I have you both here," Mr. Collymore said, stopping me in my tracks. "I need to pick two of my students to represent our school at the county art fair next month, and I was thinking of asking you two,"

His words hung in the air and I found my gaze drifting back over to Sonali to see her reaction.

"I have no objections," Sonali said, turning off the sink. "As long as the fair isn't on a Tuesday I should be able to do it."

"It sounds like fun," I smiled.

"Of course, make sure to get permission from your parents. Monty, here's the information flier," Mr. Collymore said, walking over to me and handing me a piece of paper. "And Sonali, I'll email you the details, alright?"

Sonali nodded.

"Alright I'll finish cleaning up, you guys should go ahead and get home," He said walking us to the door. "I'll see you two tomorrow, get some rest."

Once Sonali and I were both out the door, he closed it behind us, going back to sit at his desk that sat across from the door.

"What was your name? I know Mr. Collymore just said it a moment ago, but I wasn't paying attention," Sonali said, turning to face me.

She wants to know my name. "Uh, it's Monty, and you're Sonali, right?"

"Are you sure that's your name? You sounded a little hesitant," She nodded with a closed-lipped smile.

I felt the tension leave my body, that one joke made me feel more comfortable in her presence. "Yeah, I'm sure, or at least I sure do hope it's my name. I'd hate to find out that my parents have been lying to me all these years."

Sonali laughed, and I smiled. I didn't want this interaction to end. I wanted to keep talking to her. Something about her was magnetic. And if this was the first time I'd seen her this year, there was a chance that I won't see her again until the art fair. I didn't want that to be the next time I saw her.

"Hey so," I paused, trying to come up with a logical reason as to why I would be inviting her. "I mean, if we're going to do this art fair thing together, we might as well hang out and get to know each other. Some friends and I are going to the amusement park this weekend, you should come." I rambled on, not knowing when to stop talking. "Of course, you don't have to if you don't want to, no pressure at all, and if you have other plans that's completely fine too—"

"Sure," She said, cutting me off. "Sounds like fun. Not like I have anything better to do or anyone else to hang out with."

Her response seemed backhanded, as if she was only saying yes because she was lonely with no one else to hang out with. Like, she had no other option than to say yes. But even still, I didn't quite care what her reason might have been for doing so, I was just happy she said yes. "Awesome!" I exclaimed.

She laughed again. "Here, you can text me the details, I'll give you my number."

"Oh, uh, yeah, of course," I rambled, pulling my phone out from the side pocket of my backpack.

We stood in the hallway and I wasn't sure if this was where our interaction would end, or if there were more words that either she or I wanted to say. I just knew that whatever was happening now was awkward.

"It was nice meeting you. I should be heading out now, so I guess I'll text you later," She said, grabbing something out of the side pocket of her backpack. It looked almost like an umbrella cover, and she slid off the cover, revealing a bunch of small sticks and a band that held them together.

Sonali took off the band, and the small sticks clicked together as they fell. It was completely white, with a black grip at the top accompanied by a wrist loop, and about a foot of red color at the bottom, with a sort of white ball connected to the end of it.

I looked at the cane, and then at Sonali, and that was when it clicked in my brain.

"You're blind?" I asked without thinking.

She stared at me wide-eyed, and I immediately slapped my hand over my mouth.

"I'm so sorry I wasn't trying to—"

She started laughing, and I tilted my head at her, wondering what it was I had said that would have made her laugh.

"You're just now noticing that?" she said, raising an eyebrow. "Yep, I'm blind. Well, blind enough. I'm not completely blind. Oh, sorry for laughing, it's just that I've never had someone ask me straight up like that, people usually tend to dance around the question. It was refreshing to hear, if I'm being honest."

"You're welcome?" I hesitated. "I'm sorry I really don't know how to respond to that."

"That's alright, you don't have to respond. I'll see you this weekend, make sure to text me the details. See you, Monty!" She walked down the hallway, sweeping her cane in front of her from left to right.

I stood and watched her walk away, trying to process the conversation for myself we just had. I didn't quite know how to feel, but I did know that I was incredibly embarrassed by our conversation and that it would be the only thing I thought about for the remainder of my afternoon.

November 15th, 2022

My sister pulled up to the curb, and I unbuckled my seatbelt. The sidewalk teemed with people, most being parents accompanied by little children stomping on the fall leaves scattered across the pavement.

"Do you have everything?" Savannah asked, turning around in her seat. "Cause I'm not turning back around."

I opened the car door, and stepped out, grabbing the paperboard portfolios that I had sat in the seat beside me. "Yeah, I have everything, Sav." I went to close the car door but she interrupted.

"Okay, don't text me if you need anything because I

won't answer,"

I rolled my eyes. "Don't worry, I won't. Be safe on your way home," I closed the door after saying goodbye, not giving her the chance to tease me again before leaving.

I set the portfolios down, adjusting my grip on the handles as I scanned the crowd for Sonali. Finally, I spotted her standing against the wall of the building, holding her cane straight up with both hands resting on top of it and the portfolio leaning against the wall beside her. She wore a floppy sun hat that fell over the top half of her face, covering it.

I jogged over to her, slowing to a stop as I got closer, noticing the sunglasses she was wearing underneath the sun hat as she looked up towards the sky.

"Hi."

She turned to look at me, a smile falling across her face. "Hey."

"Is Mr. Colleymore here?" I asked scanning the crowd once again.

Sonali shook her head, pulling apart the pieces of her cane and folding them together. "I'm not sure, but can we head in anyways? I'm not the biggest fan of crowds."

"Yeah, me either," I said. "Do you need help at all?" I asked. "Sighted guide?"

She nodded, grabbing the portfolios from against the wall. She stuck out her hand feeling the air for a second before laughing. "Where is your elbow?"

"Oh!" I said. I reached out and grabbed her hand gently, guiding it to my arm before letting go. "Over here, sorry."

She grabbed my elbow, and I couldn't help but feel a little uncomfortable with the physical touch. "It's no biggie, you don't need to apologize or anything."

We moved through the crowd and into the building, Sonali walking a step behind me. The ceilings were low and the tiles were a faded white, black smudges and scratches on the floor beneath us, from years of wear and tear.

I followed the sign set out down the hall and leading into the school's cafeteria. There was a stage at the back of the room and tables and display boards set out around the border of the room. I scanned the room from the doorway, looking for Mr. Colleymore, not being able to find him in the cafeteria.

I went over to the table right inside the doorway, seeing an older lady sitting there with an information sheet.

"Hi," I said. "We're here to help our art teacher out with the art fair, but we aren't sure where he is or where we're supposed to go."

The lady smiled at me, grabbing the glasses that were hanging around her neck and putting them on. "What school are you from?" She asked, grabbing the information packet and flipping through the pages.

"Summerville High School," Sonali said.

She hummed, flipping through the packet pages. "So Mr. Colleymore hasn't signed in yet, so it doesn't look like he's here. It is getting a bit close to the opening time though. If you guys can just show me your school IDs, I can go ahead and let y'all in so you can start getting set up."

"Okay," I said, setting down the portfolio's against my leg. I showed the lady my ID, and Sonali showed her ID to the lady as well.

"Alright, you guys are going to be at booth twenty-four. That's going to be on the wall by the stage, right over there," She said pointing. "Here are your exhibitor lanyards," She said, holding them out to us. I took both of them, tapping Sonali's arm lightly with the lanyards so she could take one of them for herself. "I'll be over here if you need anything."

"Okay, thank you," Sonali said.

"Alright let's head over then," I added, picking the portfolio's back up.

We headed over to the twenty-fourth booth. It was a small table with a sign that had our booth number and our school name, displayed on top of a white table cloth, and a felt display board behind the table.

I set the portfolio's down next to the table, taking the ones that Sonali held as well.

"What are we supposed to do?" Sonali asked.

I shrugged, turning away to start taking the pieces out of the portfolio's.

"Monty?"

I turned, remembering that Sonali couldn't see. "Oh, sorry. Um, I guess since Mr. Colleymore isn't here yet we should just start getting set up like the lady at the table said," I said.

Sonali nodded, looking around for a moment. "I can take things out of the portfolios if you want to pin them up on the display." She said, stepping forward and reaching for the edge of the table.

"Sure," I said, taking the art out of one of the portfolios.

I grabbed the pins stuck in the corner of the display board, beginning to pin pieces up as I tried to come up with a topic of conversation to fill the uncomfortable silence.

"What do you like to draw?" Sonali asked, filling the silence before I had the chance to.

"I kind of draw a bit of everything, but I like realism a lot. I mostly draw flowers, sometimes people," I said. "You do abstract right?"

Sonali nodded. "Mhm, finger painting. I used to do a lot of spray and oil painting. I really liked doing landscapes. But, I had to stop doing those a while ago." Her face went dark for a moment, before going back to her usual neutral expression.

As I pinned up the pieces of art from Mr. Colleymore's classes, I wondered how she had lost her vision, and what it was like. I couldn't wrap my head around the idea of painting without vision. Having no way of seeing the work I was creating. What would be the point of creating a piece of work you couldn't see? I had a feeling that it was a question I shouldn't ask, so I stayed quiet.

I turned to look at Sonali, watching the way she ran her fingers along the edge of the portfolio's, searching for the loops with her hands to open them. I found myself forgetting that she was blind, seeing how she moved confidently through Mr.Colleymore's room at school. Previously I had thought that blindness would be obvious to the surrounding people. That there would be a sort of obvious helplessness. However, that seemed to be my own ignorance.

"Hi kids," I turned to see Mr. Colleymore walking over to our table. "Sorry I was so late getting here, there was really bad traffic."

"That's alright," Sonali said. "The lady at the table over there let us in to get things set up, so we went ahead and got started."

Mr.Colleymore nodded, looking over to where I stood at the display wall. "I didn't know if there was a certain way you wanted them pinned up, so I kind of just started putting them up as we got them out of the portfolios." I chuckled awkwardly.

"Oh, uh," He paused. "Yeah actually, I wanted it to be sorted by graduating class, so the seniors pieces at the top, and the underclassmen near to bottom." He came over to where I stood, and started taking down the few pieces I had already put up. "Once the pieces are all hung up and the gallery has opened to everyone I just need you two to watch the table so I can talk to the other teachers and artists around."

"Oh, so we're just gonna sit here?" Sonali asked. There was a bit of a bitter tone to her voice, and I could tell she wasn't the biggest fan of sitting with nothing to do. I wondered if there was something that I could do to entertain her. I didn't want her to be bored, I wanted her to enjoy the time we were spending together.

Mr. Colleymore nodded as he grabbed one of my portrait pieces to pin to the board. "If people have any questions you guys will answer them. And you'll also use the stamp if any kids come by with the scavenger hunt page."

"Where's the stamp?" I asked.

"It's over here," Sonali said, as she began to feel around the table. "Somewhere, I had it in my hands earlier." Her eyebrows creased, almost as if she was squinting her eyes to try and see if that would help her find the stamp.

I walked over to her, looking over her shoulder to try and find the stamp she was looking for. "Oh, it's here," I said, picking up one of the art pieces and finding it underneath.

Sonali laughed, tucking a piece of hair behind her ear, and I smiled as I watched her, noticing the lily of the valley earrings she had dangling from her ears. Said to symbolize a return of happiness, they were often believed to have formed from the tears of Eve.

"Okay," Mr.Colleymore said, getting both Sonali and I to turn our heads to look at him. "I sorted all of the art pieces into piles so you guys can get them hung up. I'm going to go over and officially check in. I'll be back soon."

"Okay," We said in unison.

I took the senior art pieces, and started pinning them up, Sonali taking a seat in one of the chairs at the table.

"I never got the chance to ask you. Did you have fun when we went to the amusement park last month?" I said.

Sonali turned in her chair to face me, smiling widely. "I did! It was a lot of fun. I was wondering though how you all met Alaska though, her being the only girl of the group and all."

"Oh, Leo and Noah and Allie all met in freshman year. So, it was basically a package deal when I became friends with Leo last year."

She nodded, smiling. "Your friends are super nice."

"You like them?"

She nodded. "I do! I haven't really had any friends since I moved here, so it's super fun to hang out with you guys. I'm still learning your voices but I would love to hang out together again."

I hummed, trying to think if we had anything planned. "We're all pretty busy these days. I know Allie is finishing up the marching band season. And Noah is working on a photography assignment from the photographer he wants to work under when he graduates," I paused for a moment, trying to think of when we would all be hanging out next, unsure if Sonali would be comfortable hanging out with just me, and too anxious to ask what she thought about the idea. "Leo is having a party for Noah's birthday over winter break, I think that's when we have anything planned. I can text you the details if you want to go."

Sonali nodded. "Yeah, I'd love to."

"Cool," I smiled.

"Cool," She chuckled.

I didn't say anything else as I finished hanging up the posters on the display board behind us. She didn't speak either, staying silent as I sat down beside her.

As people began to trickle in from outside, I sat beside Sonali, finding myself looking at her again, trying to figure out how I would paint her. Eventually, I took my sketchbook out of my bag and began sketching Sonali. I thought if I could establish how I would sketch her, I would be able to figure out how I would paint her. She wasn't sitting at an easel or doing anything particularly interesting. Maybe if I could draw her idly, it would make showcasing her dynamics easier. Her hair was drawn with fast long strokes, and large highlights to try and showcase how shiny her hair was.

Kids would stop by about every twenty minutes or so, and when they did I would stop drawing to stamp their scavenger hunt while Sonali made conversation with them.

We sat in a comfortable silence, only speaking when we were spoken to by people coming to look at our school's art. It was a kind of silence where neither one of us thought there were any more words that needed to be said. We just enjoyed each other's company, not bothering to think of a conversation to fill the empty air and the slow-passing time.

In only an hour, I filled an entire sketchbook page with her, trying my best to figure out the best way to draw her, each drawing not quite coming out the way I wanted it to. The sketches looked too clean, the strokes too confident on the page. But, that was how she appeared to me. She sat with her shoulders back, and had an understanding of the world that I didn't. I thought about her eyes, and her features. I wondered what I was missing that was making the drawings not seem to look the way I wanted them to.

I trusted that it would be something I'd figure out eventually, and I hoped that when I did I would be able to show it to her somehow, even without her actually being able to see it, I wanted to find a way to show her none-the-less.

December 27th, 2022

I wasn't the biggest fan of large parties, but when Sonali agreed to go, I knew I would have fun if she were there. However I don't think I understood what a "big party" was. There were people everywhere, and I wasn't prepared for this kind of party.

Sonali wasn't either. She thought it would be a smaller party, and because of that she didn't bring her cane, hoping that she would be able to navigate with the little vision she had left.

When we walked in and found the environment to be a lot more chaotic than expected, Sonali squinted and bit her bottom lip. She seemed to regret immaturely leaving her cane at home, so I did my best to guide her in its place, the echoing of music preventing her from hearing her surroundings.

After both of us experienced the disorienting lights and overwhelming noise inside of the house, we both decided to sit in the backyard by the bonfire.

I sat in the lawn chair beside Sonali, watching her as she looked at the fire intensely. It made her skin glow, and when the wood crackled it reflected in her eyes like fireworks. I couldn't pull my eyes away from her. She was captivated by the fire, and I by her. These past few months have been filled with nothing but my growing feelings for her. And I wasn't quite sure what I was supposed to do about it. She hadn't moved in a good few minutes, unable to tear her gaze away from the fire.

"Is the fire really that interesting?" I asked.

Sonali looked up at me for a moment, before turning her attention back with a nod. "Yeah, it is. It's one of the few things I can see y'know? And when I'm able to see it on a larger scale than the candles in my parent's room, it's nice. I think it's beautiful."

I looked at the fire, the colors bleeding up from the wood in wisps of red, orange, and yellow. Despite how beautiful Sonali thought the fire to be, I preferred to look at her.

I wanted to tell her. I wanted her to know how beautiful she is. I needed her to know that I thought she was beautiful. I wanted her to look at me, but she couldn't tear her eyes away from the fire. I couldn't see it the way that she did, but I wished maybe the shadows I casted were more interesting, so that she would look at me instead.

I turned the can of beer in my hands hesitantly, before taking a large swig of it and turning to Sonali.

"Sonali," I started.

She looked up at me, turning her attention away from the fire. She turned her body to face me. "What's up?"

"I just wanted to let you know," I started. "It's not really that important or anything, but I think you're beautiful."

"Oh, thank—"

"Like, I can't stop thinking about how I want to paint you," I said, cutting her off. "When I saw you in the art room for the first time, I was in shock, because you were just so beautiful." I paused. "Sonali, please let me do a portrait for you."

She looked at me wide-eyed, a bit of confusion scrunched between her brows. "I would be okay with that, but I don't know how satisfying that would be. Since I wouldn't even be able to look at the portrait."

I shook my head. "That's okay, I'm not looking for that kind of validation or anything. I just think it would be really cool if other people could see you the way that I see you. Painted in rainbows."

I watched her, and she smiled. Maybe it was because of the alcohol but her cheeks and ears were red. The fire reflected in her eyes, orange and yellow reflected against dark eyes turning them gold. I felt warm inside, and I think that something struck me like lightning. "I think I like you."

I paused, my heart rate jumping. "Wait, I didn't

mean to say that!" I said waving my arms around in the air.

She turned to me, the fire casting a shadow across the side of her face. "You like me?" She asked.

I swallowed, my throat suddenly dry. "I mean, I think I do?"

"What do you mean 'you think?'" She asked, crossing her arms.

I thought about it for a moment, trying to remember what caused me to blurt it out. "I mean, I can't remember the last time I ever thought about someone this much. When I look at you, I feel calm. It's like all of the tension leaves my body and I instantly relax. I've never experienced that before."

She put her hands over her face, covering her cheeks and her eyes, but I could still see the red covering her ears underneath her hair. "Don't look at me—" she murmured.

I sat silently, not knowing how to respond. Or what I wanted to say. She took a few deep breaths, her shoulders rising and falling methodically.

"Okay." She sighed.

"Okay?" I asked.

"Okay, let's go on a date then," She paused, smiling while she looked down at her lap. " I don't really know how I feel, but, if it's you, I want to try."

"You want to try?" I asked. "Dating me?"

She shook her head. "Don't misunderstand. A single date. Just a date, not a relationship."

"Oh," I whispered. "I didn't mean to make assumptions."

She shook her head. "It's okay, sorry I wasn't clear."

"So, you want to try? Like a trial run or something?"

She nodded. "I do."

I reached out her tapping the back of her fist with

my finger gently. She flinched at first at the sudden touch, but then she flipped her hand over and held mine. Her hands were cold despite us being by the bonfire, and she was shaking a bit.

"Are you okay?" I asked.

She stared at me for a moment, before breaking into laughter, and leaning forward into my hands. Her laughter was contagious, so when she started laughing I couldn't help but laugh too. At myself, and at her. At us both for the way this conversation went about. I couldn't help but laugh.

Her laughter died down, and she scooted her chair closer to mine, cautiously wrapping her hands around my arm and resting her head on my shoulder. "Is this okay?"

I froze in my chair, willing myself not to move an inch. "Yes."

"So are you going to plan the date or am I?"

I started to ramble without thinking. "I'll plan it! Okay, uh, where do you want to go? And what do you want to do? Wait, I should say thank you first. Sonali, thank you for going on a date with me. I'll make sure to treat you with the utmost respect and—"

"Monty," She chuckled.

"Yes?"

"Just be quiet and watch the fire with me."

"Oh, uh, sure," I said.

I sat stiffly for a while, not wanting to move with her head on my shoulder. I wanted to stay like this. Huddled together as we ignored the living chaos around us. Just leaning against each other as we watched the fire in our own little bubble.

However, after a bit of time, I got used to the feeling, and relaxed into her body, fitting mine next to hers and resting my head on top of hers.

December 29th, 2022

I sat at my desk, my hands in my hair and my drawing board folded up, as I tried to sketch Sonali out on the paper. No matter how I tried I couldn't properly capture her features or the way she seemed to spread color and light everywhere she walked.

Savannah walked into my room and fell onto my bed, ignoring me as she walked past.

I ignored her and continued to work on the sketch, erasing and redrawing over and over again.

Before long, I looked over at Savannah, to find her looking at my phone with a smirk on her face. "Hey!" I exclaimed, getting up and snatching my phone from her sticky fingers. "How many times have I told you not to go through my stuff?"

Ignoring my question she said, "Who's Sonali?"

I rolled my eyes and sat back down at my desk, leaving my phone in my lap so she couldn't get to it again. "What does it matter to you?" I mumbled.

"Uh, because she messaged you yesterday morning asking about what you guys are going to do for your date, and you haven't responded," She said, leaning against the wall with one of my pillows in her lap.

"How do you keep finding out the password to my phone?" I sighed, grabbing my phone from my lap to change the password again.

She shrugged while laughing, and just said, "How many times is it going to take you to come up with a good password?"

"Whether my password is good or bad shouldn't matter," I bickered. "Regardless of the quality of my password you shouldn't be going through my phone and being nosey."

She chuckled and threw the pillow she was holding at my feet. "I'm your sister, being nosey is my job."

I rolled my eyes, something that I couldn't help but do a lot whenever I'm around her. "I don't understand what you get out of tormenting me," I questioned sitting next to her on my bed.

She shrugged, not saying anything. Leaving me to think in silence.

"What would you do?" I asked.

"What do you mean, "What would I do?" She asked.

"If you were going on a date with someone you really liked."

"Is your memory really that bad?" She chuckled. "I flirt and I have fun with people, but I don't date. I won't be of any help to you."

I flopped over, grabbed a pillow, and put it over my face groaning. "I really hate you sometimes,"

Savannah gasped dramatically, clutching her chest as if I had just killed a puppy. "How could you? Your own sister? And all because her commitment issues prevent her from having a partner?"

I rolled over onto my stomach laughing. "My hate for you has nothing to do with you being a flirt and a hookup."

"Fair point," She said. There was a long moment of silence, before she said, "Listen, I may not have any idea as to what a date is hypothetically supposed to look like, but I do know that you always come up with great ideas. I'm sure you'll find the answer somewhere."

I sat up from where I was laying, waiting for her to say more as she fiddled with the rings on her hand.

"But, I don't think it's a good idea to ignore her message just because you don't know the answer to the question she is asking. It's not fair to her, and it might make her anxious too. Which, I don't think anyone deserves."

I thought for a moment about her words, before

throwing a pillow at her. "Y'know, I really hate it when you're right."

"Well, I do have a talent for critical thinking, unlike you," She chuckled.

I shoved her with my elbow and laughed. "Oh, shut up,"

Savannah and I sat there laughing, and I couldn't help but be grateful to her despite her idiocy. After all, she gave me the answer to the question that Sonali was asking.

I pulled out my phone and opened my messages with Sonali, rereading her message before responding.

> *Sonali: What did you want to do for our date? And when did you want to do it?*
> *Monty: Why don't we go to a museum? And maybe dinner?*

I sat and waited for her response, nervous about what she might say.

> *Sonali: Sure, just make sure you find a museum with accommodations for me, and let's do Chinese food for dinner if you're cool with that.*
> *Monty: Sounds good, I'll let you know later what days would work best*
> *Sonali: Alright, ttyl Monty :)*

I smiled, relieved that the idea went over well with Sonali.

I could hear Savannah giggling, and I looked over to see her sitting there with a smug look on her face. "You really like her, huh?"

"What?" I said.

"I can see it on your face," She said.

I smiled down at my phone. "I do. I think that I really do like her."

January 1st, 2022
As we walked through the exhibits, I spent more time looking at Sonali than I did look at the exhibits.

I had been up late at night the past couple nights, trying to find a museum that we could enjoy, and that had accessibility features that would compensate for Sonali's blindness. Eventually I found a space museum that had accessibility key cards that would play audio recordings of descriptions of the exhibits.

Every time she used the accessibility card to hear the audio recordings, her eyes widened ever so slightly, lighting up her face with a dim glow, and the grip she had on my elbow tightened. She leaned forward towards the sound, almost as if she was trying to jump out of her own skin at the sound of the descriptions used. Every time she heard the beeping to signal the start of the recording, she would look at me to confirm that I was also hearing what she was. It was like her chest opened up and her heart climbed up to nap on her shoulder. For the first time, I was able to feel her emotions through her body language and facial expressions. That was the first time she had seemed to truly open up to me.

We ate lunch in the cafeteria, with Savannah and Raelyn, who had driven us and decided to hang out while we went on our date. The food unexpectedly seemed to be a part of the museum itself. They had star-shaped fruit and chicken nuggets. With solar system kabobs made of fruits, and constellation pizza with pepperoni mapping out constellations along them. We ate mostly in silence, using the time to decompress from the first few hours of excitement and regather our energy.

And now we waited in line for the planetarium,

the final part of the tour. I stood next to Sonali, her hand on my elbow, and the other twisting her hair between her fingers. Savannah and Raelyn stood behind us, periodically laughing at whatever it was they were looking at.

The line began to move, and as we walked through the doors into the planetarium a museum worker stood at the entrance, greeting everyone as they came in.

"Welcome! Come on in, and watch your step along the stairs as you enter the planetarium," She said.

Sonali turned to me. "This is a planetarium?"

I nodded. "It is."

Her face darkened, and her gaze fell to her feet. "Oh."

"Do you not like planetariums?" My entire body tensed.

She shook her head as we walked in and found our seats. "It's not that I don't, they can just be a bit disorientating, and sometimes I can't even see what's going on on the screen," She said.

"I'm so sorry, I should've thought more! You said you could see light and shadows so I just thought that—"

"It's fine," Sonali said sitting down in the seat I had led her to. "I really don't mind, and who knows, maybe I will be able to *see* something."

The excitement that she had earlier in the day had left her face. It was replaced with an emotionless expression and once again I didn't know what she was thinking anymore.

The lights dimmed, and the presentation video began to play on the screen that domed over us. The seats had reclined backs, pointing our gazes up at the sky where the video played. I looked at Sonali.

After the video finished playing the screen was rolled up and the whole room went dark. Sonali grabbed the edge of my sleeve tightly.

After a few seconds, dramatic symphonic orchestra music began to play, the ceiling lighting up with bright specks of white.

Sonali let go of me and sat up, staring up at the lights, with her heart seeming to reveal itself again. The white lights from the dome reflected off of her brown eyes, making them shimmer the same way as the lights.

My chest tightened as her expression changed, stareing up at the dome in complete awe.

"Can you see them?" I asked.

She nodded.

I sighed and leaned over, resting my forehead against her shoulder with a sigh. "I really like you," I whispered.

Her shoulders tensed up, the hand she had held on to my sleeve letting go and finding itsit's way back into her lap. "It's embarrassing if you keep saying it," I wasn't looking, but I could hear the discomfort in her voice.

It felt like someone cut the wrong wire on a ticking time bomb, and sparks were starting, setting fire to everything around it. "I'm sorry,"

She shook her head at me, trying her best to smile. "... It's just because we're in public. It's embarrassing."

I smiled for a moment, finding this side of her that I had never seen to be just as captivating as the others. I lifted my head as the lights turned on and people began to file out of the planetarium. Sonali and I however stayed seated.

I got to see another side of her, a side that I still thought was so beautiful. Another reason for me to like her. I think that I had gotten a little closer to her that day. Because she smiled at me with such sincerity. I wondered if it was possible for someone with so many mysteries to be so kind. Because usually the uncertainty of mysterious people prevents me from getting closer. But the closer I've gotten, the more I've wanted to know. Because the only thing I've found hidden within her is flowers that have been hidden in the shadows, for so long it seems they've begun to wilt and harbor distrust for nature. I hoped that I could show them that the world around them was worth relying on. And worth growing around.

January 3rd, 2023

I walked into Mr. Collymore's class, hoping to see Sonali, but all I saw was Mr. Collymore standing in the middle of the classroom, his hands on his hips and back turned to the door while he looked at the easels set up around the room.

I walked into his room and over to where he stood. "Hi, Mr. Colleymore. What are you thinking?" I asked.

"Oh, Monty, hello," he said. "I'm just trying to figure out how I want to arrange the classroom for class tomorrow, we're going to start doing self-portraits tomorrow, and I want to make sure you guys have a good setup with your easel and a mirror. Do you have any ideas?"

I looked around the classroom, the easels laid out in a circle are facing inwards towards a platform in the middle of the room.

A counter with sinks wrapped around the walls of the classroom, the surface covered in all different kinds of things. There were clay pieces drying, palettes, and paint brushes, and some of the pottery wheels were stored on top of the counter.

"If you clear off the counter you could line the easels up along the counter and put the mirrors on the counter," I said.

Mr. Collymore shook his head. "I don't think I can fit enough easels like that, and I have nowhere else to put a lot of the things I have on the counter."

"Then I guess to keep the current layout and clip the mirrors to the sides of easels?" I suggested. "It's not ideal and they might fall and break but it might work?"

He paced around the classroom, his hand on his chin as he pondered my suggestion before sighing. "I guess it'll have to work. Though I was hoping for it to be able to feel a bit more private for the artists, this will have to do." He disappeared into the storage room, reappearing holding a plastic container with small circular mirrors piled inside of it. "Monty. Help me put these up, will you?"

"Sure," I nodded, walking over to him and grabbing a handful of mirrors.

As I put up the mirrors I looked around the room, trying to find what had painted Sonali in rainbows that day. I wondered if it was the suncatcher hung by the window or the drying racks that were covered in various layers of colorful paint and watercolors. The AP art projects were gone, so there was no way of me confirming that it had been those.

There was *nothing*. Nothing in this room sparkled the way that she did that day.

At the time I hadn't thought about Sonali's personality much, I just knew that both she and her paintings were beautiful and I wanted to get to know her. I wanted to meet the artist behind the work, something I had no desire to do before. I just wanted to see what might have influenced the pieces that she made. I wanted so desperately to be in the same class as her and to watch her paint again.

She looked the most confident when she was standing at that easel in the middle row third from the right. That was when her colors shone through, and maybe that would be where her feelings shone too. When her arms were covered in paint she was so focused on creating the right texture of brushstrokes.

If I wanted to have any hope of understanding her, I had a feeling that I needed to understand why she painted. And what she painted. I needed to find the version of her that I had met that day in the art room.

"Mr. Collymore?" I said. "Can I ask you a question about Sonali?"

"I'm not sure I'll be able to give you an answer, but sure go ahead," He said. "I know you guys are friends so I'm sure you have no ill will towards her with the questions you ask. At least I'm hoping you wouldn't."

"No no! Of course not!" I exclaimed, waving my hands in front of me. "I would never."

He didn't respond, just left the silence in the air, giving me the room to ask him questions.

"What's Sonali like in class?" I asked.

Mr. Collymore hummed from the other side of the classroom, thinking of what I assumed to be his answer. "Well, Sonali is quiet, and doesn't really talk to her classmates. She has a habit of ignoring people when they try to talk to her, but that's mostly the fault of her classmates for not saying her name."

He tapped a pencil against the palm of his hand. "Sonali almost sits in her own bubble within my classroom. And within it, the others can't reach her and she can bend the rules to my assignments however she wants." He chuckled. "Though, I'm sure part of the blame for that falls on me for allowing her to do so."

"So she doesn't have friends?" I asked, sitting down after finishing putting up my share of mirrors.

Mr. Collymore shook his head. "She didn't have any friends as far as I know until she met you. She seemed content with that though. But then you introduced her to some of your friends, right? After that happened I feel like I noticed her drifting off into space a bit more during class. She would look in whatever direction she could hear conversation from, and listen with a blank look on her face."

I nodded. "There was something about her that was different that day I met her for the first time. I can't seem to pinpoint what it is that's different about her now vs. when I saw her in the art room for the first time in October."

Mr. Collymore sat beside me, tracing the edge of the canvas set up at one of the easels. "Did you ever think that maybe she isn't different?" He asked.

"What do you mean?" I said.

"Well, it's like when people say not to judge a book by its cover. Sure, what you saw of her in the art room is probably a part of her in some way or another. But I'm sure that wasn't really her in her truest form."

"But I thought you said that people are always their truest selves when they are doing what they love, and Sonali loves to paint."

"I also said when we did our interview portraits that what you see on the outside isn't always what is all there is to see. People idealize themselves in front of others, and when people become infatuated, they lose their awareness of what they actually feel."

I sat for a second, looking around the room trying to find clues as to what I meant in between the cracks of paint on the walls. "I don't get it," I said.

My. Collymore chuckled and put a hand on my shoulder. "Try this then. Watch her paint."

"What?"

"Now that you have gotten to know her, ask her to paint again, and then think to yourself. Think about what is different, and what is the same, if anything is the same."

"But, what could possibly be different?" I asked.

Mr. Collymore sighed, and I could tell that he was getting tired of trying to explain it to me. "Just trust me, Monty. I've watched you, and I've watched her. I have a feeling I know what is going to change your thoughts.”

My phone buzzed, and I pulled it out to see a text from my sister telling me she was here.

I said goodbye to Mr. Collymore and walked over to the amphitheater where she was parked to pick me up.

I got in the passenger side and my sister immediately flicked me in the side of the head. “What's up loser?” She started to drive.

I rolled my eyes and ignored her, leaning against my elbow and looking out the window, as I tried to recreate that image of Sonali in my head from when I had first met her. But for whatever reason, the pieces didn't connect, and I couldn't reform that image of her. So, I sat wondering what it is that had changed, all the way up until I got home.

January 7th, 2023

I tried my hardest to paint her once again. Trying to capture that side profile of her sitting at her easel, with rainbows and light pouring out of her like watercolor, but none of the lines connected the way I saw them that day. And my strokes created sheets of color stacked over one another, rather than a smooth blend. My paper was starting to flake away from itself, beading up on the paper and clinging to my brush.

Savannah barged into my room, slamming my bedroom door behind her, and falling like a stone onto my bed with a drawn out groan.

I ignored her, doing my best to wipe off the watercolor I had painted across the page by mistake upon her entering. While trying to wipe it off, I could feel the wood beneath the towel that I held, and when I lifted it up I had rubbed a hole through my paper.

I tore my paper from my sketchbook and balled it up in my fist and threw it behind me, hearing Savannah yelp as it hit her in the shoulder.

"Hey!" She said,

I ignored her.

"Aren't you going to ask me what's wrong?" She said kicking my chair.

"Hey!" I said turning around. "I'm trying to work on an art piece for my portfolio right now, can't it wait? I don't want nor have the time to deal with your nonsense."

"It's not nonsense! I need relationship advice," She groaned, grabbing my chair and pulling it away from my desk.

I stood up, and sat next to her on my bed, glaring. "If I help you will you leave me alone?"

She nodded, her eyes begging me to help her.

I sighed and rubbed my hands over my face. "Fine, what did you do?"

"What makes you think it's my fault?!" She elbowed me in the side.

I grabbed her arm from my side and pushed it away from me. "Because it's always you,"

"Well, Raelyn got all pissy because I didn't tell them I was going to go out for the night," Savannah said, pulling her legs up and setting her chin on her knees. "When I shouldn't have to report my whereabouts to them anyways."

I crossed my legs and put my hands in my lap, doing my best to read Savannah's facial expressions. "Well, how do you feel?"

"I'm confused because it's not like this hasn't happened before," Savannah said. "I go out for the night without saying anything all the time, and they've never been upset like this before."

"Maybe it did upset them but they didn't want to tell you," I said.

"But, do they communicate with me about other things that upset them? What made them think they couldn't tell me about that?"

I let the silence hang in the air, thinking for a moment. "Maybe it isn't about the fact that you stayed out without saying anything." I asked.

"What do you mean?"

"Maybe you're missing part of what happened. I doubt Raelyn just decided to be mad about something she usually wouldn't care about. Did you maybe have plans with them and forget? Is there any significance to the date?" I said.

Savannah shrugged, her face unchanging along with her opinion.

"I think you should try and figure out what you're missing. You're immediately getting upset with them thinking they're being unreasonable. But you need to remember how flawed you are. Yes she is flawed but so are you.

"If you ignore your own flaws, or view yourself as flawless, then you might do that to others as well." I paused, thinking about my own life for a split moment. "Then you'll be putting people on pedestals. And if you put the wrong person on a pedestal you could end up getting hurt."

Savannah was quiet for a moment, her brows furrowed as I watched the gears turn in her head, each word I said slowly processing.

"I hate that you're right," She mumbled, crossing her arms.

"I always am," I said standing up and sitting back down at my desk. "Now out, I have stuff to do,"

Savannah stood up, stopping in the doorway. "Hey," I turned to look at her. "You too," She said. "Don't put people on pedestals."

I turned and smiled at her, acknowledging the worry she had written in the space between her eyebrows. "I won't, don't worry." The words tasted somehow bitter on my tongue.

I sat, unmoving, *thinking*. Thinking about Sonali and if I had noticed any of her flaws, and decided I liked her despite them. And I didn't, because I couldn't see any sort of flaws.

January 9th, 2023

I sat in the library in the corner by the graphic novels, with Leo and Sonali after school. Leo was next to me, and then Sonali sat on the other side of the table.

I listened to her computer read out what she was typing as she worked on the presentation for our english project. The computer "spoke" at a speed too fast for me to comprehend on any levels, and I wondered for a moment if Sonali was even able to understand what it was saying. But every time I looked up from what I was writing her lips were pressed in a thin line, and I could see the focus in her eyes as she typed, the computer reading out the letters as she did so.

The more we worked, the less time I spent actually working and the more time I spent staring at Sonali. I could see her pores on her nose, and her mascara had begun to clump up on her eyelashes. The arms on her hairs stood up and her skin was covered in goosebumps as the AC turned on above where we sat in the library.

Her hair was messy and dry, and she seemed to me uncomfortable in the clothes that she was wearing, constantly tugging on the neckline of the shirt.

Leo elbowed me in the side. "Hey, focus, this is due tomorrow so stop staring."

Sonali looked up from what she was doing. "What is Monty staring at?"

"Oh he was just—" I put a hand over Leo's mouth, hitting him on the head with my notebook.

"I wasn't staring at anything," I said glaring at Leo. "Just zoning out is all. Let's keep working, alright?"

Sonali didn't respond, she looked as if she was deciding whether or not she wanted to believe me. I really hoped that she would, because I wouldn't have an explanation if she didn't.

"I agree I don't think we should be getting distracted right now," She said.

I nodded and mumbled, "Right, sorry."

We got back to work on the presentation, bouncing ideas off of each other and adding on to the points that each other brought up.

We were almost done with the presentation when someone's phone buzzed making the whole table vibrate.

We realized it was Sonali's phone when the all too familiar voice started repeating the same phrase over and over, neither me nor Leo able to make out what the words were.

Sonali answered the phone and stood up as she started gathering her things. "Hey," She said, pausing as the voice on the other line said a few words. "Okay dad. Yeah, I'll be out soon."

Leo and I both stood up, taking Sonali's phone call as our cue to start heading out as well.

Still unable to tear my eyes away from Sonali.

"Yeah, I'll see you in a bit, bye," She said, hanging up and putting her phone in her pocket. "Yeah my dad's here so I gotta go."

"That's alright," Leo said, putting on his backpack. "We were at a good stopping point anyways," He said. "We can call and finish it up later tonight if no one has anything else to do," He said.

I nodded. "I'm good to finish it up later."

"Yeah, I can too. I just have to do a few things when I get home but after that it is fine," She said, unfolding her cane and starting to walk towards the library exit.

"Sounds good," Leo added, holding the door to the library open.

"Okay, my dad parked at the front of the school so I'm this way," Sonali said.

"Okay," I said, grabbing her hand. "I'll see you, text me when you get home alright?"

She nodded, giving my hand a quick squeeze before letting go. "Kay, bye you guys."

Leo and I turned, him and I heading to the senior parking lot while Sonali went the opposite way to the front of the school.

"You really like her, huh?" Leo asked.

"What?" I said looking up.

"I said you really like her, don't you?"

I didn't respond. I just shrugged, keeping my eyes on the ground.

"Monty?" Leo asked. "What's that face for?"

"I think, maybe, I was wrong…" I said. "Or something."

Leo stared at me, concern written in the way he scrunched up his nose. "What do you mean you think you were wrong?"

"I thought I liked her, but…" I stopped, not knowing how to phrase what I was trying to say.

"Monty…"

"Don't get me wrong Sonali is an amazing friend and I love the time we spend together. I just think that maybe I liked the idea of her. The idea of the rainbow painted girl in the art room. But now my initial perception of her is clashing with who she actually is as I get closer to her."

I recalled each interaction I've had with her since meeting. I thought of how she would run her fingers through her hair. How she would fiddle with her bangs trying to get them to lay perfectly on her head.

"I thought that she was this sweet sparkling girl. But, she's a lot more blunt than I thought she would be. I think it was the idea of loving her that I liked. I think I kind of put her on a pedestal without realizing it, and I'm only just now realizing how human we both are. Maybe."

"Wow, that's— that's a lot," Leo said, opening the door that led outside. He seemed to be thinking, his eyebrows pointed down as he thought. He seemed a bit disappointed, and I wondered if he was sad for Sonali, in the same way that I was.

"I don't think it's possible to fall in love with someone in a few months," I paused. "And even if it was possible I don't think I'm capable of loving people in the way that most need to be loved."

"What are you going to do?" Leo asked.

"I mean, I have to tell her because that's obviously not fair to her. But, when? And how? I don't know. Plus, I'm not even sure yet. I think I still have to think some more."

"Well, make sure you do it when you know, because… if you let this linger it won't turn out very well." Leo paused, looking at me. "You know what I mean don't you?"

I nodded, as we walked over to his car. "I do."

"Good," He unlocked his car and got in, not saying anything else. I don't think there was anything else that needed saying, but still made the air around us feel heavy. Probably because we both knew the topic at hand was something that held a lot of weight. And I wasn't exactly known for being strong.

"Thanks for driving me home," I said.

"Yeah no worries. I'm here for you man, alright?" Leo said.

I nodded, getting into the car with Leo silently. I

thought of what I had spent the past couple months doing. I spent time with Sonali. Watching movies, studying together. I hung out with her as friends, but I think I admired her a bit too much to treat her like one. I mistook my admiration for romantic feelings. I should have realized something was wrong. I had no desire to kiss her. I didn't know then, but I understand now. It was time for me to be honest with her, and with myself.

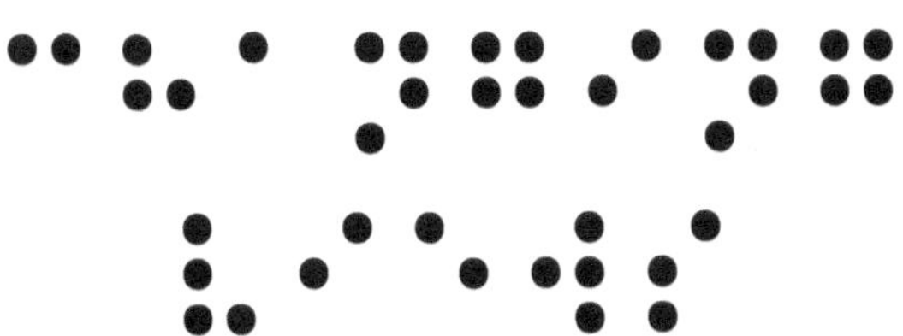

Sonali

Changing Views (Sonali)

November 15th, 2022
I didn't have to see him to know he was beautiful.
His voice sounded the way that fleece feels— soft, and ever
so slightly raspy. I liked his voice, it made me feel safe
whenever we were together. He had the hands of an artist,
dry and cracked from paint water. I couldn't make out a
lot of his features, but his hair was dark, short, and curly.
I learned through our texts that he has a lobe piercing on
his left ear. His eyes greyish blue. He paints to preserve
memories that he can only be a part of for a moment. His
way of revisiting important moments in his life. He paints
like the world is a time capsule and he is trying to record its
history hidden in his brush strokes. He likes history, with a
specific interest in The Salem Witch Trials. Savannah, his
older sister. is twenty-one and does college from home. He
likes morning glories, and how they only ever open up to
the sun; their beauty is something that the night sky would
never get to see.

He told me about flower language. How morning
glories were a symbol of everything that is temporary. The

way they die each night only to be revived each morning is a representation of mortality. I never thought I would relate to a flower, but the way he talked about them made me want to paint them. Pluck them from the cracks in the sidewalk and lay their petals in my paintings, hidden beneath the color. A secret in the painting that you would only know through touching its surface. Feeling the shape of the petal beneath the layers of paint. He told me about how morning glories are resilient, rooting themselves between cracks in pavement and underneath houses.

I wanted to be like that. I wanted to root myself somewhere that fit me perfectly, a crack in the pavement that I could fight my way out of. I wanted the space to open up to the sun each day, even if only for a little while.

When I first met him a month prior, his voice was shaky as he talked to me. But despite his clear nervousness, he still made an effort to talk. I thought maybe it might have been because he didn't know me very well that made him so nervous. But when we met that weekend to go to the amusement park with his friends, his voice shook just as much as it had the first day we met. Even now, as we had been setting up for the art fair, his voice wouldn't seem to settle into a steady rhythm.

After setting up the art displays, we sat in silence for the most part. I would talk to the kids that stopped by while Monty would stamp their sheets. I thought that Monty would be good with kids, but he didn't really seem to know how to talk to them, so I did my best to do so while Monty did the part that I couldn't.

"Hey!" I looked up to see a few shadows standing in front of the table. "We came to say hi to you guys!" The voice said.

I heard Monty's chair scrape against the floor as he stood up, and I heard his footsteps walk around to the other side of the table. "Hi guys, I didn't think I'd see you here,"

He said. "I thought you guys were hanging out today."

"Hi Sonali!" Someone exclaimed coming around to the side of the table and wrapping an arm around my shoulders, causing me to flinch at the sudden touch. Goosebumps ran down my arm as I tried to figure out whose arm was around my neck. It took me a moment to recognize their voices, but it seemed that Monty's friends had stopped by to say hi.

"Hi Alaska," I smiled. "I didn't know you guys were coming."

"I didn't either," Monty chuckled. "What are you guys doing here?"

"We thought you might be bored," Noah said.

"What Noah is trying to say is that *we* were the bored ones," Leo added.

"Yeah," Alaska agreed. "In my opinion, there's only so much entertainment video games can offer."

"Hey!" Leo and Noah exclaimed in sync.

"Don't be like that," Noah said. "You were the one having the most fun out of the three of us."

"Yeah, don't try and act like you don't enjoy a good video game or two," Leo added.

I stayed quiet, wondering if they would realize they were talking about games with someone who couldn't exactly play them.

"I'd rather hang out with Sonali than either one of you guys," Alaska said, squeezing me. "Boys, am I right?" She leaned her head against mine.

"Yep, boys," I chuckled.

"Sonali, I was actually wondering if you would be a model for me? I need a model for my clothing designs for my portfolio," Alaska said.

"Oh? So you're definitely going to school for fashion design?" Monty asked.

Alaska hummed for a moment, thinking. "Nah, I

still don't know yet, but I'm gonna prepare a portfolio and apply to some schools just in case the whole internship thing doesn't work out."

"That's really cool, Alaska. I wish I knew what I wanted to do," I said, trying to hide my anxiety between laughs.

"Don't even sweat it, Sonali. I'm sure you'll figure it out soon," Alaska added, giving me a quick squeeze.

"Yeah, I'm sure you could do anything you wanted to," Leo added. "I mean, you're super talented, you could figure anything out if you—" Leo yelped, groaning in pain as if he had been hit.

"Leo, be quiet," Noah murmured.

I thought for a moment, before laughing at what I had realized to be their attempts to be sensitive to me. These people who hadn't known me for very long, treated me like they had known me for years. With the same gentleness of drizzling rain.

"He's fine Noah. He's just trying to make me feel better," I said.

"There's always a chance! Who knows, maybe you'll find yourself being a nascar driver or something," Leo grumbled, glaring at Noah.

I sat listening to this group of friends bicker and laugh. Their voices weaved together, washing away my loneliness with a wave of color.

December 12th, 2022

I sat on the exam table, running my hands back and forth over the powdery texture of the paper pulled over the cushions. The air conditioning buzzed above my head, and I could hear my mom bouncing her heel up and down in the corner.

I sighed and ran my hands through my hair. "Could you stop that?" I asked. "My vision has barely changed since I was fifteen. I doubt it's changed much."

"I know, I know, but still," My mom said.

I heard the tapping of her heel stop when the door to the exam room creaked open, my optometrist coming in and shutting it behind her.

I turned towards the noise, a blurry figure of gray to my left in the dim room. "Give it to me straight doc, am I dying?" I asked, adjusting my glasses.

She chuckled, and I let out the breath I had been holding. Every year I have made that joke, and every year she has laughed. The only time she didn't was when I was twelve, and we realized that my vision had rapidly deteriorated.

"Still quite the comedian I see," She said.

"Still quite the lackluster doctor I see," I mimicked what she said, looking her up and down. "How many years have I been telling you to bedazzle your lab coat?"

"And how many years have I been telling you that I can't?" She chuckled.

"At least two," I paused. "So how are the eyes?"

"They're fine, a little worse, but again your vision has really slowed down its degeneration rate three years ago," Dr. Regardo said.

I zoned out to the sound of her voice, the recap of my eyesight boring me at every appointment. It was stuff I already knew, and it was stuff my mom also already knew. I don't know why she felt the need to repeat herself at every appointment, drowning me in the same words that she spoke every year over and over again.

After she finished talking, my mom and I left Dr. Regardo's office. I listened to the sound of the AC. It's hum fading in and out as we took the elevator to the ground floor.

"The least you could do is pay attention when she's talking you know," My mom said.

"What's the point? My vision is getting worse. I know that— you know that, there's no point in stressing myself out about it every year. I'd rather spend my time working on how to get into art school," I said.

"Nali, I'm just saying—"

"Can you just drop it?" I asked, not wanting to talk about the thing that isolated me from my peers in middle school.

My mom sighed and I could hear the frustration as she did. I expected some sort of retort. A lecture about my attitude, but she just stayed quiet.

The doors opened, and I stepped inside to see a familiar silhouette standing in the corner.

"Sonali!" She exclaimed.

"Alaska hi!" I said leaning in for a hug. "What are you doing here?" I asked.

"Oh, uh, nothing, just a doctor's appointment," she said.

"Who's this?" My mom asked.

"A friend," I said. "We met last month when I went to the amusement park with some friends."

"Hello, it's nice to meet you, I'm Alaska," She said.

"It's lovely to meet you too, I'm Nali's mom,"

I thought for a moment about the building.

"Hey, Alaska, what are you doing here? This is one of the specialty buildings, so there's no general medicine here?" I was a little worried, wondering what she was doing in this building. I hoped she was okay, but the people who came here usually weren't. The third floor is the ophthalmologist, and I think the fifth floor has a wing for eating disorder treatment.

"Oh, uh, I was at the orthopedics." Ah, the fourth floor. "I was having back problems but turns out I just have the posture of a shrimp," She laughed. "Well, um, my mom parked outside so this is my stop." She stepped past me and out of the elevator. "I'll see you at school later?"

"Um, yeah sure, I'll see you!" I said waving goodbye as her figure disappeared into the building lobby, the elevator doors closing behind her.

"She seems skittish," My mom accused.

I turned to her and scowled. "Maa, really? You just met her, stop being so judgy of my friends," I said.

"I wasn't judging her, I was just making an observation." She huffed. "We were on parking level two right?" She asked.

I sighed. "Yep."

"Hey, I don't need you giving me any of that attitude missy," She said pressing the button for parking level two. There was that attitude check I was waiting for.

I stayed silent, keeping my reaction to myself.

When we got in the car, I collapsed my cane, putting it back into its sleeve, the silence hanging heavy in the air.

After some time on the road, I decided to speak up. "I'm sorry for being rude,." I leaned my head onto the window of the car.

My mom sighed, "I'm sorry too. I know it doesn't bother you as much, but as your mother I can't help but be scared for your health. I want you to be healthy."

"I know, but I wish you would remember that just because I can't see that well it doesn't mean I'm not healthy," I murmured under my breath, realizing that once again it seems my words wouldn't be getting through to her once again.

She sighed again, and I rolled my eyes at the theme of silence in the day. I just rolled the window down and rested my head in my arms. I closed my eyes, making the few spots of the world that I could see go black. I felt the breeze from the highway pull through my hair, tugging on both the roots and the ends of it. The chilly weather tickled, leaving goosebumps running up my arms. But, I didn't mind the cold all that much. I felt more aware in the cold than in the heat, and the sky always brightened up when the sun reflected the white of snow. What the surprisingly warm December lacked in temperature, it made up for with a cold wind that made my skin tingle.

I fell asleep leaning out the window, and when I woke up again it was around noon, and I was sitting in the parking lot of the school, my mom shaking my shoulder so she could roll up the window.

December 27th, 2022

An arm wrapped around me and pulled me close, startling me awake. A bit against them.

"Hey, wait Sonali, it's just me," they said, grabbing my hand. "It's Monty."

"Monty?" I immediately relaxed, squeezing his hand with mine. Feeling the cold wind, and the warmth of fire, I realized that I had fallen asleep by the bonfire in Leo's backyard. "Jeez, you scared me."

"I'm sorry I really wasn't trying to," he said.

I could feel a line on his skin that was raised and tight, like scar tissue. "You have a scar?"

"I do," He flipped his hand over in mine.

I traced the scar with my fingers from my other hand. His hand shook a bit before he pulled away, chuckling.

"That tickles," he said.

"Oh, I'm sorry," I said, putting my hands in my lap. "I could just feel a scar, so I couldn't help it I guess."

"It's okay! I'm not mad," He said.

I couldn't see much, just a vague shadow of his figure lit by the firelight. His shadow didn't move an inch. It didn't shift; he remained quiet and still. As did I.

All I could think much of was our conversation

earlier in the night, and all that did was make me nervous. I talked big earlier, but I think it might have just been the alcohol talking. And now I couldn't even imagine any reason as to why he would ever want to paint me.

It's not like I'd be able to see it, so I really didn't see the point. He was nervous and tense; I was scared and confused. The previously relaxed and comfortable atmosphere went out like a candle. All that was left was smoke, dancing in the air as it tried to escape itself.

I sat back in the lawn chair, tracing the edges of the fire's light with the shadows my fingers casted in the air.

"What are you doing?" Monty asked.

"Trying to remember its shape," I said. "So that I can maybe paint it later."

"That's really interesting," Monty said. "I really love the way you paint."

I turned to him and stared while chuckling. "For real? Why?"

"Because it tells a story. Something that I've never been able to do with my art." He paused as if to give me the room to talk, but I just sat quietly, waiting for him to tell me more. "It's like, with the way I paint, I capture a moment. I transfer a single moment of time to a canvas so that it can be remembered forever. But, it's just one moment. Your paintings don't capture just a moment, they capture the whole story."

I didn't understand what he meant, and I didn't think it was something that I'd be able to understand anyways. I think if I wanted to understand his words, I would need to be able to see the difference between his paintings and mine. But that isn't something I'm able to do.

I looked down, turning my fingers over each other in my lap. "I really don't get it."

"Get what?" He asked.

"Why you like me." He didn't respond, he just

sat there silently, and I could feel my ears start to burn. "Are you just not going to say anything? I'm being honest and telling you my feelings here but you're not saying anything."

"I'm sorry!" He exclaimed, grabbing my hands. I flinched at the sudden touch, my body freezing completely. "I'm not trying to ignore you, I promise! I'm just trying to find the words to describe it to you in a way you'll understand. Because I can't describe to you how you make me feel because that won't mean anything to you," He said. He squeezed my hands tightly, and though I couldn't tell for sure, I could feel his eyes on me. "I promise that I really do like you. I just don't have the resources to express to you why I do. But, I want to find the resources that will help me make you see— or well understand and comprehend why I like you."

I couldn't help but stare, trying to make out any of his features or any bits of his expression. I couldn't help but laugh at how desperately he talked.

"I don't want you to have to doubt my feelings for you," He said.

"I'm sorry," I sighed. "I shouldn't have said what I said the way I said it." I thought for a moment, trying to find the right words instead of just saying whatever happened to pop into my head. "I just can't really wrap my head around this. I know I said we could try going on a date but…" I paused and pulled my hand out of his, shaking my head to reset my thoughts. "I don't want to be relied on."

"Then I'll make sure I won't," He said. "Listen, I'm not expecting you to believe me right away. And if you don't want to go on a date with me, we don't have to. But I do have feelings for you. I won't do anything you don't want me to do. I want it to be on your terms."

I covered my face with my hands thinking. "I want to try, but I'm nervous."

"Okay, then, it doesn't have to be anything serious, we can just hangout and try doing things couples do," He paused. "Would that be okay with you?"

I shrugged. "I… I don't know if I'm being honest."

"That's okay, I won't force you or anything."

I pulled my hair to cover my ears, pulled my hood over my head, and tightened the strings to cover my face. I groaned and leaned back into the chair. "You're too nice,"

"I'm… glad you think so?" He said hesitantly.

I could feel my heart beating, it felt like it was going to force my ribcage open, freeing all of the butterflies that I kept in there.

Strangely, it was like that quick nap by the fire reset my perception of Monty, and I somehow thought him to be so much more bright than he was before.

"I don't know what to do with myself around you," I said. "You make me feel embarrassed."

He laughed, and I couldn't help but glare in his direction. "You want to know a secret?" He asked. He didn't give me enough time to respond before saying, "You make me embarrassed too."

I smiled at his words. They made me feel good about myself, something that I hadn't experienced in a while. I liked how he described his feelings for me. They sounded too good to be true, and I wondered if maybe I was lying to myself in order to feel better.

January 1st, 2023

I was a little nervous about my date with Monty. Or more accurately, I was terrified. After all, he had proposed going to a museum, but most museums don't cater to me.

I sat on my bed, waiting for him to pick me up, obsessively running my fingers through my hair and my hands over my legs.

I had already spent twenty minutes just trying

to pick out what to wear, and with Monty on his way, I couldn't keep changing my outfit. I didn't have time to change again, and I was too anxious to check my phone. All I could do, all I was able to do was wait. Wait and hope that he didn't stand me up despite the fact that he was a half hour late to our agreed-upon time.

I couldn't help but worry, maybe he really did decide that I wasn't worth it after all. He thought about the idea of making sure that wherever we go would have accommodations for me and he gave up. He decided it was too much of a hassle for him to deal with. And I wouldn't be able to blame him because sometimes it's too much of a hassle and I don't want to deal with it. I was so sure that he had blown me off, and I was ready to give up on the idea of a date. I felt the watch on my wrist, running my hands over the face of it, reading the braille on its face. Two more minutes. Two more minutes and I would give up. I would change out of these clothes, take off the makeup my mom helped me put on, and bundle up in bed to watch true crime for the rest of the night.

The bell rang and I froze, waiting to see if my mom called me to come downstairs. It felt like my heart stopped, anticipating some sort of answer from whatever god watches over this world that I wasn't abandoned. That he did in fact show up.

"Sonali!" My mom called. "Monty is here!"

I jumped up from my bed and ran out of my bedroom, slamming my knee against my bookcase as I did. "Dammit!" I grunted.

I hobbled down the hallway and towards the front of the house. Past the kitchen and into the living room where I could see my mom's figure standing with Monty.

"Nali, language," My mom warned, pulling on my ear.

"Ow ow ow!" I whined. "Okay okay, I got it, stop!"

My mom let go of my ear, her hand falling onto my shoulder. "Make sure to bring my girl home by eleven."

Monty cleared his throat, his voice shaking as he spoke. "Yes of course Ms. Roa, I promise to bring her home on time."

"Alright, be safe, I love you," My mom said, kissing my cheek. "Are you sure you don't want to bring your cane?" She whispered.

I kissed her cheek and took a step forward, reaching out my hand and finding Monty's elbow. "Monty learned how to do sighted guide a while ago, I'll be fine," I said. "I love you Maa, see you when I get home."

"Uh, have a good night!" Monty said to my mom as I dragged him out of the house.

I shut the door behind us and sighed, getting a better grip on his elbow. "Sorry about her. She has no sense of anything,"

I stood on the porch with Monty for a moment.

"You're late," I said. "Why?"

"Savannah," He groaned. "She wasn't ready to go, and neither was Raelyn, her friend. Neither of them will walk around with us, don't worry. They're just our ride and then they'll hang out on their own."

"A text would have been nice."

"I'm really sorry."

I didn't respond, I just smiled, not being able to stay mad at him for long. Birds were chirping, and the air was cold and damp. I couldn't make out any lights or shadows. Everything was dark.

"Is it foggy?" I asked.

"Very, how did you know?" He asked, beginning to walk down the three steps of my porch.

"When it's foggy the airflow is different, and all of the lights and shadows that I can see get all fuzzy and everything blends together. Basically eliminating any vision that I do have."

He stopped, nine steps across the sidewalk that led to the driveway. "Did you want to grab your cane?" He asked.

I shook my head. "It won't be an issue once we're inside,"

"Okay, if you're sure," He said.

He walked me down the driveway and to his sister's car.

"Sup, lovebirds," I heard his sister say from the driver's side.

"Get in losers we're going shopping!" I heard a voice exclaim from the seat in front of me.

I looked at Monty for a brief moment, before turning my attention to the person sitting in front of me as Savannah pulled out of the driveway. "Hi Savannah, how are you?" I asked.

"I'm good thank you for asking," Savannah said.

"Who is in the passenger seat?" I asked.

"Hi!" I heard the same voice again, and I heard a shift in movement accompanied by a gasp. "Yo! Are you okay? Why are your eyes shaking so much? It looks kind of cool. Ow! Savannah what was that for?!"

"Stop trying to befriend the high schooler," Savannah said. "This is my friend Raelyn, they're stupid so don't mind them."

"Hey!" Raelyn exclaimed.

"I like your name," I said, turning my attention back to Raelyn in an attempt to stop them from any more playful bickering.

"Thanks, I picked it out myself," They said. "But for real though, what's up with the eyes? Is it something I can learn how to do?"

"Raelyn!" Monty exclaimed. "You're being rude!"

"How? All I'm doing is asking about her eyes!"

I couldn't help but laugh at their reaction. "I just have nystagmus. It's an eye disease that makes my eyes shake."

"Oh, so you really are blind?" Raelyn said. "I didn't think Savannah was saying you were actually blind I thought she was just saying you're oblivious. My bad man,"

I smiled and laughed again, their reaction is quite refreshing compared to reactions I've gotten in the past. It reminded me of how Monty reacted, and I wondered if both him and his sister had a talent for surrounding themselves with people who could surprise me in ways others couldn't. I thought maybe it was something about the way they were raised that drew them together. "The nystagmus isn't what makes me blind, but it's no biggie, really. I've heard a lot worse."

I made small talk with Savannah and Raelyn in the car on the way to the museum. We talked about school, and our favorite Indian foods. Monty sat quietly beside me, his faint shadow fidgeting every few minutes.

When we got to the parking lot, I got out of the car and waited for Monty to walk around the car and offer me his elbow.

Once he did we started walking through the parking lot to the front door of the museum, Raelyn asking me questions about sighted-guide as we walked.

Monty stayed quiet, and he seemed tense, his arm barely moving as I held it.

Once we made it inside and got into line was when he finally said something.

"Once we get our tickets and are able to go in and everything, Savannah and Raelyn are going to split up from us and go do their own thing, but we'll meet up for lunch and for the event at the end of the day. Is that okay with you?”

I nodded. “What’s the event at the end of the day?”

“Uh, I want it to be a surprise if that’s alright.”

“Okay, if that’s what you want,” I said, as we walked up to the counter.

“Hi, I need two starlight tickets please, and an accessibility pass for the audio play-throughs,” Monty said.

“Yep of course,” the person behind the desk said. “That’ll be thirty dollars each, so sixty total. The starlight package includes a free pass into one interactive exhibit, and a free meal and dessert pass in the cafeteria. And the—”

“No! Please don’t say that thing that they do at the end of the day!” Monty said, cutting the person behind the desk off. “It’s supposed to be a surprise,”

The person laughed, and said, “Of course, will it be cash or card?”

“I’ll pay for both of them with cash,” I said, pulling out my wallet.

“Alright—”

“No! You will not. I’m gonna pay, okay?” Monty said.

“I don’t think that’s fair—”

“You can pay for our next date, how does that sound?” Monty asked, cutting me off.

“Oh, so we’re already having a second date now are we?” I asked.

“No! I mean, well yes. I would like to definitely, but I’m not going to force you or anything,” He rambled.

I couldn’t help but laugh, relaxing as soon as I realized that the cause of his silence was his nervousness. “I was just joking,” I said, nudging him in the side with my elbow. I turned to the shadow behind the desk. “I guess he’s paying then,”

“Alright sir, will it be cash or card?” the person

behind the desk asked again. I could hear the smile in her voice, and I was so grateful to be able to do this.

"It'll be card."

"Okay, go ahead and insert it right here, and once you pay here are your wristbands and your guide and card for the audio play-throughs, and to your left over there is going to be the sample site. That way you can test it and make sure your card is working and you know how to use the system." She said.

After Monty paid, we stepped off the side and put our wristbands on while waiting for Savannah and Raelyn to buy their tickets.

As soon as Savannah and Raelyn stepped over to where we stood, Monty handed me the guide for the audio playthroughs for the exhibits, and I ran my hands over the braille that was on the brochure.

"Okay, Raelyn and I are going to go ahead and do our own thing," Savannah said, her voice getting farther away as she spoke.

"See you," Monty said.

I waved goodbye to them as I watched their figures walk away, and once they had left I stood with Monty in the silence that was left behind, neither of us moving. Even after I finished reading the guide to the audio play-through card, not a word was said.

It was a shared understanding of not knowing what to do or where to go from where it is that we were right now. I imagined it in a painting, swirls of gray wrapping around two pillars of color, sharing a mutual agreement about the swirls. One pillar would be made of gradients of muted greens and pinks, the other… I couldn't think of the colors needed for the other pillar in this hypothetical painting. I just knew that it would keep the swirls of gray as the focus, almost as if the two pillars of color were people standing in the eye of a hurricane.

Silence has always scared me, and sure I could hear what was going on around me. The sound of people's footsteps, and the whispering of voices. But even as I held onto Monty's elbow, he was eerily quiet. I refused to look up from the ground, or unclench my jaw. I was afraid of him slipping away if I let go even fo9r a moment.

"Hey, Sonali?"

I looked up and smiled, relieved to hear the sound of his voice from beside me. "Yeah?"

"Do you want to test out the audio playthrough card?" He asked.

"Oh, yeah," I held the card up and turned it in my fingers, finding the side that had the braille on it. I reached my hand out to feel for the edge of the display and found the notch in the corner. The notch extended to a divet in the exhibit, creating a line to the center of the display, right around where my belly button was. It led to what appeared to be a card slit, and along the top of it was braille that read "Audio Play-through card scanner, please insert card. Remove the card when the scanner begins to beep."

I found the slit in the scanner, found the edge of the card opposite to the braille, and put it in the card. For a moment nothing happened. But after a few seconds, the scanner beeped.

I pulled out my card and an audio recording started to play from somewhere above me, perhaps higher on the wall, there were speakers.

"Thank you for using our Accessible Audio Recordings Program. Your card appears to be functioning properly, so please continue to use it as you tour the museum. Each exhibit has a card scanner located four feet from the ground. Whenever a card is used it will play a recording similar to this one, and at the end of each recording will be a ding, to signal the end of the audio recording. It is recommended to find where the card

scanner is in relation to your body to make them easier
to find throughout The Exploratory Star Museum, an
interactive museum that has exhibits related to anything
you could ever want to know about space. If you at any
point have any questions feel free to find one of our
employees, and we will do our best to answer the questions
you have. Thank you for coming, and we hope you enjoy
your visit."

I stood frozen, not really knowing how to react. I
had never experienced something like this. It seemed that
such an accessible place had been right under my nose this
entire time and I wasn't even the one who found it.

I looked at Monty, trying to find some sort of
clue in the smudge of his body, telling why he put in the
effort to find this. I tried to find some reason as to why he
even bothered. I had told him to find a museum that had
accommodations, but I didn't think he would be able to find
this. A museum so accommodating right under my nose. I
didn't think that something like this could exist. If I had

"Wow, you really went all out," I breathed.

"What do you mean?" He asked.

"I mean you really went and found a museum that
would be enjoyable to me," I said. "I didn't think it was
possible."

"Why didn't you think it would be possible?" He
asked.

I shrugged. "I think I spent so long alone, I didn't
really understand what kind of accommodations are out in
the world."

"Well you aren't alone anymore."

I, for a moment, shrugged off his words, not
seeing the significance. However, I thought back to when
he invited me to the amusement park. A place where the
experience you had was based on what you felt. The wind
in your face, and then the lap bar rested against your thighs.

The smell of fireworks and the sound of music. Despite the chaotic environment that didn't offer much room for me to walk, I got to experience the attractions there. And the people. His friends, that I hoped to soon be able to call my own.

I laughed at him reaching out and finding his elbow. "You really are something else."

"What is that even supposed to mean?" He said as we began to walk away from the test exhibit and towards the lobby exit.

I shook my head and chuckled, wrapping my hand a bit tighter around his elbow. "It means I really don't know what colors I would paint you in."

He laughed, as we walked towards the first exhibit. "That doesn't help me understand any better."

I thought for a moment, stopping in my tracks to try and find the right words. "I just mean that, if I were to paint you, I don't know what color I'd paint you as. Because you aren't really just one color, but there isn't one color that I can see you as either."

I tried to think about the way I would explain to him. His raspy and kind voice and his warm skin. Whether I would carve lines or swirls into the canvas. Add glitter to the canvas or use metallic paint. I couldn't decide whether or not I would use everything to paint him, or nothing at all.

"Are you talking about auras or something?" He asked.

I shook my head. "To an extent? But it's more like, I'm trying to paint you in a way that'll show you the parts of yourself you can't see, but I don't know how I would do that."

He shook his head. "Yeah, I still don't think I understand."

I shrugged. "That's okay, making you understand wasn't really my goal anyways. I'm just rambling about the weird thoughts I have going on in my head."

We walked in silence for the remainder of the exhibit, and I was reminded of the bonfire. I wondered if painting it would offer me any sort of hint as to how it is that I would want to paint Monty. I hoped it would.

January 2nd, 2023

I walked into Mr. Collymore's room, no greeting needed from either me or the shadow at his desk. I just grabbed my apron, and sat at my easel silently. I grabbed a palette and a paint from underneath the easel and began to paint. I ran my fingers over the canvas, feeling the texture of the fabric and the sharp edges of the folded over corners. The strong smell of alcohol and oil filled the room. There was a slight breeze coming in from the right of my body, making the hair on my arms stand. There was probably a small crack in the window by Mr. Colleymore's desk, to ventilate the room while I worked with the oil paints.

I don't know how long I was painting for, but I know that the shadows casted by the sun grew longer as I continued to paint.

The watered down paint dripped down the canvas and onto the edge of the easel as I spread it across the surface with my hands. I felt the edge of the canvas, grabbing a bit of black paint in my hand and spreading it across the edge of it, giving the work a black frame to it.

Mr. Collymore stood up from his chair and I could hear his footsteps walking over to where I stood. He stayed quiet for a moment, not saying anything and just looking at the piece that I was working on.

I sat, waiting for what his thoughts would be about the piece. I was attempting to paint what I could not see. And he was there to talk with me as I did.

"It's pretty. What is it? Kind of looks like…" He paused, thinking. "Fire, maybe? Or even a sunset?"

I shook my head. "You were right the first time," I picked up the canvas, and tilted it, to see the shapes of the shadows casted by the excess amount of paint that remained piled onto its surface. "It's a bonfire."

"It looks lovely," He said.

"Thank you," I smiled, setting the canvas back down into the easel. "What color do you think I should use for my fingerprint?" I asked him.

He hummed for a moment, before tapping a bottle of paint against my hand. "I think white would stand out the most on this piece."

"What does the piece mean to you?" He asked.

I shrugged. "It's just something I saw one night. I hadn't seen fire quite like it." I think the thing that made the fire different was the company I was with when I sat in front of it. There was someone holding my hand, and I could feel the warmth in his hands, somehow it felt nicer than the warmth from the fire.

"I definitely think you got your meaning across."

I rolled my eyes. "You said you think it was a sunset."

"That was my second guess, thank you. Even if it was my first guess, would that have been a bad thing? It's abstract art, so it's going to be up for interpretation no matter what you do to it. For the person looking to be able to find their own meaning within the work."

I nodded, not bothering to tell him that I still wished I had the capabilities for painting things other than abstract art. I opened the bottle of paint and smudged some of the white paint onto my thumb, before pressing it into the top left corner of the canvas.

"Sonali," He started. "Have you considered art school?"

I took off my apron and folded it in my lap as I sat up on the stool in front of my easel. "I mean, I haven't not considered it. However I'm not quite sure I'd be able to do that. Most schools usually require a realism course, and I obviously can't do that."

"Well I was thinking of recommending you to apply to the Rhode Island School of Design. That's the school I went to, and I think you would really love it there if you went," He said. "I'd be able to help you with the application, send in a letter or recommendation, and even talk to the admin there and help assist you in getting in."

I shrugged. "I don't know, because if I apply, the chances of me getting in are high purely because of my blindness. I don't want to be accepted into the college if the only reason they did it was to improve their diversity rating, y'know?" asked. "Or because I talked my way in to the school through an alumni."

"I understand, but I really do think you would love it there. If you could at least give it some thought…?" He trailed off.

"Okay, I can do that," I nodded, knowing that for the most part, it was a lie.

"Amazing."

I could hear the smile in his voice, and it scared me a little bit. I didn't even know if going to college at all was something I wanted to do. He sounded so excited to hear me even just consider it, that I couldn't help but feel bad for deceiving him with a lie of false hope. The last thing I wanted to do was disappoint the teacher who has been supporting me for the past four years. Especially after he would stay after for multiple hours to help me relearn how to paint after my vision started to fade quicker.

"Sonali?" I turned, a shadow standing in the doorway. "I thought I heard you!"

I sat silently and thoughtlessly for a moment before I realized who it was. "Oh, hi Noah," I said standing up. "What are you doing here?"

"I just got out of the photography club," He said. "What are you doing here? I thought the art club meets on Mondays."

"They do, I just can't paint at home so sometimes I stay after to paint in here," I said.

"It's nice to see you Noah," Mr. Colleymore said, the sound of papers rustling filling the silence that was hanging awkwardly in the air. "It's been a while, I miss seeing you and your artwork in my classroom."

I turned. "You draw, Noah?"

"I used to."

"He was good too. He won a couple of awards with his works," Mr. Colleymore said. "But—"

"Ultimately I decided that it wasn't for me, despite Mr. Colleymore insisting upon the apparent natural talent I had for the skill."

I went to hang up my apron, before going over to the sink to wash my hands while Noah and Mr. Colleymore talked, catching up with each other like cousins meeting for the first time in years. I couldn't help but resent Noah for a moment, thinking about what he could've done if he had stuck with it. I had never seen his art, but if Mr. Colleymore spoke highly of it, then I'm sure he was good at it. I thought about how none of my art had won any awards at all.

"Have you applied for university yet?" Mr. Collymore asked.

"Nope, but I am applying to be a photographer's assistant once I graduate," Noah said.

"That's great," Mr. Collymore sighed. "I was worried you wouldn't be doing anything after you graduate."

Noah laughed, and so did I.

"What's so funny?" Mr. Collymore asked.

"It's just that Noah is the most future driven out of everyone in our group, I don't even know if anyone else we know has any sort of plans for the future at all," I said sitting back at my stool beside where Noah was perched.

Noah hummed, thinking. "I'm pretty sure Alaska wants to go school in Paris for fashion design or to intern under an already established designer." He paused. "Or something."

"That's cool," I said. "I had no idea that she had such big plans."

"You aren't the only one, Alaska keeps a lot to herself so it's no surprise that you wouldn't know."

My fingers felt tight, and I cracked my knuckles in my lap looking down at my hands. "It must be nice, knowing what you want to do with your life," I said. "I don't think I'm even ready to leave high school yet."

"I think you should do whatever it is that you want to do," Mr. Collymore said.

I rolled my eyes. "That's what every teacher says, and it's the least helpful thing ever."

"That and the 'where do you see yourself in five years?' question." Noah mimicked.

I watched Mr. Colleymore's shadow move across the room. "Sonali, do you want to do something with art in your future?"

I shrugged. "I don't know. I just don't wanna jinx myself."

"What do you mean?" Noah asked.

I shrugged, the room going silent.

Mr. Colleymore froze where he stood, and Noah didn't move from where he sat either.

"There's a chance I won't have any vision left, five years from now."

"There's a chance you will though?" Noah asked.

I shook my head. "Whether it's five years from now or ten years from now, I'll lose all of my vision eventually. It's just a matter of how soon I want to start figuring out what I'm going to be doing once it's all gone, or if I want to spend this time enjoying what I can still do with the little vision I have left."

The silence in the air was bitter, and I could tell the two of them were racking their brains trying to figure out what to say. Trying to figure out if they should encourage me to pursue what I can still see, or if they should encourage me to prepare for the future in which I know I won't be able to.

"Is there a reason you wouldn't be able to work with art after going completely blind?" Mr. Colleymore asked.

I stood up and started grabbing my things, wanting to leave the conversation that was becoming increasingly uncomfortable to be in. I unfolded my cane, and walked towards the door, stopping and standing in the door frame for a moment. "I just don't think it's realistic for me to think that it's possible for me to be successful, without any sort of vision at all." I paused, wondering if there was anything else that needed to be said. "I'll see you guys tomorrow, don't have too much fun without me."

I left the room silently, running my fingers through my hair, shaking.

January 5th, 2023

I sat at the table in the busy cafe, my cane sat between my legs as I waited for Alaska to get back from grabbing us menus. I twisted my hair in my fingers, thinking about what I had said to Noah and Mr. Colleymore. I wondered if maybe I had hurt them, or said something rude. But I couldn't help but feel I said what needed to be said, though it might not have been phrased as well as it could've.

"Here's the menu," Alaska said. I heard her tap the counter.

"Alaska I can't read it," I reached out to push the menu towards her, only to feel my fingertips brush against the subtle raised dots. I put both hands down on the menu, dragging my fingers across it. "Wait, this is braille." I looked up at Alaska. "But, why?"

"What do you mean why?"

"Well, because it's an inconvenience, even *I* hate doing it," I said as I continued to read the menu with my fingertips.

"I'm not doing anything out of the ordinary," She said. "I'm just making sure my friend is able to enjoy something with me properly. It's bare minimum behavior."

I thought for a moment, trying to piece together what she meant, before coming to the realization that maybe I had been surrounded by the wrong kinds of people for a while. "Right…" I said my voice trailing off as I started to focus more on what was on the menu.

"What did you want to talk about?" Alaska asked. "You said you wanted to ask something right?"

I nodded. "It's kind of a personal question though, so I don't know if—"

"Oh hush," Alaska said, her voice softening into a gentle tone. "Talk to me, what's going on?"

I took a deep breath, ready to rapid fire questions.

"Have you ever liked anyone?"

"Yes."

"How many people have you liked?"

"One."

"When?"

"It was in middle school."

"What happened to the person you liked?"

That question was met by silence. I heard Alaska's chair creak as she readjusted how she was sitting.

"She moved away." Alaska's tone was sad, and I wondered if maybe she was smiling despite the sound of her voice.

"How did you know you liked her?"

Alaska hummed for a moment. I heard the ice of her drink clink against the inside of her glass. "We hadn't been friends for that long, maybe a couple years or so. As time went on, I found myself wanting more. I liked talking to her, and I wasn't uncomfortable in our relationship. I was happy hanging out with her as we were, but I couldn't help but think I wanted more. I wanted to hold her hand, feel her rest her head on my shoulder. I wanted to hug more often. Eventually I found myself wanting to kiss her."

"Did you ever tell her?" I asked.

"Ah," Alaska said. "I didn't. She broke my trust."

I turned my thumbs around each other in my lap, trying to figure out what I wanted to ask next. "So, you lost feelings for her?"

She chuckled a bit, her voice sounding a bit empty. "I didn't. It's not that simple you know? I didn't want to be in a relationship with her anymore, because I first wanted to fix the one that had been broken."

I heard Alaska move in her seat, and I turned the rings around my fingers as she talked.

"It was partially my fault. One of the few times in my life I've spoken without thinking. I never got to make things right though. She moved away before I could get the chance. And now I have too much pride to admit my mistake to her face. And I can't apologize."

I reached out, trying to find Alaska's hand on the table. My fingertips brushed against hers, before placing my hand overtop. "I hope you get your chance Alaska."

She flipped her hand over and squeezed mine in hers. "Me too." She let go and pulled her hand out of mine, sitting back in her chair. "Alright then enough about me. Why were you asking about all of this?"

"Oh right," I said. "Monty told me he likes me. We

went on a date the other day, and it was nice. But I'm not completely sure if I like him or not."

"Can you explain a bit more?" Alaska asked.

"Well, he's nice to me, and it makes me feel embarrassed, and I feel like I can't really tell how much he likes me. But… I don't know. I think I might like him, but I don't know if my feelings are real and I like him. Or if I just like the way he feels towards me. Because, maybe I don't like him. What if I just don't want to be alone, so I've convinced myself that means I need to like him in order to maintain a relationship with him. If I lose him will I lose you too? Will I lose Noah and Leo? I'm afraid."

"Do you think he won't want to be your friend anymore if you don't like him romantically? Do you really think we won't talk to you if you don't?" Alaska asked.

I nodded.

Alaska sighed, and I was nervous that maybe she was upset that I didn't believe in him. "Monty isn't like that. He's gentle and caring and an old soul. More than anything he values you a lot as a person, and I don't think he would want to lose someone he values so much, just because his feelings might not be reciprocated. And I know that Leo, Noah, and I won't abandon you either just because of that. I definitely won't. I don't want to be the only girl in this friend group again."

I didn't respond, I sat quietly trying to figure out how I wanted to respond, and how it was that I felt. I put my face in my hands and sighed. "I *want* to like him. He's shown his feelings to me so sincerely. And it made me feel good inside. And he likes me. He likes me so, I want to like him."

Alaska shook her head putting her hand on it. my shoulder. "I know you do, but I'm sure that you also know that isn't fair to him."

"I'll have to tell him, won't I?" I asked.

Alaska nodded.

"I don't want to hurt him," I cried. "He introduced me to you and Leo and Noah. And he worked so hard to find something that I would enjoy. I wish with all he's done for me I could at least return his feelings, but they just aren't there."

"I know," I heard Alaska's chair scrape against the floor, and then I felt her arms around me, squeezing me tightly. "It sucks." Her voice came slightly above me as she spoke in a sympathetic tone.

I nodded, holding her arm against my chest. "Yeah, it really does."

After I talked with Alaska, we ate pastries at the cafe, and studied for our Latin test. I thought about Monty. His kindness. His sweet voice and the pretty words he would say. I thought about how tightly he held my hand. How warm his personality is.

I remembered my lonely days in the art room, where often I would go days without talking to anyone. I was content with being everyone's acquaintance. I would get lonely sometimes, but at the time I preferred it that way.

It had only been a few months, but I felt like this small circle of friends had become the people I wanted around me. They encouraged me endlessly. They reached out and welcomed me with the same warmth that Monty gave me. They kept each other in check unapologetically.

A kind of honesty I had been too afraid to be a part of. If I shared my hopes with them the way they shared them with each other, I think I'll be able to grow in a way that I haven't been able to previously. I wanted to change; and it was time for me to start.

January 10th, 2023

Sitting on the floor of the art room, I ran my fingertips over canvas. Each piece with different textures plastered across their surfaces. Despite having sensitive fingers, I couldn't ever feel the fingerprints I left in the corner of each of my pieces of art.

I had even brought paintings I had done at home, some from when I was younger and still had some sight left. Those ones had been folded and placed in sheet protectors, all stuffed away in the garage for safekeeping for my mom.

I took one out, and it felt like the paper would rip with the least amount of force, the creases of the paper weak and ready to tear. So I put it back in the sheet protector, wondering if there would come a day I could show these pieces to people.

Mr. Colleymore sat at his desk, and I could hear the clicking of keyboards as he typed. I sat surrounded by a mess of my own creation as I waited for the others to get to the art room.

Leo and Noah arrived together, and they sat down next to each other at the table beside where I sat on the floor.

"Are you okay, Sonali?" Noah said. "I'm sorry about the other day. I should've been more sensitive about it."

I shook my head. "Don't be. I think you gave me the push I needed."

"I pushed you?" He said.

"I'm here!" I heard Alaska's voice echo from the door, and then the sound of footsteps getting closer to me. I looked up, seeing a shadow tower over me.

I stood up and sat at the same table with Noah and Leo, Alaska taking a seat beside me.

"What's this big mess?" She laughed. "There's paintings everywhere."

"That is a lovely question," Mr.Colleymore added as I heard the sound of his chair rolling over to the table.

I locked my fingers together on the table in front of

me. "I wanted your guy's help with something.

"I've been thinking a lot recently. About you guys, and about the future. About the conversation we had in the art room the other day," I said, gesturing to Noah and Mr. Colleymore. "I'm going to do it. Pursue art, I mean. Specifically, I want to teach it. I can't exactly do much about my sight, so I'm not sure how it'll go when I try but if I can, I want to teach art to kids.

"So," I said, gesturing to the mess around me. "I need to put together a portfolio, and I wanted to ask you guys to help me decide which pieces to put in it."

I turned to Mr. Colleymore. "And I wanted to ask you to help me with my application to the Rhode Island School of Design."

"I can definitely do that," He said. I could hear it in the way he spoke, that he was smiling. I didn't need sight to know that.

"Of course we'll help!" Alaska exclaimed, throwing her arms around me. "I'm super proud of you! This is exciting!"

"Yeah!" Leo said. "I don't know much about art like Alaska or Noah, but I'll help out best I can."

Alaska laughed, squeezing me tightly. "Leo, I can only draw clothes. I don't even draw their bodies, I use pre drawn model paper for designing."

"Yeah, and I gave up art a few years ago," Noah added.

I laughed, happy to be sitting at this table with these people. I was a little sad, at the fact that I couldn't share this moment with Monty, but I had to talk to him separately, and unfortunately have yet to have the chance to.

All I could do was cross my fingers. Cross my fingers, and do what I could to mold together my own future.

January 15th, 2023

I sat outside on the curb of the parking lot. Monty and I had decided to meet up after he had art club, and then his sister would take me home after. My fingertips were numb from the cold, and I was hyper aware of the group of kids I could hear a few yards away from me. They were loud, and seemed a bit rowdy. I wondered if they were listening in or if they were just gossiping to themselves. There was a slight breeze, and the air smelled damp, the way it would after it had rained.

I had my cane set between my legs, and my backpack was at my side while I waited for him. I had checked my phone a bit ago, and the art club should be getting out soon. Trying to distract myself from the yelling of the group of teenagers, I started to think of what I was going to say. How I would properly express to him all of the feelings I had.

I wanted to express my emotions just as sincerely as he had expressed them to me. I struggled a bit, wondering if it was even something I was capable of doing.

There was a gentle tap on my shoulder, and I turned as someone sat beside me.

"Hey, Sonali."

The yelling from the teenagers faded as I focused in on his voice.

"Hi, Monty," I said. "I'm sorry it took me so long to be able to talk to you. I was thinking about things. A lot."

He hummed, a light chuckled floating through the air. "Yeah, I did a good amount of thinking myself as well. And I'm glad we were able to schedule this because I needed to talk to you too."

"Oh, did you want to go first then?" I asked.

"No, I think that it should be you." He said.

I swallowed, my throat suddenly dry. I squeezed my hand around the handle of my cane, trying to steady my breathing. "That's a little scary," I chuckled. "It's kind of hard to say."

"We met up for a reason. I won't go anywhere so," I felt him nudge the hand I had resting next to me with his, not necessarily holding it, but simply putting his hand beside mine, our pinkies touching. "Take your time."

I nodded, taking another few deep breaths to prepare myself.

"So, first, I want to say thank you. You shared your feelings with me, and put in the effort to show me a planetarium that I could see. The ceiling sparkled like glitter. I haven't seen something that could shine so brightly and not hurt my eyes at the same time. The experience meant a lot to me." I paused, turning to look at him. "You mean a lot to me. I had been planning on accepting your feelings. But I came to the realization that I don't like you romantically. You liked me, and that was what I liked. Not you but instead the feelings you had for me. I wanted to like you so badly. But, I just can't." My voice dropped to a whisper the more I talked.

I heard him sigh, and shut my eyes waiting for his reaction.

"I was worried you were going to say you liked me back," He said.

"What?" I said, turning back to look at him.

"Don't get me wrong!" He exclaimed. "I do like you, but I think I mixed up how I thought I felt with how I actually feel. I thought I had feelings for you romantically, but I had talked with Savannah, and realized that wasn't really what it was. I admired you. Idolized even. You were a miracle story to me. You created beautiful and interactive art that I never could. All without sight. I put you on this pedestal without realizing it. I thought you were extraordinary for being able to paint without sight. But then I got closer to you. I learned that I had been treating you all wrong. You were never a miracle, you were only ever just human. I don't think I ever properly saw you for who you are. But I want to.

I'm sorry. Not only for not being able to see you properly, but also for playing with your feelings just because I didn't know mine."

I sat in silence for a moment, trying to properly absorb everything he had told me. I exhaled the breath I had forgotten I was holding. "I'm so relieved. I didn't want to hurt you with my response."

"And I didn't want to hurt you with my revelation."

I started to laugh, and he laughed with me. I was curling in on myself, but still my hand rested besides his.

"I guess, both of us need to pay attention to our own feelings better. And learn from it." I said. "I still want to be your friend."

"Me too." I heard the sound of a zipper. "And I also wanted to give you this. It was only after I realized how I felt, but I was finally able to do a portrait of you."

I held my hands out, and he placed a heavy canvas in my hands. It was small, but I could tell there was a lot on it purely by the weight of it. I placed my hand over the piece, finding raised lines across it.

"There's puffy paint, and then, I know you can't see with your sunglasses on, but it's a portrait of you with flowers blooming from your eyes. The background is a light blue, and I used gold leaf to make the clouds shine."

I brushed my hand against the petals that were sticking up from the canvas.

"I know you said you could see metallics, so when you're inside you might be able to see that I used gold paint to draw tears. I haven't seen you cry before, it was what completed the piece. It's like, I painted you in your most human form."

"Monty, it's beautiful." I said, gently holding it to

my chest. "Thank you for everything."

"And thank you."

I held out my hand to him, his painting in the other. "Friends?" I asked him.

He took his hand in mine, holding it in his beside us rather than shaking it like I thought he would do. "Friends."

I squeezed his hand tightly in mine, all of the anxiety washing away from my body. I felt like I had a storm bottled inside me, and the glass had finally shattered, revealing a rainbow instead of dark clouds.

I sat silently with him, holding hands in the parking lot of our high school. I was scared of the future, but excited to discover the colors it might hold. Knowing it was all so uncertain how things would turn out, I could only really hope for one thing. That I would end up here again, as the world around me changed. Hoping that whatever future I ended up having, he would be a part of, one way or another.

Timeless

Leo

<u>Timeless (Leo)</u>

October 8th, 2022

My first love was a collection of messy feelings for a messy person. I don't think he ever properly brushed his hair, he would just comb his fingers through it and let it fluff up on its own. He had the world in his eyes, the fade from the yellowish green by his pupils to the dark brown on the outer edge of his iris looked like the Earth was reflecting in his eyes. He had broad shoulders and the build of an athlete, but he never exercised.

He didn't have any confidence in anything but his photography, and he always felt more comfortable in a jacket and jeans than anything I would try and get him to wear.

The amusement park was full of the clattering of roller coaster carts and the squealing of children. You could smell different foods depending on where you were in the park. I could smell funnel cake. I sat with Allie, while the others had gone up to order lunch.

Noah had a nervous habit of hiding his face and avoiding eye contact, like the way he was doing now as he read Sonali the menu at the counter. He had his face in the menu, looking everywhere but in Sonali's eyes.

He was uncomfortable around new people, and he has never had a good grasp on understanding the emotions of others. He doesn't understand his own feelings either, and he made a habit of using me as an armrest when he was nervous. All things I've learned throughout the past four years of knowing him.

When we first met, I thought, *I'll get over him eventually.* But here we are, four years later and his smile still makes my breath get caught in my throat.

And despite my efforts to get over him, nothing worked. I've tried avoiding him, but I couldn't help but find myself back at his side. I tried dating other people, multiple times. It never worked. I wondered if things would work out if I tried by starting a physical relationship, but that wouldn't work either. I tried that more times than I can count, and the only thing that that taught me was that hook-up culture sucks, and the idea that "the only way to get over someone is to get under someone else," is a big fat lie. So instead I just put the feelings I have into a box, and do what I can to forget that they are there.

I could feel Allie's gaze on me, the sunlight reflecting off the lens of her glasses. Her hair was pulled back and she smiled softly as we sat at the table waiting for the others to get back with our lunch. Her looking at me, and me looking at him.

"You can't keep pretending that your feelings for him aren't real," She paused. "You're hurting people when you use them to push your own emotions down. You can't keep kissing other people pretending that they're him. Watching you hurt both others and yourself the way you are is really starting to get on my nerves."

I turned to her and smiled. "I wish you would stop meddling in my relationships,"

"And I wish you would stop getting into them without thinking. You're smart enough to know that what you're doing isn't good for you so why do you keep doing it?" She asked. She looked desperate. Searching for some sort of logical explanation in my facial expression.

"I don't have any particular reason. I just," I was a liar, I did have a reason but she didn't need to know that. "I guess I just like being free to flirt and sleep with whomever I like whenever I like, without having to think about my feelings too much."

"And that's exactly your problem," Allie said. "You're hurting people, they feel like you're toying with them and not taking their emotions seriously. I hadn't said anything till now, but this last time you hurt one of my friends from my marketing class. It's one thing if you and whoever you're with establish that it's just physical, but recently you really haven't been doing that. They genuinely had feelings for you, but to you it was just a game, something to distract yourself with."

I sat for a moment in silence, thinking, my gaze falling back onto Noah, Sonali, and Monty. "I told him that it wouldn't be serious. It's his fault for getting his feelings involved."

Allie huffed, snapping her fingers in my face. "Seriously! Look at me when I'm talking to you. I'm trying to have a serious conversation about your bad habits, and you can't stop gawking at the boy that you claim not to have feelings for."

I looked at Allie, before putting my face in my hands with a sigh. "But, I just…"

Allie sighed. "Listen, I'm sorry for snapping at you," She scooted closer to where I was sitting and put her hand on my shoulder. "But you're being an asshole with the way you end up treating the people you're supposed to be dating. It really sucks to watch because I know you're not a bad person, but others don't know that. So, please. Figure it out."

She stood up, and I watched her as she ran off over to the others, to help them carry the trays of food back over to the picnic bench where I sat with all of our things. I rolled my eyes at the way she lectured me, treating me like I wasn't able to make my own decisions.

Without fail, my eyes fell back onto Noah. He carried two trays of food and Sonali walked with a hand on his elbow and a drink in the other. Monty walked beside them, struggling to carry three drinks. My eyes always fell back onto Noah.

"Here's your food Leo," He said, setting the tray down in front of me.

"Oh, thanks," I said, averting my gaze.

He kept his eyes on me as he set the other tray down. "Here, Sonali, you can sit on my left, here," He said, guiding her hand to the table.

"Awesome, thank you," She said, breaking down her cane and putting it back into its drawstring bag.

"Leo, are you okay?" He asked, filling in the space between Sonali and me.

I looked up and smiled at him. "I'm perfectly fine,"

"Are you sure?" He asked again, raising an eyebrow.

I nodded, finding myself unable to find my words again.

"If you're sure," He said.

I sat silently, listening to my friends chat about pointless things while we ate. I didn't say a word, till we had all finished and everyone started throwing away their trash and putting up their trays.

"Since Noah bought everyone lunch, I'll buy everyone dinner after we leave the amusement park, how does that sound, y'all?"

"I won't turn down a free meal," Allie said, nudging Sonali with her elbow.

"Sure," Sonali said, hooking onto Allie's elbow and unfolding her cane.

"If we have the time, sure," Monty said. "Though at that point Savannah might want to come too."

"And as long as you're okay with it," Noah said.

"Yeah, I'm fine with it," I said. "So long as I don't have to pay for her."

"What do you guys want to do next?" Monty asked as we started walking.

"Can we go to the arcade?" Allie asked. I smiled. Though she hated to admit it, Allie showed the most interest in games then the rest of us ever did.

"I actually wanted to go ride more coasters," Sonali said.

"I don't really care what we do, but I want to make sure we see the fireworks show before we leave," Noah said walking ahead.

"Want to split up?" I asked.

"Nah, let's stick together," Allie said. "It'll be more fun."

"Let's start heading to the arcade and we can ride any of the coasters that we pass on the way there for Sonali, how does that sound?" Monty said.

"Sounds good," Noah said.

I listened to them discuss what to do, where to go, and in what order while keeping quiet and turning my thumbs around each other in front of me. I wasn't the biggest amusement park enjoyer, so I was content just hanging out with everyone.

As we were walking, I noticed a girl from my school sitting on a bench. I looked forward, and having already gotten behind the group, I decided to take a detour.

Her hair was pulled back into a long ponytail that

fell over her shoulder. She looked up from her phone and we made eye contact as I went to sit beside her, a confused look on her face.

"Hey! You go to Summerville right?" I tried my best to start a conversation, hoping she would respond well to it. "I go there too, I think I've seen you before."

She nodded, raising an eyebrow. "I go to Summerville, yeah. What about it?"

"I was just wondering that's all." I ran my fingers through my hair and assumed the persona of someone who knew what they were doing. "You're in my oceanography class right?"

She looked at me for a moment, her eyes squinting as she looked at me. "I don't know? Maybe?"

"Well even if you haven't seen me I've definitely seen you. I think you're really pretty, and I was wondering if we could hang out sometime together." I threw on my best smile, my chest tightening slightly.

"Leo!"

I thought I had heard Noah's voice, but I always think that. I'm sure I was imagining it, just like I always was.

"Leo!"

This time I looked up, to see him standing a few yards away, with his arms crossed in front of him and an angry look on his face.

"I guess it's time for me to go," I sighed standing up. "You don't have to give me an answer, but I'll be around if you want to hangout."

She stood up and rolled her eyes as I walked backwards towards Noah, hoping for a favorable response from the girl.

"If you paid any attention when you saw me around school, you would know that I'm taken!" She yelled. "And a lesbian!"

I could feel my face heating up, and I didn't know how to react, so I just turned around and didn't say anything else as I walked over to where Noah stood.

Once I got to where he was, he started walking, I assumed so we could get back together with the others. As we walked, I couldn't help but find myself thinking about how close his hand was to mine, and how easy it would be to hold.

"Why are you always hitting on people?" He sighed.

I shrugged, not really wanting to answer the question he had asked, afraid that the truth might come out of my mouth instead of the made up answer that I would tell everyone who asked the same question.

Noah nudged me with his elbow, his jaw set tensely and a crease forming between his eyebrows. "Are you sure you're okay? Like, really?" He asked again.

I couldn't help but laugh at him. He was oblivious to the emotions of strangers, but he could always tell when Allie or I were upset. Both she and I are the two people closest to him, always with our hearts in plain view on our sleeves. "I promise you, I'm fine," I said. "What about you? Are you good? I know you're not good with strangers so I was wondering how things were going with Sonali,"

He shrugged. "It was a little awkward at first, but she's nice, and Monty likes her, so I'm not too uncomfortable."

"That's good."

He nodded. I walked in silence next to him, tensing up every time our arms brushed against each other, being reminded that if I wanted to, I could grab his hand in mine. The screams of little kids filled the air. I could smell smoke and funnel cake along with the clanking of roller coaster carts as they zoomed past us as we walked through the amusement park.

"The others went to go ride the roller coaster already, did you want to go?" He asked as we came to a ride entrance. "I'm holding everyone's stuff if you want to."

I shook my head. "Nah, I'll pass," because I would much rather spend time sitting with Noah than sitting in the uncomfortable seat of a metal death trap. But I would never tell the others that.

I sat with Noah on the park bench, waiting by the fence of the roller coaster that the others had gone to ride.

I looked at him and he smiled at his phone, and that familiar feeling of my breath getting caught in my throat found its way back to me.

"Hey, Noah?" I asked.

He looked up. "Yeah? What's up?"

"I like you, that's all," I smiled.

He stared, and I looked down begging for him to say something. Anything.

"Thanks, I like you too." He said looking back down at his phone. "I'm really glad we're friends, y'know?"

I sighed, chuckling. "Yeah, *friends*," I tried to hide the disappointment in my voice as I said, "I'm glad too."

December 27th, 2022

I couldn't focus on the conversations happening around the circle, as people spun the bottle. I could only think about my idiocy and what it felt like to finally kiss him after four years. I couldn't help but wonder if I would have kept my feelings a secret if he wasn't straight. Alcohol made it so much easier to do the things that scared me.

Allie sat beside me on the couch, downing a bottle of vodka without any thought, and giggling at nothing.

"I don't know what you did to Noah, but he's sitting with Sonali and Monty out by your bonfire looking like a lost puppy," She said, flopping over into my lap.

"Allie, not now," I said, pushing her off of me. "I'm trying to think."

"Think about what? How you just messed this boy up in the head?" She flopped over again leaning against me, taking another drink from the bottle of vodka.

I pulled the bottle out of her hands, sighing. "You need to stop drinking, you're such a lightweight," I said, setting the bottle down on the nightstand. "Go get some water."

"No, I don't wanna," She whined.

I sighed and stood up in front of her. "Too bad, let's go."

I pulled her to her feet, and grabbed her shoulders, guiding her into the kitchen.

After making sure she was able to find the water, I opened the back deck and looked out to where Sonali, Monty, and Noah sat by the bonfire.

Sonali sat to Monty's right, her head resting on his shoulder. Noah sat to Monty's left, leaning forward in his chair with his elbows on his knees and his head in his hands, while Monty rubbed his back sympathetically.

I was on my way to the door when I felt someone fall into my back. I turned to find Allie with a can of beer.

I sighed and grabbed it from her hands, pouring it out into the nearby plant. "Seriously we didn't get that much alcohol where do you keep finding it?"

She wasn't saying anything coherent, just laughing without any real meaning to it. I pulled her arm around my neck and wandered through my house trying to find a chaperone for her while I went to grab Noah for cake.

Sitting at a table there was a girl with faded pink hair wearing one of the cheer team jackets. I walked over to her and tried to pull Allie off from around my neck.

"Hey, you're the new transfer, Titania, right?" I

asked.

She nodded. "What's up? Do you want me to leave? I know I wasn't formally invited or anything, one of the cheer team members dragged me here against my will. I'm really sorry," She said, standing up and grabbing her jacket from the back of her chair.

"No no, I really don't care about that," I said, pulling Allie from around my neck and draping her over Ita's shoulders. "I just really need someone to make sure my friend gets home safe, and all of the cheer team members are amazing so I'm trusting you by default cause I can't find anyone else."

"Wait! Don't just leave me here!" She called.

"Sorry! But I really have to go! Thanks a bunch!" I said running out of the kitchen.

I went out the back door, down the steps, and over to the bonfire.

"Hey, you guys!" I exclaimed. Noah looked up at me, before immediately looking away. "It's time to do cake and sing happy birthday. So, you guys should come inside."

Monty looked between Noah and me, as I stood there waiting awkwardly.

"Sonali is asleep, so I'm going to stay out here," Monty said, wrapping an arm around Sonali's shoulders. "But you should go with Leo," Monty said, nodding at Noah. "It's your birthday party after all."

Noah glared at Monty and stood up, looking everywhere but my face as he followed me inside the house. He lagged behind me, almost like he was afraid of walking beside me. Getting a bit impatient, I grabbed his wrist and pulled him into the kitchen where people had already started to gather.

I let go of his arm leaving him standing by the dining room table. I went to pull the cake out of the freezer and placed it on the table, lighting the candles. "Let's sing happy birthday! Ready? One, two, three, go!"

My friends began to sing happy birthday to Noah, and I stood beside him, not being able to take my eyes off of him, as he stared intently at the napkins on the table. His face was flushed, and he looked uncomfortable with me beside him.

I looked away and took a step to the side to give him more room, but I felt him grab my hand. Pulling me back to where I was originally standing beside him.

I looked down at our hands, then up at him. Despite his actions, he still wasn't looking at me. But his face was red all the way up to his ears, and he wasn't pushing me away or punching me. I thought that he would never want to see or talk to me ever again after what I pulled mere hours prior. But rather than hating me, it seemed like what I did might have affected him in a different way. He looked flustered.

"Don't be a coward and get cold feet now," He mumbled.

I chuckled to myself at the face he was making, while squeezing his hand and setting my head on his shoulder.

And for the first time since we kissed earlier that night, he looked me in the eyes. "I'm ready to hear it," He said. "I'm not going to run away from your feelings."

I couldn't help but smile at his words. And I wondered to myself why it took me so long to make a move.

December 28th, 2022

I sat at the dining room table, across from Noah. We had barely spoken since we woke up this morning. I made omelets while he slept, thinking so much I gave myself a headache. I watched him eat them, his gaze not leaving his plate for even a second. I couldn't focus on the lunch I had made for us, so I sat in silence tracing the grooves of the wooden table. I didn't know how to bring it up, and I didn't know what to do. I wanted to disappear. I felt like I didn't have the right to show my face to him. I wanted to do exactly what he told me not to. I wanted to be a coward. Tell him that I was too smashed to remember anything that happened the night before.

I wanted to forget that the kiss ever happened. I wasn't prepared for this conversation. I never thought this would be a conversation I was having and now here I was, facing the consequences of my stupid drunk actions. I wanted to put the feelings I had been keeping back in the box that I had locked them in so long ago.

"Hey, Noah?" I asked.

He flinched at my words and froze for a moment before looking up at me. "Yeah?"

"About last night," I started. "I think it would be best to just forget about it. I don't want me kissing you to have any sort of influence on your feelings about me."

I heard his chair scrape against the floor as he stood up slamming his hands on the table. "You're kidding right?" He pleaded. "Of course the kiss is going to affect me. My best friend kissed me, at a party, drunk, on my birthday." He paused, before speaking quietly. "I mean, I didn't hate it when you kissed me. In fact I kind of liked it. So, of course it's going to affect me."

I swallowed and fiddled with the napkin in my lap, unable to look up. "I just don't want to mess anything up," I whispered.

He walked around the table over to where I sat. "But Leo, I—"

He got cut off by the sound of the garage door opening.

I heard the door slam shut, and the footsteps walking from the kitchen over to the dining room. My younger brother Felix ran up to me and jumped into my lap.

"Leo! Leo! The concert Mommy and Daddy took me to was so much fun!" He exclaimed, throwing his hands in the air. "You should have come with us."

My mom and Emmett— my stepdad— turned the corner and gave me a smile. "I don't think Leo would have liked going to a concert for a little kids show," Emmett chuckled, pulling Felix out of my lap.

"Plus, he wanted to stay here and celebrate Noah's birthday," My mom said, putting a hand on Noah's shoulder. "Did you have a good birthday?"

Noah smiled and looked at my mom. "I had a great birthday. Thank you for asking Mrs. Colm, Leo planned a great birthday for me," He said. "Though, he is being a bit selfish right now. He won't take me to get ice cream like he said he would last night," Noah said, shooting me a glare.

"Wait, when did I promise that?" I asked, raising an eyebrow.

Emmett frowned at me, and so did Felix while my mom looked between Noah and I with a confused look on her face. "Now, Leo, you know better than to go back on a promise."

"Was it a pinky promise?" Felix asked tugging on the hem of Noah's shirt.

"I don't remember any—" I tried to say.

Noah nodded, answering Felix but ignoring my previous question and interrupting me. "Yeah, it was a pinky promise."

Felix looked at me with tearful eyes. "Leo, you can't break a pinky promise."

"But I didn't."

My mom took off her jacket and set it over one of the dining room chairs. "You should go take Noah for ice cream since you told him you would," She said.

I didn't remember telling Noah we would go for ice

cream, and the smirk on his face was giving away that he was indeed lying. But my parents didn't seem to notice.

"We're home now so you don't have to worry about watching the house. Take Emmett's car, and I'll take care of your dishes once we unpack, okay?" She said, grabbing the suitcase that was at her side and walking to the stairs.

"You know the rules," Emmett said, putting Felix down and going towards the stairs with my mom. "Just be home by eleven, alright?"

"Kay, thanks Emmett," I sighed and stood up grabbing Noah's arm. "C'mon, lets go," I mumbled, pulling him towards the kitchen and out the garage door.

I let go after I shut the garage door behind us. I turned to look at him, and elbowed him in the side. "That was a dirty trick,"

Noah shrugged. "You're trying to avoid talking about the kiss. After you told me not to let you regret doing it."

"I was *drunk*," I said, getting into the driver's side of Emmett's car.

"You were not *that* drunk," Noah paused, getting in the car and putting on his seat belt. "I mean, you were drunk enough, but I've seen you be much worse too."

"Whatever," I mumbled, starting the car and driving out of the garage.

"You told me you would tell me how you feel," He pestered. "So, stop avoiding it. I want to know how you feel."

I didn't respond, I just ignored all of what he said and kept driving, till we arrived at the ice cream shop a few minutes from my house.

I parked the car and took off my seatbelt, but neither of us bothered to get out of the car.

"Just talk to me," Noah said. "I can't do anything if you don't talk to me."

I sighed and turned to him, his usually warm were greyer than usual, matching the weather around us as it started to rain.

I sighed, deciding to just get it over with. Knowing his stubbornness, he would keep me here all night if that's what it took. "Okay, so I like you," I could feel my heart trying to rip itself out of my chest, and my lungs felt like they were about to pop like balloons.

"And I have liked you, for a while. For a few years now. I didn't say anything because as far as I know, you're straight."

I looked over at Noah, to see him staring with a serious look on his face.

"I was content just being your friend. I was content watching you take pictures, and laughing with Monty and Allie. I was content staying a step behind you just so I could watch you existing." I said. "I didn't want to ask for anything more, I saw no reason to do so, because I was comfortable with the way things were. But, I ruined that last night, so I'm sorry."

He didn't respond, he just stayed quiet, and I could feel myself starting to recede into my body, trying to hide within my own skin instead of living in it.

"I never really saw you as my friend," Noah started. Before I could have the chance to ask what he meant, he started to explain. "I mean, I didn't treat you the same way I treated Allie and Monty, or even now, Sonali. I've just never put you in the same categories as our friends. I felt weird whenever you bounced around relationships, for whatever reason it hurt me to see you with other people. And I preferred hanging out with you alone then in a group, unlike the others"

I watched him play with the chain of his necklace as he talked, my heart beating so fast I feared he could hear it.

" For a while, I didn't really know what you did

mean to me, I just knew you meant something different and that was all I really needed. I thought I was just closer with you than anyone else." He looked up and smiled at me. "And then you kissed me, and all of the pieces came together. It was like you opened my eyes. Everything clicked. I never considered the idea that I had feelings for you, but I developed them without even realizing it. It was like you set off a chain reaction. I thought, 'Oh, this is what that feeling is then.' You helped me realize what the feelings I had were called."

I looked at him, and I couldn't help but struggle to believe what he was saying. "So, are you saying that you have feelings for me?" I asked.

He nodded. "I think I always have, I just didn't know it," He grabbed my hands. "Listen, if you want to stay friends after this, that's okay, and I'll respect that. And I know it might not be ideal dating me, considering that I don't even know what my sexuality is," He paused as if those words had finally hit him. "I don't know what my sexuality is, but I do know that I like you. And I liked it when you kissed me. If that's enough for you, I don't want to go back to being *just* friends," He said. He looked down at our hands and nervously opened his fingers, intertwining them with mine.

I squeezed his hand and put one hand on his cheek, turning his gaze up to me. His face was hot, and my hands were shaking. "I don't think I want to go back to being just friends either, that is if you'll have me."

He put his hand over mine, holding it to his cheek. "So are we dating now then?" He asked.

I nodded in disbelief. "I guess we are." *Wow.*

"So, can I kiss you?" He said.

I stared at him, my ears burning. "Yea—"

He leaned forward and pressed his lips to mine, grabbing the back of my neck and wrapping his other arm around me. Despite all the uncertainty that awaited in our newly found relationship, there was one thing I was sure of. He kissed me, and it was a feeling that I never wanted to stop experiencing.

January 5th, 2023

I talked a big game of keeping my relationship with Noah a secret till whenever he was ready, and I was still going to hold true to that, but it didn't stop me from wanting to shout it from the rooftops. I wanted everyone to know what I spent so long not talking about. I wanted to finally be able to express my feelings about him to everyone and make sure that everyone knew.

But despite wanting that, I also liked this secret romance between the two of us. It was like trying to contain the light underneath a blanket.

"Leo!" My counselor exclaimed. "Pay attention!"

I sighed and put my elbows on his desk, setting my chin in my hands. "What?" I mumbled.

Ms. Saxe rubbed the bridge of her nose with her thumb and index finger, letting out a heavy sigh and handing me another sheet of paper. "Okay, I'll send you an email with *another* list of scholarships to go over and apply to. Can you do that for me?" She asked. "You need to look at this stuff since you won't have much help from family."

"Fine," I said, taking the piece of paper and standing up. "Are we done here?"

"Yes, go back to class, and please email me back with any questions you might have alright?" She pleaded.

I didn't respond, just walked out of her office and back to my class, the sun reflecting against the hallway floors creating spotlights of dust that floated in the air.

I walked back into my classroom, and set back down next to Monty, putting my lab glasses back on.

"What did Ms. Saxe want you for this time?" He

asked, using an eyedropper to mix two chemicals on a laminated sheet of paper.

I shook my head while putting on my gloves. "Just more college stuff."

"That's good then right?" He showed me the paper.

"I mean, sure, but I don't even know if I want to go to college," I wrote the reaction caused by the chemicals down on the paper in front of me. "It's a scam anyways so what's the point?"

"I guess that's true," Monty said.

We sat in silence for a bit, working through the chemistry lab quickly as we sat at the counter by the window. When we finished the lab, I sat quietly staring at the clouds in the sky behind the glass. I tried my best to make out any of the possible shapes that were there, but it was almost impossible when the clouds were laid out like a grey blanket across the sky.

"So, hypothetically," Monty began. I turned to him, raising an eyebrow. It was a habit of his to ask 'hypothetical' questions. Everytime he did I easily deciphered what he was actually trying to say. "If there was someone you liked, and they didn't necessarily say they liked you, but said you could go on a date, and then the date went well, but now you're stuck wondering whether or not that means you're in a relationship, what would you do?"

I smirked, a certain someone that he was probably thinking about coming to mind. "Well," I said, pausing dramatically. "Hypothetically, I would do my best to give them space to think. Just because you go on a date with someone, it doesn't mean you're dating. She's probably trying to figure things out for herself. Give her time."

Monty sat quietly, looking at his lap and twisting his hands within each other.

"I like Sonali," He said.

"I know."

"Wait, what? How did you know?" He said, his eyes widening.

I looked him up and down, sitting back in the chair and crossing my arms. "Well, you aren't exactly the most secretive person. You have a really bad poker face too and anyone who looked at you would be able to see that."

"I know I'm bad at hiding stuff but I didn't know I was that bad at it."

"I'm surprised you didn't know how obvious you are," I said.

I thought for a moment, remembering how I watched them stumble among each other at the amusement park in November as Monty learned how to use a sighted guide.

"I know you want her to know how much you like her, and I know that you want to spend time with her cause you're friends, but even then it might be hard on her."

He nodded. "I'm just worried about it seeming like I'm trying to sway her decision one way or another. I don't want her to feel pressured by my advances or lack thereof."

"Well, that is definitely a problem," I looked around the room, then back to Monty scanning him for any sort of clue as to what he could do to win her heart. "Hm… I'm really sorry Monty. You could ask her what she wants from you until she figures out her feelings, but that might upset her too. I honestly think you're just going to have to live with the discomfort for a little bit. I've been a bit of a flirt so, you know I'm not exactly fit for actual relationship advice."

"I know that," He said, jabbing me in the elbow. "Just wanted to see what kind of advice you could give."

"Everyone start packing up the bell is going to ring in one minute!" The teacher exclaimed.

I rolled my eyes and elbowed him back. "Are you satisfied then?"

He nodded standing up and grabbing our papers to go hand them over to the teacher. "I am. You give good advice. I think I know what to do now."

He went to give our papers to the teacher, and then right afterward, left the room without a second glance. I admired him for being able to just tell people about his feelings and even ask for their opinions on them. All I wanted was to be able to at least hold his hand in front of our friends, but I couldn't do that, and despite how much it hurt I was going to do my best to make sure that what happened to me never happened to him.

I left class and started walking down to my next class. I could feel butterflies buzzing in my chest knowing that I would be able to see Noah as I walked down this hall. I usually found him at his locker with a blank face. And when I saw exactly that, I couldn't help but smile.

I walked up behind him, and put my hands over his eyes, making him jump.

"Guess who?" I laughed.

He grabbed my hands and pulled them away from his face. He turned around and rolled his eyes with a small smile on his face. "Hi Leo."

I pulled him in for a quick hug, the way I always would, and his whole body tensed up in my arms. When I pulled away I felt a stab of pain in my chest as his eyes darted around us, checking to see if there just so happened to be anyone watching.

Instead of a wandering eye from a stranger, we were met by Allie throwing her arms over both of our shoulders with a loud groan.

"The day is almost over," She sighed. "I just want to go home."

"Agreed," I said. "Don't you have that cheer thing after school today?" I asked.

Allie scowled, her expression going dark. "Don't remind me," She mumbled, looking away. "You know who is going to be there."

"I'm sorry again Allie for what happened," I sighed. "I didn't know that Ita, the girl you knew from middle school, and Titania, the new transfer, were the same person."

She shrugged, trying to brush it off. "It's whatever, I would have met her eventually when the competition cheer season started. It was inevitable."

Noah nodded. "Is it hard seeing her after all of this time?"

"Harder than you could possibly know," Allie said. She let go of our shoulders after a quick squeeze. "I gotta go, I'll see you guys later, bye!" She said before walking away.

"See you!" I said.

Noah waved goodbye and shut his locker turning to me. "Ready to go?"

I nodded. "We have our playing test today right?" I asked.

Noah sighed. "Don't remind me, there's no way I'll pass. I haven't practiced outside of class all winter break," He said.

"You'll be fine," I said.

The conversation fell quiet as we walked to Philharmonic Orchestra, and I couldn't help but look down, his hand swinging with mine. I wanted to grab his hand. It was a different kind of wanting than before. Before I was longing for something that was so far out of reach from me. It wasn't just about me wanting to hold his hand. It was about the relationship that I wanted with him that would allow me to hold his hand and now I have that relationship with him. Holding his hand is something both physically and emotionally within my grasp. And despite how much it hurt not to, I knew that I would be able to hold it when I gave him a ride home today, so I just let out a sigh and waited patiently for those last two hours of school to pass.

January 8th, 2023

I walked up to the front porch of Noah's house, and paced in a small circle. I wasn't sure if I should text Noah to tell him I was here, or if I should knock. Usually I would just text him, but this time it's a date, and I wanted to conduct myself in a way befitting of that. I wiped the sweat from my hands and knocked on the door, it immediately being opened by Noah's Pa.

"Leo!" He exclaimed, holding the door open for me to come in. "Hi, how are you doing?" He asked, hugging me.

"I'm doing well, thank you!" I said. "It's nice to see you again."

I looked around Noah's house, it looked the same as the last time I had visited. The only thing seemingly different is the absence of Noah's moms blanket that would sit on the couch whenever she came back home to visit.

I heard a yelp and a loud thud, before Noah came stumbling down the hallway. "Hi!" He said. He ran his hands through his hair and stood by the hallway, not moving to come over to where I stood, just standing stiffly by the door.

I smiled. His hair was messy and his face was flushed. "Are you okay? What was that noise?" I asked, walking over and grabbing his hands.

He pulled his hands out of mine and tucked them into the pocket of his hoodie. There was an ache in my chest at the way he avoided my touch. I couldn't tell if it was because we were in front of his Pa or because of some other reason that he had yet to tell me. "I'm fine, I just fell, that's all," He murmured, looking away from me.

I looked him up and down, he looked frazzled, worry written in the furrow of his brow. "Noah?" I said quietly.

Noah didn't look at me. He just walked past me and over to where his pa stood. "Can we have pizza tonight before you go to bingo?" He asked.

"Yeah sure, that sounds like a good plan," Pa said. "I'll go order it now," He said walking down the hall to the kitchen.

Noah turned to me, walking over and grabbing my arm. "I need to talk to you," He said, dragging me behind him towards his room.

He pulled me into his room and shut the door behind me.

"Noah, are you—"

"I don't know if I can do this," Noah interrupted, sitting down at the foot of his bed.

"Oh," I said. I kneeled in front of him and grabbed his hands. "Are you okay? Do you want to talk about it?"

Noah wouldn't look me in the eye, just stared down at my hands holding his. "I'm scared. I'm sure I have no reason to be, but I can't help it." Noah said. "I don't want him to hate me. I don't want anyone to hate me."

"If you don't want to, you don't have to. It's your choice, I'll support you either way." I asked.

Noah shook his head, silence filling the air between us.

"Are you going to?" I asked, standing up and sitting beside him. "Do you want to?"

He shrugged. "I don't know! I'm scared. I don't want to have to hide it. I want to be able to be with you properly. But I can't stop thinking about the 'what-ifs.'"

I nodded. "Is there anything that I can do?" I asked. I put my hand on his knee, rubbing circles with my thumb, trying to comfort him in any way I could.

He shrugged again. "I don't know. I don't know what I'm gonna do."

I wrapped my arms around him and pulled him into my chest. I pet his hair and hummed quietly. He leaned in, his breath shaky.

"I'm here for you. Whatever you decide to do, I'll support you the best I can." I whispered.

He nodded into my chest, and I set my cheek against his hair.

There was a knock on the door, and Noah put his hands against my chest and pushed himself away from me as the door opened.

"Hey boys," Noah's Pa said. "I ordered pizza." He stood in silence, waiting for a response from either of us.

But Noah sat silently, and the words that I needed to say were getting caught in my throat between the words that I wanted to say.

I looked at Noah, but he just kept his eyes down, and I could see him shaking slightly. He said he would tell his Pa today before he left for bingo, but nothing along those lines was being spoken between the two.

A selfish part of me wanted to say it instead. To rip off the bandaid for him. Show that there really was no reason for him to hide. I wanted to be able to show how much I liked him.

But despite my feelings, being outed was probably one of the worst things that a queer person could do to another queer person. So rather than trying to fill the silence with useless chatter, I stayed quiet. Because I knew if I opened my mouth there's a chance I would say the wrong thing.

"Are you boys alright?" Pa asked from the doorway.

We're okay, I thought. I wanted to answer his question. To tell him that everything was okay and we would just hangout and play games till the pizza came, so that he would leave us alone and I could hold Noah in my arms again. To make him feel safe.

I noticed that, along with Noah it seemed I also couldn't peel my eyes away from his bed. Unable to make eye contact or to speak.

"I guess, I'll just," He paused. "Leave you boys alone then," Noah's Pa said, grabbing the door handle. "I'll just be in the living room, I'll let you know when pizza is here," He said, before closing the door.

When the door clicked shut, Noah flinched, and looked back up towards the door. His eyes seemed to flicker for a moment, like he was trying to decide what it was that he wanted to do next.

And then he stood up, grabbing my hand and dragging me behind him once again. "Pa, wait!" He exclaimed.

"Noah—" I exclaimed wincing as his nails dug into my wrist as he dragged me behind him into the hallway.

His Pa turned around to look at Noah. "What's up?" He asked.

Noah stood, frozen in place but refusing to let go of my wrist. I could feel him shaking as he held on to me, and he squeezed his eyes shut as he attempted to keep his tears in his eyes.

I didn't move. Again we were at a stand still of no one saying a word. I couldn't peel my eyes away from Noah as I watched him try to find the words to tell his Pa.

He took a few deep breaths, before looking up. The grip he had on my wrist loosened, and he let go, taking a step forward and turning back to look at me. Noah looked at me and smiled, the corners of his mouth barely curling up.

"Noah?" I whispered.

He shook his head at me. "I think I have to do this by myself."

I looked at his Pa, who stood with a confused look on his, and then back at Noah.

"Are you sure?" I asked.

He nodded, and walked over to me, brushing his hand against mine. "Just, go back to my room, I'll come get you in a bit."

I stood for a moment, my feet frozen where I stood. Noah gave me a gentle nudge, and I found the strength in my legs to leave the hallway and go back into Noah's room.

I turned to look at Noah, and I saw him mouth words that I wasn't able to make out before he shut the door behind me, leaving me to wait inside of his room.

I thought about maybe sitting down, but decided against it, and instead started to pace. I couldn't stop thinking about it. *What do I do if things go badly? How can I protect him from what might happen? I can't. There's nothing I can do. In this situation, I have no power. All I can do is wait where he told me to, and hope for the best. I didn't hold any power.*

I sat against the wall beside the door, trying to see if I could make out the words being said from Noah's living room. I couldn't make anything out.

I started to disconnect from reality. I wasn't prepared for what could happen. I was scared. But knowing that Noah was probably terrified, made it easier to stay at least a little calm.

All I could do was wait, and I was never known for being patient.

Time had passed. I didn't know how much. It could've been minutes, or hours.

But as I was pacing his room, I heard the door open from behind me. I turned to see Noah standing in the door frame. His cheeks were red and wet with tears, and he stood holding one of his arms in the other. His Pa stood behind him, with a hand on his shoulder and a smile on his face. I hoped that that was a good sign.

"Noah?" I asked, walking over.

Noah smiled at me.

"I told him," Noah said. He looked relieved, but also like there was still something he didn't have answers on. "About me, and about you. He said he wanted to ask you something." And it seemed Pa's opinion on us dating was what we still didn't know about.

Noah's Pa looked between the two of us for a moment. "So you're dating, Noah?"

I nodded, turning my thumbs around each other. "I am."

"And you like him?" Pa asked, turning to Noah and nodding at me.

Noah's face turned red, the color crawling up his ears and over the back of his neck. "Yes, I like him. I really like him, Pa. I just told you that I do."

"And you," Noah's Pa started as he turned to me. "Do you like Noah?"

I nodded. "I definitely do. I like him a whole lot. So much. I can't express to you how much I do."

There was silence, and I stood with Noah, both of us holding our breath waiting for any sort of reaction from his Pa that would tell us whether or not he approved of us being together or not. All old people were the same in that it was hard to tell what they were thinking based on the look on their face, and Noah's Pa was no exception to that rule.

I couldn't pull my eyes away from Noah's Pa. I was looking for a sign in his expression. Noah however couldn't pull his eyes away from the floor. I think he was afraid of what he might see if he looked up and turned to face his Pa.

"Okay."

Noah looked up, and then turned to him. "Okay?"

"Okay," His Pa said. "So long as you two like each

other, and you treat each other right, I don't care. All I care about is that you're safe, and you're loved."

Noah let out a loud sigh, and leaned into me, before falling to his knees. "I was so scared,"

I sat down on the floor next to him and held his hand tightly. "Me too," I said, letting out the breath I had been holding.

Noah's Pa walked over and kneeled down to us, groaning. "I'm too old for this." He looked between the two of us. "Noah, you're my grandson, I love you, no matter what you do or who you love."

I watched them talk, the words that Noah's Pa was saying becoming irrelevant to me. In this house, raised by these people, Noah was taught to approach people with kindness. As Noah and his Pa hugged, it hit me. That thing that he was raised with that I would never get the chance to experience. In this moment I was remembering all of the ways I was different from him.

But us both sitting here on the floor, fought those thoughts off, reminding me more so of all the ways we were the same.

"Noah?" I looked up at him, breaking my train of thought. "What's wrong?"

"What do you mean? Everything's—" I felt a tear fall down my cheek. "Oh," I chuckled. "Sorry, I don't know why I'm crying," I quickly wiped my face, trying to keep the emotions inside of me where they belonged.

Noah pulled me into a tight hug, squeezing my shoulders. "I know," He said softly, running his fingers through my hair. "I know you were scared too, it's okay."

His words cut deeply, and out of it came the feelings I didn't even know I had.

I wrapped my arms around him, hugging him tightly, and a sob escaping from my lips. I had been trying to stay calm, for Noah's sake. To be a pillar of support for him, but I couldn't have helped wanting his Pa's approval. Now that I had it, all of the tension left my body.

Noah's Pa wrapped his arms around me and Noah.

"Thank you," I cried. "Pa, I promise I'll treat him well. I'll take care of him." I thought back to the way I had behaved before. Remembering all of the people I would pick up and then leave behind. "I'll treasure him."

Noah's Pa smiled at me, before putting a hand on my head and ruffling my hair. "I know. You'll protect him, right?"

I nodded, another sob escaping me as I sat on the floor of Noah's room.

Noah hugged me tightly, before letting go and grabbing my hands. "Hey, Leo?"

I looked up at him, wondering what it was that he would say now.

"Thank you for being patient with me. Thank you for liking me."

I grabbed his hands in mine, squeezing them tightly. "Of course, this was for you. This was your moment. This wasn't about me, it was about you." I reminded him. "I would be a horrible person if I didn't let you take your time with it and do it on your own terms."

When I saw him smile after getting to come out on his own time, on his own terms, it made all of the heart ache I had felt worth it. The years I spent pining one-sidedly. The impatient feeling I would get when I couldn't hold him when I wanted to, all of those feelings dissipated.

We sat on the floor, and we laughed, and we smiled, as Noah's Pa hugged him. And again. I wondered why I hadn't done this sooner.

February 14th, 2023

I sat in chemistry, doing a similar lab to the one we had done the month before. My hair was longer now, curls constantly falling into my field of vision. I had to use a couple of bobby pins from one of the girls in class to pin my hair back.

The girl I sat with had freckles across her nose and her hair fell in front of her goggles haphazardly while I mixed the chemicals on the laminated sheet.

She wouldn't stop staring at me, and she wasn't doing any of the work either. She just smiled and hummed as I did the work by myself.

I rolled my eyes and put the eyedropper back down in the beaker and sat back in my seat crossing my arms. "Are you going to help at all?" I asked.

The girl looked at me, like she had been suddenly snapped out of a daze. "Oh? But you're so good at it!" she whined. "Plus I'm scared I'll get burned or something."

I sat there silently for a few moments, before sighing and grabbing the dropper again. "Whatever," I mumbled.

"Yay!" The girl clapped. "I've always loved how considerate you are."

I ignored her, trying to just focus on the work in front of me.

"You know I really like you, Leo," She said. "I mean you're always so nice to everyone, and you make everyone smile."

"That's what you think."

"Oh c'mon," She whined. "Let's hangout, kay? I want to hangout with you again."

That was when I realized that she was one of the girls I had hooked up with earlier in the year. She was also someone who had been known for hooking up with people, and so we both hooked up a couple of times, and I felt a pit of regret in my stomach.

"I don't do that anymore," I said. "I have a boyfriend."

She immediately backed off putting her hands in the air. "Oh really? I didn't know, sorry Leo!"

I shrugged. "It's okay, since you didn't know."

She smiled, and the look in her eyes had softened. "I'm happy for you, Leo. I really am."

"Thanks, but can you actually help me with this assignment now?" I chuckled. "Oh, and, I'm sorry for what I did. I wasn't considerate of anyone's feelings during that time in my life."

She shrugged. "Nah, I don't care, it was fun for me. And, I guess I can help you with the assignment."

"Cool."

We worked on the assignment for the rest of class. She didn't invade my privacy or get too close like she had been, but she asked me questions about Noah a couple of times, congratulating me following the mini conversations we had about him. I had a feeling that maybe she was in a similar situation to what I was in, with one-side pining and boxed up feelings. Using other people to push away her own emotions.

We chatted back and forth. We told each other the little things about the people we liked. We talked about our experience with hookup culture, both the good and the bad parts. I thought about proposing that she be honest with herself and the person she liked. But I didn't say anything, knowing from experience that she needed to realize on her own.

When class was over I walked over to Monty's desk and he was packing up his things when his phone buzzed. I watched him pick it up and smile before putting it in his bag.

"Sonali?" I asked.

He nodded.

"How is that going, by the way?" I started to walk towards the door slowly, looking back as he began to fall instep beside me.

"It's going well, we are really close friends now," He said. "We've had bumps in the road but it's been good mostly."

As we walked over to them, I saw Allie standing with Noah by the lockers. I walked over and leaned down beside him, and blew softly beside his ear.

He yelped, slapping his hand over his ear as he turned around, revealing that he was holding flowers in his hands. He scowled when he saw me, proceeding to kick me in the shin.

I winced and jumped back, grabbing my shin. "That hurt!"

"Well, you scared me!" He bickered.

We made eye contact, and I smiled at him, causing a smile to appear on his face as well, before we both broke out into laughter along with Allie and Monty.

He laughed with me, before shoving the flowers into my hands. "Here, happy Valentine's Day," he murmured, rolling his eyes.

"Wait, for real?" I asked. I looked down at the flowers, all of them different shades and hues of red, orange, blue, and purple. "I thought you hated Valentine's Day."

Noah's face turned red, and Allie laughed, throwing an arm around his shoulder. "Yeah he does. But he wanted to do something for you since he knew you liked it."

Noah turned around and kicked Allie in the shin. "Don't speak for me!" He laughed. "I was getting to it!"

I smiled at him, looking between him and the flowers before pulling him away from his bickering with Allie and into a hug.

"Thank you, Noah," I said.

He stood frozen for a moment hugging me back. "Yeah, yeah, whatever." He mumbled.

"Stop being gross," Allie laughed.

I looked over Noah's shoulder at her and stuck my tongue out at her, while she just rolled her eyes.

Noah pulled away from me, his hand slipping down and into mine. "We should get going," he said.

I nodded. "Are we all still on for dinner later?" I asked.

Allie nodded. "Mhm."

"Yup all set!" Monty said. "Sonali is all good too, She texted me about it."

"Okay, cool!" I said. "We should get going to orchestra,"

"Bye you guys!" Allie said as Noah and I started walking away.

I waved goodbye to them, turning my focus back to Noah as we got farther away.

"Are you excited for the spring concert next month?" I asked.

He nodded. "I am, My mom will be back in time to see it. Oh, and I forgot to tell you, but I got approved to intern with a photographer once I graduate."

My heart fluttered for him. I was excited to see both his mom and what he would do with his photos in the future."Both of those are super exciting!" I exclaimed. "I'm proud of you."

He smiled, his cheeks brightening. "Thank you!"

We walked into the orchestra room and set our stuff down by our chairs before heading to the instrument lockers together to get my violin.

"How did the modeling gig go yesterday?" Noah asked.

I shrugged. "It was really weird, but they were super nice and helped explain everything to me since I was so nervous,"

"Think you'll keep doing it?"

I shook my head. "I don't think so, at least, not full time. I still want to be able to work at the book shop."

"Right, that makes sense. I'm excited to see the photos they took, but I doubt they're better than my photos of you."

"Ah cocky I see," I said, grabbing my violin case.

I followed him as he went to grab his cello and bow from the rack. I set my violin by my things, and then went over to where he sat, unable to keep myself from smiling. We talked about sweet nothings while he pulled out his sheet music. He looked up and smiled at me as we talked. His hand instinctively found mine and I couldn't help but get a bubbling in my chest.

I stood holding his hand, knowing that I no longer had to hold myself back from reaching out to grab it. Because I knew that if I did, he would wrap his fingers with mine, look at me and smile.

And though it had taken so long to get here, everytime I felt his warmth, I smiled, knowing that all the years pining was worth the wait.

Pictures of You

Noah

Pictures of You (Noah)

June 15th, 2019

The first thing I learned when I picked up a camera was to photograph change. That way after something is erased, there remains a memory of what something once was.

The second thing I learned was to take pictures of my favorite things because there was no telling what could happen to them.

So when I started taking photos, one of the first things I ever took a photo of was my best friend, Leo.

I walked up to his porch and heard screaming from inside.

I was about to knock on the door when Leo flung it open and slammed it behind him.

He looked at me, tears streaming down his face smudging the rainbows he had painted on his cheeks. He looked at me his whole face tight before his gaze softened and he took a shaky breath. He ran his fingers through his hair, the corners of his mouth curling into what looked like an attempt at a smile.

"Leo, are you-" I asked, reaching out to him.

"I'm good!" He exclaimed walking past me. I turned to see him facing me, wiping the tears from his cheeks. "Let's go, before we're late!" He smiled widely, but his voice wouldn't stop shaking.

"...Okay," I said walking down his porch and back to Pa's car.

"Hey, how are you doing Leo?" Pa asked when we got in the car.

"I'm great! How are you?" Leo asked him climbing into the back seat after me.

"I'm good, thank you for asking."

After Leo and I put on our seatbelts, I looked at him looking at his phone, a picture of him and his parents from last year pulled up.

"Leo?" I whispered. I nudged him gently with my elbow.

He looked at me, his eyes glossy with tears.

He set his head on my shoulder, grabbing my hand and holding it in his lap.

"I told my parents why I wanted to go to the parade," He said.

"That's great then, right?" I said.

"My mom is happy for me, but my dad? Not so much," He hiccuped and buried his face in my arm. "I think they're going to get a divorce. Can I stay at your place tonight? I'm… scared to go back home."

I nodded, squeezing his hand. "Of course, you can. You know you're always welcome there, right Pa?" I asked, looking at Pa in the rearview mirror.

"Of course," he said.

Leo let go of my hand, wrapped his arms around my shoulders, and sobbed into my neck. I put one hand around his waist and the other on the back of his head, combing my fingers through his hair. "Don't worry, I'm here." I paused.

"You'll always have a friend as long as you have me."

He chuckled bitterly, "Thanks, I'm glad."

We sat in silence for the rest of the car ride, before we started hearing the sound of cheering and music.

I nudged Leo. "Hey! Look!" I said pointing out the window.

He lifted his head to peek out of the window, his face lighting up when he saw the various pride flags being held by all different kinds of people. I watched him scramble to pull a flag out from behind his back and tie it around his neck as my Pa came to a stop.

"You guys will have to get out here and walk the rest of the way," He said. "I'll drop you off and then go find a cafe to hang out in. So, just text me if you need anything alright? I'll be right around the corner."

"Okay," I said, opening the car door. "I love you, we'll be safe." I looked at Leo, who seemed a bit hesitant to get out of the car. "C'mon," I said, holding my hand out to him. "It'll be fine, I'll stay with you."

He nodded, grabbing my hand and getting out of the car behind me.

He walked a step behind me as we walked closer to the parade. I held his hand tightly, making sure not to let go.

The sun was bright, and the flags made the streets look like a sea of color flooding into the city, people's voices ringing and echoing off of the buildings around us.

I pulled Leo up to the fence that blocked off the road, and turned to see him standing still with his eyes on the ground, his previous excitement shrinking into himself and turning to fear. He was still shaking.

I grabbed his shoulders and shook him gently. "Leo!" I exclaimed letting out a loud laugh.

"Look at where you are!" I said gesturing to the crowd around us before setting my hands back on his shoulders. "You're safe here, do you hear me? You're safe."

I saw something click in his eyes, and he looked around us, before nodding. "Yeah, you're right, I am, aren't I?" He said with a breath of relief. He took my hands off of his shoulders and held them tightly in his.

I nodded. "You are."

He smiled, looking down before he brought his gaze back up to meet mine. He wouldn't look away, and I felt trapped in his eyes, the colors of the rainbows around us reflecting in them. I couldn't pull my eyes away from his. I felt like I couldn't, or rather I shouldn't. There was something that kept my gaze locked on him. I guessed I wasn't immune to his magnetic personality and abilities.

He opened his mouth like he had something to say, but before he could someone on the other side of the roadblock interrupted his thought.

"You're quite young!" An older man exclaimed looking at us. "Are you two dating?" He asked, looking between me and Leo.

"Oh, no, I'm just here for moral support," I said, letting go of Leo's hands. I looked at him smiling. Leo was great, and I would always be ready to support him from the sidelines. But if I could avoid it, I didn't want to do anything that could make me stand out.

"Ah, well then you must have yourself a really good friend young man," He said, turning his attention to Leo.

Leo looked at me and smiled. "Yeah, I do."

"Did you want a hug? I'm giving them out," he said.

That was when both Leo and I finally noticed the man's shirt. Written on it were three simple words that made Leo's eyes well up with tears.

'Free Dad Hugs.'

I looked at Leo to see what he would say in response. But instead of any words coming out, he just let out a sob and covered his mouth.

"Oh, come here," The man said, holding out his arms over the fence.

Leo walked towards the man, and as soon as he pulled Leo into a hug, I saw his face relax as he let out all of the tears and cries he must have been holding up until that point.

He completely relaxed into the man's arms, hugging him tightly and desperately, like he wanted that moment to last forever and he would never have to let go.

I held my camera up and snapped a photo of them together.

Leo had relief and pain washed over his face, and the man just whispered quiet nothings to Leo, telling him how everything was going to be okay in the end.

It was only after they pulled away from each other that I saw the man was crying too.

After the man left, Leo's mood had been drastically lifted. He was incredibly happy, and despite the tear stains down his cheeks, he was glowing.

After the parade was over, we were walking to the cafe Pa said he would meet us at, and Leo was excitedly rambling about how fun he had when I decided to interrupt him.

"Hey, Leo? Did you have something to tell me earlier?" I asked.

He gave me a confused look. "Earlier when?"

"Y'know, before you got a hug from that guy," I said. "When we were holding hands."

He looked down quickly, red creeping up his cheeks and over his ears. "It was nothing!" He said looking up at me and waving his hands dismissively.

"Are you sure?" I asked.

He nodded. "I'm sure! It wasn't important."

I stayed silent for a moment, questioning his

response, before shrugging. "I mean if you're sure."

"I'm sure," He paused for a moment before continuing to ramble about the parade.

I had a feeling that it wasn't nothing like he said it was and that it was more important than he seemed to be making it out to be. But I didn't want to ruin his good mood by continuing to press the issue.

So, I just watched him, and smiled at him smiling. Sure that he's bound to tell me what he was thinking that day eventually.

December 27th, 2022

I made the horrible mistake of letting Leo throw me a party for my birthday. What else was I supposed to do? Say no?

I sat on his bed while he rummaged through his closet throwing clothes here and there. I leaned back and sighed, wondering how long it would take for him to change.

He hummed to himself, and I watched him carefully as he stepped over the mess of clothes he had created around him, hoping that he wouldn't fall and snap his neck.

I crossed my legs beneath me and put my hands in my lap. "Leo, I'm not so sure about this after all… I know I said you could, but I don't know anymore."

"Well, it's too late!" He exclaimed. I covered my eyes as he pulled his shirt over his head, uncomfortable where I sat. "Everyone is already on their way."

There was a pause. "Noah, you're never going to get a girlfriend if you're too embarrassed to look at someone who is the same gender as you." He paused. "You won't get a boyfriend like that either. Especially a boyfriend."

I took my hands off from over my face and grabbed one of his pillows before chucking it at him. "Shut up!"

I laughed. "I have no interest in that stuff right now, remember?"

He rolled his eyes at me, as he looked in the mirror adjusting the collar of his shirt. "Yeah, yeah I know."

He turned around to face me, putting his hands on his hips and shifting his wait to his left leg. "Thoughts on the outfit? It's your birthday so I want to do my best."

I looked him up and down. He was wearing black slacks and a short sleeve button down that he had only tucked in on one side. The collar of the button down was embroidered with flowers, and he had the first few buttons of his shirt undone.

I went over to him, and grabbed his collar pulling him closer to where I stood. "If this is a party for me the least you could do is be decent," I grumbled as I buttoned up his shirt.

He looked up at me, his eyes wide.

"What?" I said after a moment of silence.

"Nothing, I just wasn't expecting that," He said.

I rolled my hands into fists and gently pushed him away from me. "People are going to start showing up soon right?"

He nodded, still silent.

"I'll go downstairs so that people can be let in, just make sure that nothing too crazy happens, okay?" I asked him.

He nodded. "Don't worry, I'm a great host, and I'll keep an eye on everyone."

"Good." I nodded and turned onto my heel to walk downstairs.

I know I had told him that the party was a bad idea, but a part of me was looking forward to it. I couldn't help but fear the idea of anything bad happening, but I looked forward to experiencing something I have yet to experience. And the fact that Leo was throwing the party?

It was the best part.

The party had been going well despite the slowly increasing smell of body odor, and the varying degrees of sobriety. I sat with a circle of kids who I had never met before. Some with familiar faces, and others complete strangers. I was dragged into this stupid game by Leo, who had already had a couple of drinks. I'm glad no one was smoking, but with his younger brother's asthma, the no smoking rule was a staple of Leo's house parties. There weren't as many people as he could have invited, but there were enough around to make me anxious. If it weren't for me, I'm sure the party would be bigger and louder. But despite Leo obviously watering down his usual shenanigans, it was the most people I had been around. And I didn't even get the comfort of sitting beside my best friend who had thrown the party *for me*.

There was a tap on my shoulder as a girl with dirty blonde hair sat beside me. "Hey, it's your turn."

"Oh, uh. Right," I looked across the circle and saw Leo sitting with both a girl and a guy hanging over him as he flirted with them drunkenly.

I rolled my eyes and looked away, squeezing my hands into tight fists. It was a party he was throwing for me, and instead of spending the party with me, he spent it throwing himself at the other guests.

I leaned forward and spun the stupid bottle that was sitting in the middle of the living room. In the time it had taken to get me, Leo had already gone into that closet twice. Once with a girl when he spun the bottle, and again with a guy when the boy spun it.

The bottle spun to a stop, pointing across the circle to a girl with faded pink hair. I stayed sitting, not really knowing what to say, and unable to move.

The girl with pink hair sighed and stood up. "I'm going to go get a drink," She said, as she walked away.

The girl next to me chuckled and put her hand on my shoulder sending shivers down my arm. "That means you get to spin again," She said.

"Oh, are you sure?" I said. "I don't think that's fair maybe the next person should-"

"Just go!" She said, nudging me in the side with her elbow.

I sighed and grabbed the bottle, spinning it again.

This time it slowed to a stop, pointing at Leo.

"We haven't even gotten all the way around the circle and he's already going in there a third time?" She exclaimed.

I locked eyes with Leo. Before he could get any ideas, I looked down at my lap, waiting for him to tell me to spin it again. He would laugh and say something about how he would never kiss his best friend. And I would quietly leave the circle without drawing any attention to myself.

I was waiting for him to say it, but nothing of the sort came out of his mouth. Instead, I looked back up to see him giggling, prying the boy and girl off of his arms as he stood up.

"Guess it's us," He said, walking over and grabbing my hand. "Let's go."

He pulled me up from where I was sitting, and I could hear the cheering and the whistles of the other people in the circle. He dragged me behind him, out of his living room and down the hallway.

"Wait, Leo, we aren't seriously going to—" I stammered as he opened the closet door.

He shook his head and held a finger up to his mouth while making a shushing sound. "We're just humoring them," He whispered before shoving me into the closet.

I ran into the back wall of the closet as he closed the door behind him before turning and facing me.

I looked up at the mistletoe that was tied to the closet rod, before looking back down to find him staring at me.

"What?" I mumbled looking away. "Why are you looking at me like that?"

He shook his head laughing. "It's nothing," He said, putting his head against my chest. He stayed like that for a moment, before pulling away and smirking at me. "Your heart is beating really fast."

"It's… it's because you were walking so damn fast when you dragged me over here," I said.

He laughed, and I couldn't help but smile. "You're so uptight all of the time," He said. "You should let loose every once in a while. Have fun."

I shook my head. "If your definition of having fun means flirting with everything that walks I'll pass."

He raised an eyebrow. "Are you mad?"

"Yes!" I exclaimed. I realized that I said it a bit loudly, and cleared my throat. "I want you to find someone you like. Someone you genuinely have feelings for. You're not treating yourself or your partners with the respect you deserve." I looked down. "It's frustrating." There was a moment of silence.

"Who says I don't have feelings for someone?" He asked bitterly.

I looked up at him, my chest tightening. "*You* have feelings for somebody?" I asked.

He nodded. "Unfortunately, they're really dense. So they aren't picking up on any of the signals I'm so clearly sending."

I thought for a moment, trying to find the right words to say before Leo broke my train of thought.

"What? Jealous?" He smirked.

"I am *not* jealous!" I mumbled.

"I think you're jealous," Leo hummed.

I rolled my eyes. "What do I have to be jealous of?"

Leo thought for a moment before shrugging and leaning back against the door. "I don't know, you tell me. What are you jealous of?"

I sighed and ran my fingers through my hair. "I don't know," I said. "Maybe, the fact that you treat me differently from everyone else?"

My heart started beating faster. Before I could even think about them, the words were coming out of my mouth like a broken dam.

"You flirt with all of your friends except for Sonali, Allie, Monty, and I. Are we not close enough? Why do you keep us at arms length? Or, maybe I'm jealous that you're able to be comfortable playing a game like this. That you can relax around people so easily. Maybe I'm jealous because others are drawn to you? Maybe I'm jealous because you're able to recognize your own feelings?" I paused. "No, I'm *definitely* jealous because you're able to recognize your own feelings." I sighed.

The silence hung in the air like a tight rubber band. One wrong move and it would snap.

"I had no idea, I made you feel so many things…" Leo said, grabbing my hand. "I'm… I'm really sorry, Noah."

I sighed, unable to stay angry at him for more than a moment, but also unable to say anything either.

"You…" He looked up at me, I could see that his cheeks were red through the strips of light being let in from the hallway. "You make me feel things like that too." He whispered.

I looked away, and we stood there for a moment with his eyes on me and mine on the wall. "What is that supposed to mean?" I mumbled. My hand was getting sweaty holding his but I was too nervous to move. I was terrified that he could hear how fast my heart was beating.

His hand shifted in mine, and he interlaced our fingers together, pulling my gaze away from the wall and down to his.

His gaze was intense, and his cheeks were flushed. "I'm going to do something. The only reason I think I'm going to be able to do it is because I'm drunk," He said, his voice shaking.

My heart jumped inside my chest. Even though I wanted to, I couldn't tear my eyes away from his. His hand was shaking in mine, and his voice came out quiet and nervous.

"So, tomorrow, you can't let me blame it on the alcohol and say that it didn't mean anything, okay? Don't let me take this back and don't let me forget. I'll make sure to tell you properly when I'm sober." He said. In just a moment, he went from nervous to determined.

And even though I had no idea what he was about to do, because it was him, I couldn't say no. But I couldn't speak either, so instead, I just nodded, and waited for whatever it was he was going to do.

He finally let go of my hand, before he brought his hands up to the back of my neck, pulling me down and pressing his lips against mine, and then pulling away again before I had any time to react.

He and I stared at each other for a moment, before it clicked in my head what he had meant.

"Leo, do you—" I started.

"Okay! I think we've been in here long enough!" He interrupted me, laughing awkwardly as he opened the closet door. "I'm going to go back now! This was fun, bye Noah!" He said. He waved to me, avoiding eye contact, before walking out of the closet and back down the hallway to the living room.

I stood in the closet for a couple of minutes, unable to move, as I replayed the past four years I had spent beside him.

Oh.

Oh.

I closed the closet door behind me as I exited. The faces around me blurred as I walked past the people in the hallways. I walked down the hallway towards the kitchen, and out the back door. My feet started feeling heavy as I made way over to where Monty sat with Sonali. I sat down beside them, staring at the bright glow of the bonfire.

Monty leaned forward to look at me, the music from inside playing in the back of my head.

"Leo kissed me," I said looking at Monty.

"Oh shoot," Monty said, looking between Sonali and me.He blinked a few times, confusion washing over his face "What are you going to do?"

"I don't know," I said, putting my face in my hands. "I really don't know."

December 28th, 2022

Leo looked at me, his face so red I imagined it would be hot to the touch. "So, are you saying that you have feelings for me?" He asked.

I nodded. "I think I always have, I just didn't know it," I grabbed his hands in mine tightly. "Listen, if you want to stay friends after this, that's okay, and I'll respect that. I know it might not be ideal dating me, considering that I don't even know what my sexuality is," I paused, the idea of my sexuality having come out of my mouth before even being a thought in my mind. "I don't know what my sexuality is, but I do know that I like you. And if that's enough for you, I don't want to go back to being *just* friends," I looked down at our hands holding each other, and slowly opened my hands, interlacing our fingers together.

He placed a hand on my cheek and turned my face

up to look at him. "I don't think I want to go back to being just friends either, that is if you'll have me."

I put my hand over the one he had against my cheek. "So are we dating now then?"

He nodded. "I guess we are."

"So, can I kiss you?" I impulsively.

"Yea—"

I kissed him. With one hand on the back of his neck and the other around his waist; without thinking I kissed him. I hadn't even given him enough time to completely respond to my question, about whether or not it was okay for me to kiss him. The moment I was given the littlest bit of a sign that it was okay to do so, I did it. I lost all of my willpower the moment he kissed me the night before. The kiss I gave him held years of feeling that I wasn't even aware I had. I wanted to kiss him, I wanted to show him. I wanted him to know that my feelings despite even having known they were there were real. I didn't want him to doubt me.

But the moment I heard laughing, and opened my eyes to see people walking past our car, I grabbed his shoulders and pushed him away from me, looking down at the center console, afraid to look up and find them looking. It was as if the butterflies in my chest had finally been freed from their cage only to be trapped in a net that awaited them.

And it was suffocating.

"Noah!"

I looked up to see Leo looking at me, his hands rubbing my arms gently as he shook me back to reality.

I let go of him and sat back in my seat hiding my face in my hands. "I'm sorry, I didn't mean to— I didn't mean—" I started.

"Noah," He said, pulling my hands from my face. "It's okay, I get it, I understand."

I sighed and put my hands on the back of my head, closing my eyes and looking down. "I just… I don't want…" I pulled on the ends of my hair, recoiling into myself. "I'm afraid of being stared at."

Leo sat quietly, and I couldn't help but second-guess his decision to date me. "Well," He started. "If they do stare, let's make sure to give them a show."

I looked up at him, leaning close. "No no no! I don't— I don't want to be watched," I said. "Let's just, I don't want other people to know either!" I said. I grabbed his hand, rubbing my thumb over the top of it. "Can we please just… keep it a secret? Can we just stay 'us'? I'm sorry, but… I need time," I whispered.

"Noah," Leo said, grabbing my chin and making me look at him. "Of course, we can. We don't have to do anything you don't want to do. I waited years to tell you, I will wait for however long it is that you need in order to tell others."

"I'm sorry."

"Noah!" Leo exclaimed, grabbing my face with both of his hands. "It is okay, I get it. You're allowed to be afraid, and I understand why you would be. I was in the closet once too you know. You can take your time with this, and I'll do my best to support you okay?"

I sat silently, before nodding.

My phone rang.

Picking it up I saw that it was my Pa calling, and after three rings I answered.

"Hello?" I said, putting my phone up to my ear.

"Hey Noah, are you going to be home soon? Your mom is leaving today, remember?"

Shit.

"Right, I'm on my way home now, I'm really sorry I'll be there soon," I looked up to see Leo already starting the car.

"Alright, just be safe on your way back, see you when you get home, bye Noah," My Pa said.

"See you at home Pa, I love you," I said before hanging up.

"You need to go home right?" Leo asked.

I nodded. "Yeah, my mom is going back." I put my seatbelt back on.

"Oh that's right, let's get you home," Leo said, pulling out of the parking lot.

I watched him drive as we made our way over to my house, he drove with one hand on the wheel, and his other on the center console. The rain that began to fall around us filled the world with static, everything else going quiet around it. The sticky feeling of uncertainty was washed clean, and my head cleared, thinking only of the person sitting beside me. The rain created a protective barrier around the car we were in and protected us from anything that could possibly make our feelings waiver.

I set my arm on the console beside his, pressing my arm against his, and nudging his hand with mine, he nudged back, and I hooked my pinky with him, turning to look out the window as my ears burned.

I was scared of people, and of myself. But I knew that I could find safety. It didn't matter if I lost sight of my feelings in the fog of others, I knew that if I had him I'd be able to find those feelings again. So as the raindrops clattered against the car roof, I closed my eyes, trying to remember the warmth of his touch.

I sat in my driveway in Leo's car, my pinky hooked with his, and the rain falling heavily around us. I didn't want to get out of the car. I didn't want to leave this safe little bubble I had with him. But he unhooked his pinky from mine and unbuckled his seat belt reaching into the back seat and grabbing an umbrella.

"C'mon," He said, getting out of the car and

opening the umbrella. "I'll walk you to your door, is that alright?"

I nodded, and got out of the car, running through the pouring rain around the car to meet him under the umbrella. I crashed into him, and we both stood there laughing, just existing against each other.

He handed me the umbrella and held my hand as we walked up to my porch.

I walked onto the porch and closed the umbrella, holding it in front of me with both hands wrapped around the handle.

"When will I see you again my dear Cinderella?" He gasped, grabbing both of my hands in his. He was smirking, and I couldn't help but roll my eyes.

"I don't know my dear prince, but the clock strikes…" I paused, trying to remember the time. "Four p.m., and so I must go."

"What is your name?" He asked.

I rolled my eyes and pulled my hands from his. "I haven't the time! I really must go!"

He didn't respond, just looked at me, with a stupid grin on his face until the both of us started laughing.

"I won't see you till school starts back up again right?" He asked.

I nodded. "Yeah, I've just got some stuff to finish up. I'm going to an event, and then doing a photoshoot with Allie for my photography portfolio and design school for her. Plus I gotta help Pa with some things around the house after my mom leaves."

"Alright, well," He said, taking my hand and kissing the top of it. "Until we meet again."

I turned away, trying to hide from him the embarrassing expression I knew I was wearing. After a moment, I looked behind me expecting him to have already walked away. As soon as I looked he pulled me into a hug. He held me so tightly that I thought he didn't plan on letting go. But I had no intention of letting go either. I wanted to stay here with him. I wanted so much from this newfound relationship with these feelings I wasn't aware I had until the party.

"I don't want to let go," He said, burying his face in my chest.

"Me either," I sighed.

We stayed like that for a few moments longer, before I pulled away knowing that I couldn't keep my Pa or mom waiting much longer.

"Bye," I said, as he started to walk away, his hand slowly slipping from mine. "Get home safe."

"I will. Tell your mom and Pa that I said hi," He said running to his car. He grabbed the handle and pulled the door open, waving to me with his other hand and giving me a dopey grin. "Bye! See you at school Noah!" After that, he got in the car and shut the door behind him. I watched as he started the car, and drove out of my driveway. My eyes followed him as he drove down my street, all the way until his car disappeared behind the corner.

Then I turned, and opened my door, to see my mom's suitcases by the door. I had spent most of my life raised by Pa, so I wasn't close with her. Which, I didn't mind. We texted regularly and that was enough for me considering she was usually hundreds of miles away. I figured I would tell her about Leo at some point. But not before she went back to the UK. I hope I'll have the confidence to tell her when she visits next.

The news was playing on the TV, and my Pa sat in the living room. The smell of mom's cooking was coming from the kitchen along with the sound of laughter as Pa and Mom talked across the house at each other.

I took off my shoes and walked into the kitchen to

see my Pa and my mom standing at the island, with a few pots and pans simmering on the stove, cooking a meal for more people than mouths we had to feed.

"I'm home," I said, walking over to stand next to my mom.

"Hi Noah," My mom said, pulling me into a hug.

"Look who finally decided to come home," My Pa chuckled from the living room.

I laughed with him, my mom keeping an arm around my shoulder. "Sorry, I did intend to be home sooner I swear."

"What's with the umbrella?" My mom asked.

I looked down at the navy blue umbrella with a broken rod that was still in my hand. "Oh, it's Leo's, I forgot to give it back," I paused, thinking maybe I should call him to come back and get it. But I was hit with a wave of fear of my mom or Pa seeing him, and somehow knowing that something was up. "I can give it back to him on Tuesday when we get back to school from winter break."

"Okay," My mom said. "Well, we still have a little bit of time before dinner, do you want to do anything?"

"Um," I said, my brain beginning to turn in circles. "Nothing in particular, but I might go to my room and just relax for a bit if that's okay."

"Sure," My mom said, kissing the top of my head. "I'll call for you when dinner is ready."

"Okay, thanks," I said.

When I walked into the living room, I saw a rainbow on the TV out of the corner of my eye. I looked at the TV, frozen in place as my eyes were drawn to the screen.

"Clothing brands hire queer models to promote diversity."

I looked to my Pa for his thoughts, but before I got

the chance to read the emotions on his face, he changed
the channel. It was such a small gesture, but it made my
stomach drop to my feet. I couldn't help but think that
maybe it meant something more.

I walked down the hall towards the garage, and
went into my room, closing and locking the door behind
me.

I turned on my TV and opened up youtube, going
to the search bar. I hesitated for a moment, wondering how
much and how far I wanted to dive in trying to figure out
what my sexuality is.

The idea in itself terrified me. There were so many
sexualities and genders, and it was something I had never
considered until now. I couldn't figure out for the life of
me whether or not I would even be able to find what I was
looking for.

I mean, I never considered dating any of the girls
I've seen or met.

But I never considered the idea that I would like a
guy either, my best friend no less. It's not that I couldn't
imagine myself with a guy or a girl, I think I could date
either, but I wasn't sure if I only exclusively liked guys
either.

I twisted the remote in my hands thinking, before
noticing the picture on my wall of Monty, Leo, Alaska,
and me from the end of last school year. I stood next to
Leo, with his arm thrown over my shoulder. I looked stiff
and awkward. I used to think I looked uncomfortable, but
looking at it now with the context that I have, I don't look
uncomfortable at all. I just look flustered.

I turned the remote back into my hands normally,
and looked between the screen and my hand, as I began
typing.

'Guide to sexuality'

'How to know what your sexuality is'

'You like someone but what does that mean for you'
'The difference between gender, sexuality,
presentation, and pronouns'
'The history of the LGBTQ+ community'
'Fetishization of MLM relationships in media'
'Fetishization of lesbians in media'
'The Stonewall Riots'
'Heartbreaking facts about the LGBTQ+
community'

I had barely gone that deep into my video search, but already my head was beginning to ache. There was so much information to absorb, and there seemed to be a lot of bad things that happened to people like my friends. Stuff that I didn't really pay much mind to until now.

'Countries that are unsafe for queer people to visit'
'Gay man murdered'
'Lesbian couple kidnapped and raped outside of a
gay bar'

The more I searched the more I found, and I could feel my heart swelling, trying to escape my chest and run away from me. I turned off my TV before I could dig myself a further grave. I climbed up my ladder and fell into bed, pulling my blanket around me. I pulled my knees up and wrapped my arms around them, trying to drown myself in the layers of blankets that I had on my bed.

Identifying as part of the LGBTQ+ community is enough to get me killed, and putting a label on my identity is just putting a target on my back for those looking to prey on certain types of people. But, not labeling myself at all just means that I have to put myself through all the emotional heartache of hiding who I am, as well as hiding my identity. It also means that I would be putting Leo through heartache too, for having to hide his relationship even though he is already out of the closet to essentially everyone.

It doesn't matter what I choose to do, my life is in danger anyways. What if Pa or mom is against it? I know that they were okay with me going to pride to support Leo, but what if it's different if the gay one is me? I don't want to get kicked out of my house. I don't want to become another statistic. But I don't want to trap Leo into something secretive when he doesn't have to be if he doesn't want to.

I just want to like him without those feelings putting his life or mine in danger. I didn't fully realize that my life was something that would be in danger.

I'm... so scared. And there's nothing I can even do. There are going to be people who want to hurt us no matter what. I am completely powerless in protecting him. I won't be able to do anything even if I tried. I'm trapped. And there are people who will never be willing to allow us to love without reservation or fear.

"Noah!" I looked up at the sound of my mom's voice carrying through the house. "Time for dinner!"

I looked over at the clock, it felt like no time had passed at all as the clock displayed the time 7:18 p.m.. I unwrapped myself from the blanket, and climbed down my ladder. The door knob jiggled as she tried to open the door.

"Noah? Why is your door loc—" She began.

I cut her off by unlocking and opening my door, making her flinch and jump as I opened the door. "I was just changing."

She raised an eyebrow, and looked me up and down. She shifted her weight to one leg and put her hand on her hip, blocking my doorway. "But you're wearing the same clothes you came home in."

"Oh, uh," I started. I couldn't find the words, or come up with an excuse fast enough. I couldn't think of any excuse that would make sense for me to say. All I could think was, *she knows.* I didn't even know what it was that I thought she knew, but I knew it would be something that she would never forgive me for. It was this irrational thought of her being able to see right through me, and not liking what it is that I am currently hiding.

My mom started to laugh, and I felt all the tension I was holding in my body pool into my stomach. "I'm just teasing," She said, patting my shoulder. "C'mon, let's go eat."

I nodded and followed her out of my room and to the kitchen.

My Pa had just recently switched out the tablecloth, the one with the fall leaves having been replaced with a light blue tablecloth that had snowflakes of different sizes scattered over the blue in no particular pattern.

I sat down on the side of the table by the back door, my mom sat across from me and my Pa sat between the two of us.

I stared at my plate, none of the food looking any sort of appetizing, and my stomach started to twist into knots as I sat with my family. I felt like an animal carcass sitting at a table with vultures, who were waiting for me to croak before eating me alive.

"Noah?" My mom asked. "Aren't you going to eat honey?" She said before taking a bite of the corn and peas my Pa made.

I shrugged. "I'm not hungry, and I don't really feel good either."

"Do you need any medicine?" My Pa asked.

"No, I'm sure it'll go away soon. But," I pushed my plate away from me. "I don't think it's a good idea for me to eat right now, so I'll eat later."

"Are you sure? Not even a bite?" My mom asked.

"I'm sure."

My Pa nodded thoughtfully, pointing his fork at me. "You better make sure to eat later."

"I will."

"Oh!" My mom exclaimed, clapping her hands together and looking over at me. "How was your sleepover with Leo? Did you guys have fun?"

I tried to swallow, but my throat was dried and seemed to stick to itself. "Yeah, we had fun. Hung out with some friends, and played some games."

"Good good, I'm glad you had fun."

The table went silent as my mom and Pa continued to eat.

I folded my arms over my stomach and looked at the clock hanging above the entryway. I watched the hands tick by, zoning out and trying to detach from the feelings that were spreading across my body, trying to stop them from getting further than they had already gone.

It felt like I had been struck by some sort of sickness. It started in my stomach, and then spread to my lungs, crawling up my throat and stealing my ability to talk and eat. I was sure it would soon spread to my brain and my heart, using my emotions against me and tearing my body apart from the inside out. And I had no control over it.

I could hear my mom and Pa's voices, murmuring like I was underwater. Drowning in muddy black waters in front of them with nowhere to go. They watched as I did, with no intention to save me. They didn't want to dirty themselves by following me into that dark ocean, with no bottom in sight.

Time passed in a fog, and I lost track of myself in the time it took to drive with my mom to the airport. My mom sat beside me, Pa on the other side of her as we waited at the airport gate. My mom and Pa laughed, but I sat silently, picking at the skin along the edge of my nails.

"Noah?" My mom said putting a hand over mine. "Are you okay sweetie? Does your stomach still hurt?"

I smiled and shook my head. "No, I'm okay."

"Are you sure?" Pa asked leaning forward to look at me. "You've seemed off ever since you came back from Leo's."

Oh, yeah, that's right. Along with all of this, there's Leo. I shrugged. "I'm just thinking about stuff. And I forgot to tell you earlier but Leo told me to tell you that he says hi."

My mom chuckled and my Pa smiled. "I like that boy," My mom said sitting back. "Despite being younger than you it seems he's done a great job taking care of you while I've been gone."

"Yeah, Leo is amazing," I nodded.

"He's so sweet and polite," My mom said, turning to my Pa.

"Yes, the young man always insists on helping with the dishes when we have dinner together," Pa said, crossing his arms. "He won't ever let me do anything for him while he's here. He's such a busybody I can't help but worry."

My mom nodded thoughtfully, sitting silently for a moment before putting a hand on my shoulder. "Make sure that you keep Leo in your life alright? He's a great friend to you, and I think you need to keep someone like him in your life."

There was a pang in my chest at my mom's words. She called him my friend, and up until today, I did too. But I can't help but wonder if this relationship is worth it for him. I wonder if maybe he deserves better.I'm going to weigh him down with my uncertainty; maybe he deserves to be with someone who is out of the closet, and more like him than I am.

"I think you're good for him too," My mom said, interrupting my train of thought.

I turned to her, shaking my head. "I really don't think so."

My mom shook her head and hit me on the back of

my head with a gentle knock. "You balance each other out. Everyone needs someone who fills in the gaps where it is that they are lacking. And everyone needs someone to pour their strengths into."

"You're not making any sense Mom," I said.

My mom stood up at the sound of the overhead speaker calling for her gate. "Maybe I'm not, but I'm sure you'll get it one day. Maybe when you have kids."

I couldn't tell if she knew the truth and was trying to be subtle about it, or if she was oblivious and just doing the mom thing where they tell you random philosophical things that don't make sense to anyone.

I walked with my mom and Pa to the gate, stopping before my mom had to board.

She hugged Pa first. "Bye dad, take care of my kid alright?"

Pa nodded, wacking me aggressively on the back. "Don't worry, I've got him. I've been taking care of him for a while. know what I'm doing by now."

My mom laughed before turning to me. She exhaled and pulled me into a hug, squeezing so tight that I was having trouble breathing. "I'm going to miss you. I'll be back for spring break, so make sure to text and make good choices alright?" She pulled away, cupping my face in her hands.

"Have I ever given you a reason to make an unexpected trip back home before?" I asked.

My mom laughed, before leaning forward and kissing my forehead. She had tears running down her face at this point, a normal occurrence by now. It didn't phase her or me when it happened anymore. It just became another part of our goodbyes.

"You haven't," She said softly, pulling me into another hug. "I love you, take care."

"I love you too Mom, text me when you land

okay?" I requested.

She nodded. "Bye, Noah."

"Bye, Mom."

My mom turned around and started heading towards the gate, when I ran up to her and grabbed her arm pulling her back.

"Wait, Mom, I—" I cut myself off, looking up at the tears still streaming down her face. "I…"

"What is it Noah?" She asked, putting her hand over mine.

I shook my head and smiled. "No, it's okay. It's nothing," I said, letting go of her arm. "You should go now. Don't want to miss your flight."

My mom's brows furrowed in the center of her forehead and she looked at me. "Are you sure Noah?"

"Positive, now go," I said, pushing her towards her gate.

"Okay, okay, bye I love you!" She tried to give me another hug.

I wriggled out of her arms and continued to push her toward the gate. "We already did goodbyes, we don't need to do them again. Mom, just go," I laughed.

She laughed with me, broken sobs escaping between each hiccup. "Okay okay!"

I watched my mom give her ticket to the airline employee, and I watched as she walked through the doorway and down the terminal, disappearing behind the corner.

My mom had left for the term, and with her went my last opportunity for months to tell her in person about Leo and me.

January 5th, 2023

I got into the passenger seat of Leo's car and was immediately wrapped in a tight hug. Leo took a deep breath into my shoulder. He was shaking.

"Are you alright?" I asked rubbing his back.

He nodded. "Yeah, I just wanted to hold you," He said.

My heart jumped in my chest, and that tingly feeling found it's way back into my stomach. I pulled away from him and covered my face with my hands. "Stop… saying embarrassing things,"

"Sorry sorry," he chuckled.

He started the car, and for a little bit, we drove in silence, his hand over the top of mine.

"Do you want to maybe go on a date?" He asked.

I looked down at my lap, avoiding his eyes. "Where? And when?"

He hummed, for a moment thinking. "Sunday?"

"Sure, why not?" I said. "What do you want to do?"

"I know it's cliche but we could do dinner and a movie?" He asked.

I flipped my hand over and rubbed the back of his hand with my thumb. "I'll have to check with Pa, but yeah, it sounds like a nice idea."

"Sounds good. And you don't have to worry about anything cause I'll make sure to plan everything. We can have a nice date on a Sunday night, and it'll be perfect. I promise," Leo said. "Is there anything you want to do? Anywhere you want to go?"

I shrugged, and tension was building in my chest, my breath getting caught in my throat. "I don't know if I'm being honest," I pulled my hand out of his and folded my hands together, squeezing them tightly in my lap. "Just because, I don't want to put us in danger. I don't want…" I paused. "I don't want to get hurt," I murmured.

He stayed silent for a moment, not taking his eyes off the road to look at me. "Yeah," He said. I looked up at him, the tears welling up in my eyes and my stomach dropping down to my feet. "It's scary, huh?"

I choked on my voice, and grabbed his hand off of the center console holding it tightly. "It is. I'm… I'm really scared, Leo," I cried.

Leo rubbed the back of my hand with his thumb. "Why don't we do a home date then? We can order pizza, and watch a movie in a pillow fort. That way, we won't have to be afraid." He suggested.

I nodded, humming. "Yes, I'm sorry," I held his hand to my forehead, my hands shaking. "I'm sorry, I'm sorry, I'm sorry."

"Hey, stop that," He said. "Why are you apologizing?"

"Because, I basically dragged you back into the closet with me because I don't want to tell people."

"Oh, be quiet," He said, chuckling sympathetically. "That's not what this is about. You're acting as if I wouldn't understand what you're going through when I went through the same thing you did. You watched me go through it. You let me lean on you for support when things were bad. Your whole family was there for me, when mine wasn't. I know it's hard, realizing that we could die just from loving each other." He went silent for a moment, grim thoughts seeming to hang in the air around us. "It really does suck."

I nodded, my sobs escaping between coughing.

When we stopped at a red light, Leo grabbed my hand and pulled it towards him, leaning down to kiss the back of it. "It really does suck. It's terrifying, but I'm going to do what I can to protect you." Leo intertwined his fingers with mine and pulled my hand into his lap.

"Our relationship is going to be hard, but I want this. I want you. I've wanted to be with you for years. I knew what I was signing up for when I started to develop feelings for you." . "But, I hope you know that there are a lot of good people in this world too. Allie, Monty, and

Sonali, they're all good people. We've watched each other struggle and we've protected each other as well from the things that we could."

I wiped my eyes with my hands. "I should tell my Pa."

"Wait, what?" Leo said. "Are you sure? That's really soon and I don't want you to feel any kind of pressure to come-out before you're completely ready."

I shook my head. "I'm definitely not ready. But I also know that he'll be accepting. I mean, he took you and I to a pride parade. I know that…" I paused for a moment, the fear I felt making me second guess my trust in someone I've known my whole life. "I want to be able to be proud of dating you without any sort of fears. It may take time but I think this is a good place for me to start."

"I mean, if you're sure," Leo said. "But only if you're one hundred percent positive you want to do this."

I nodded. "I'm sure. You know me, I'd rather rip the band-aid off then peel it off slowly." I turned to him. "Let's have our date at my house. I can properly introduce you."

"But I already know your Pa," Leo said.

"I know, but I want to introduce you to him as my boyfriend," I said quietly.

I saw Leo smile as he drove, his emotions painted across his face. "Okay."

"We can have the date at my house and I can introduce you as my boyfriend to Pa before he leaves for bingo that night."

"Sounds good," He said. "But are you sure you want to do this?"

I nodded and pulled my hand that was holding his towards myself, and kissed the back of his hand. "I want to be with you Leo, without fear. So, I'm going to do what I can to get there," I paused, my face and neck heating up. "Y'know, because I like you."

Leo chuckled and squeezed my hand tightly in his. "I like you too."

I didn't usually make a habit of acting on impulse, but as the old saying goes. People will do crazy things for love.

"I don't want to regret any of the time we spend together just because of a fear of what could happen when we are together. It isn't fair."

"I just," Leo paused. "...don't want you to think you have to come out to him, y'know? It should be on your own terms, not just because you think you should because of me."

I thought for a moment. With his words I couldn't help but second guess myself and wonder who it is I was doing this for. Was it for him? So that he wouldn't have to go back into the closet with me? Or was I doing it for myself, so that I could feel at ease and be comfortable holding my boyfriend's hand in my home? Of course, the answer was obvious.

"Coming out is for me, but it's also for us. I think with my Pa it'll be easy," I said. "I'm scared of how he'll react, but I also know what his feelings are overall, so I don't want to be scared of someone when I know that they're going to show support, I think…" I stopped. "It's not fair to my Pa. For me to have so little faith in him, I mean."

Leo hummed and nodded thoughtfully while he drove. "Yeah, I suppose that makes sense." He stopped, his expression darkening for just a moment. "I guess, it's just hard for me to see how you're ready to come out so quickly, because it was different for me."

I looked down, the memory of him leaving his house in tears flashing through my head. "Oh… right…" I said.

"Do you think you want to come out to more

people?" He asked.

I squeezed his hand and shook my head. "That…
I…I can't do that." I said quietly.

He didn't respond, just rubbed the back of my hand
with his thumb and played soft music as we pulled into my
neighborhood and turned onto my street.

"That's okay," He finally said, pulling into my
driveway. He parked the car and looked over to my house
for a moment, before turning to me and pulling me in for a
kiss. "I think the whole secret romance thing might be kind
of fun."

I rolled my eyes and slapped his arm. "Oh hush," I
said unbuckling my seatbelt. "Don't make it weird."

"I didn't do anything of the sort."

I got out of his car and grabbed my bag from the
backseat, closing the door behind me. He rolled down his
window and I leaned onto the edge of it. "Bye, thank you
for taking me home."

"I'll drive you home any day if it means that I get to
see your face," He said with a smug look on his face.

I covered my face with my hands and chuckled,
my cheeks turning red behind my hands. "You're such an
idiot."

"But you like me so I can't be that much of an
idiot."

I rolled my eyes and took my arms off the edge
of the window. "Okay I really have to go now, so stop
flirting."

"Okay okay," he said. "So, I'll see you on Sunday
then?"

I nodded. "Get home safe."

"I will. Goodbye, Noah."

He rolled up his window and I watched him pull out
of my driveway from the porch of my house. I unlocked
the door and saw Pa sitting in the living room watching the

news. "Welcome home, how was school?" He asked.

I took off my shoes, the smell of ham trailing down the hall into the living room, giving me a clue to what we would be having for dinner. I fell into the couch next to him, the exhaustion from the school day hitting me as I sunk into the couch, a part of me wanting it to swallow me whole.

"It was the same as it always is," I said. "Can Leo come over Sunday?"

"Of course, Leo is always welcome here," Pa said.

I turned my face away from my Pa, not being able to help the stupid grin from spreading over my face. "Cool."

I was overwhelmingly aware of the fact that coming out in a lot of cases was dangerous. I couldn't even begin to fathom what it was like for those who never got to come home to a warm meal again after coming out. A mix of gratitude for my upbringing and pity for those who didn't experience something so warm swirled in my stomach, clashing and burning each other when the two of them mixed.

"Noah," Pa said.

"Hm?" I said not bothering to look up.

"Your mom messaged me."

"She did?" I turned to Pa. "What about?"

Pa shook his head. "She's worried about you," Pa said. "Which tells me that I was right to also be worried."

I shrugged, trying to think up an excuse that would satisfy him. "I mean, I need to retake my physics test."

"You know that's not what I mean," Pa said.

"I'm just a little stressed right now," I said, trying my best not to give too much away. "I just have a lot on my plate so I'm trying to both handle all of that stuff and still maintain my personal relationships with people."

He raised an eyebrow, trying to get me to confess

more, but I kept my mouth shut, knowing that I would dig myself a bigger hole if I opened it.

"Okay, well just let me know if you need anything alright?" He asked.

I nodded and smiled, knowing that what I was saying was only half true, and that my Pa probably wasn't prepared for what's to come. But that was okay, because I don't think I was prepared either.

January 8th, 2023

I had talked a big game to Leo about coming out to my Pa by myself, but now that I was sitting beside him on the couch, with sweat forming along my hairline. Pa sat silently, and as did I, with my hands in fists on my lap.

"What did you need to talk about with me so badly?" He asked.

My head was running in circles, replaying over and over every interaction that I had ever had with my Pa and my mom, overanalyzing them, looking for the signs that would lead to my downfall. I thought about my Pa changing the channel when the news was running an LGBTQ+ story. And I thought about if I could really do this.

"This is hard to talk about, huh?" He said sitting back in the chair. "Well, I'm not going anywhere, okay? Whenever you find the words, I'll be right here."

I ran my fingers through my hair and tried my best to steady my breathing. I thought about the feeling of his hand in mine. His thumb rubbing against the side of my hand.

I was raised by my Pa, and knowing it was possible for things to end had me running circles in my head. I thought maybe it would be better to just say it. To spit it out and get it over with. But every time I tried to open my mouth it was like there was a blockage in my throat preventing the words from coming out.

"Sorry," I whispered, having finally managed to say something. I was trying to hold back my tears, and the one thing I needed to say, I was struggling to do so. "I'm scared."

Pa was silent, before he turned to look at me, resting a hand on my shoulder. "Does this have to do with Leo at all?"

My shoulders tensed underneath his hand, and unable to say anything more I just nodded silently, looking at my lap to avoid seeing whatever reaction could be painted across his face.

"Things have seemed a little different between you two recently," He said. "I didn't know if you were fighting or what. I just knew that you seemed to have a lot on your mind, and a lot you wanted to say. Even your mom is wondering if maybe something happened. She said it seemed like you had something you wanted to tell her. Is there?"

I nodded.

"Can you look at me, Noah?"

I lifted my head and turned to him. My entire body relaxed when I saw the wrinkles in his reassuring smile.

"I like boys," I whispered.

"Are you gay then?" He asked.

I shrugged. "I don't really know. I've liked girls before, but whether I'm gay or straight, the label isn't exactly important to me." I said.

"So then the thing going on with Leo…"

I nodded. "We're dating, Pa."

Pa pulled me into a hug, rubbing my back comfortingly. "Thank you for telling me, Noah. I'm happy for you."

I hid my face in his chest, holding him tightly and trying not to let him see my face.

"I'm glad you were able to find someone that really appreciates you." He paused. "Honestly, it's about time. I had a feeling that maybe Leo liked you, but I could never be sure, so I never said anything."

I laughed into his chest before pulling away from him and smiling at him as he smiled at me.

He wiped the tears from my face and brushed my hair back out of my face. "Noah, I love you okay? You could be a unicorn for all I care, you're still family."

I nodded. "Pa, thank you," I tried to speak, but my voice came out soft and strained, as if the words stuck in my throat had scraped the sides of it on their way out. "I love you."

"And I love you." He said, standing up. "I want to talk to Leo now, though. Do you mind?"

I shook my head and stood up beside him. I followed him down the hall and towards my bedroom door.

I had taken my first step towards being okay with my identity. It was probably the hardest out of all of the future ones to come. And it hurt to do, but I don't think I would change it. Because I don't think I would be here holding hands with this person if I did. Discovering parts of myself that I didn't know had existed. Discovering the feelings that I didn't know I had. And it's all thanks to that stupid party that I didn't even want him to throw. And that silly drunken kiss.

Temporary Goodbyes

Titania

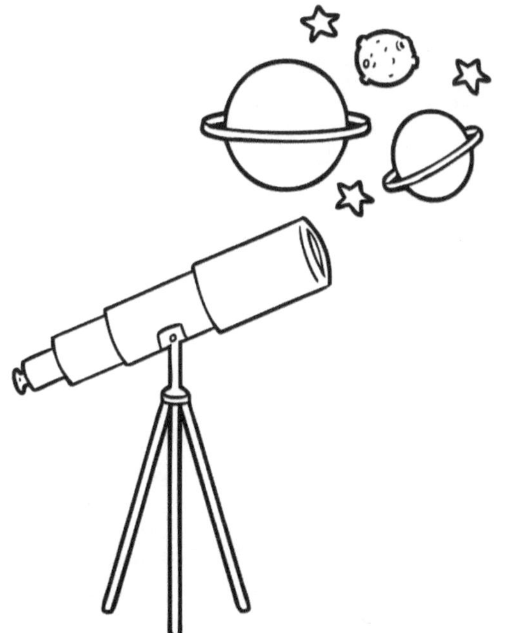

<u>Temporary Goodbyes (Ita)</u>

December 13th, 2018

I didn't think that the hospital could be so colorful. I walked down the hallway with my mom a step behind me. It didn't smell the way you would expect a hospital to smell. It didn't smell like saline, or like chemicals, it just smelt like a clean house.

There was art work hanging from the walls between doorways, and bright banners hung from bulletin boards on the doors of patients' rooms. The floor tiles were in a pattern of mellow colors, with white stripes going down the sides of each hallway with the stripes underneath. Three tiles of grey, one of a dull teal, a dusted pink, another of the teal, and then the pattern repeated itself all down the hallway.

My mom put her hand on my back and leaned down to me. "There's the nurse's station, go ask for directions over there, alright? I'm going to wait in the waiting room. I'll be there when you're done," She said.

I turned. "Wait, you're not leaving me are you?" I said, grabbing her arm. "No, no, I can't just—"

My mom pulled my hand off of her, interrupting my train of thought when she said, "This is something you have to do on your own."

"But," I said. "I don't want to, I'm scared."

My mom sighed, kneeling down in front of me. She looked me up and down, then started to smooth out my hair, brushing her fingers through the end of it. "We've been over this. Ita, I can't hold your hand. You need to be brave. I want you to understand the world around you on a deeper level, and you can't do that if you're always looking down." She stood up. "I'm going to go wait in the waiting room at the end of the hall, okay?"

I nodded, and stood motionless matching my mom as she walked down the hallway and around the corner to the waiting room.

I turned on my heel and groaned, looking towards the nurse's station. A few nurses sat at the counter in front of computers, talking amongst themselves and writing things down in binders. I sighed and walked up to the counter, tightening the grip I had on the bouquet of flowers I was holding.

"Um," I started to talk, none of the nurses turned to look at me. "Sorry to bother you, I'm just uh," I avoided eye contact, not knowing which nurse to look at. "I'm looking for my friend, I'm just trying to visit."

There was no response, and they continued to talk to one another not noticing me standing by them, as I peeked behind the side of the counter to try and get their attention.

"I just don't know what we're supposed to do, y'know?" One of the nurses said. "This pay isn't sustainable for my family, but… who is going to take care of these kids if I quit now? We're already understaffed enough as it is. I think these kids deserve better than that, y'know?"

"I get what you mean. I can survive off of this income, but it just isn't enough for me to live off of, especially if I wanted to support a family in the future. I have to think about stuff like that." A nurse with a deeper voice said.

"Um," I said again, taking a step behind the counter. "I'm trying to find my friend, and I was hoping to get some help." I said putting my school ID on the counter and pushing it over for them to see.

"Okay! Where is your mom?" The nurse with the deeper said standing up.

"She's in the waiting room by the elevator, she said I needed to do this on my own."

She looked at me suspiciously, before turning to the other nurses, who responded to her facial expressions with shrugs. "Do you know what wing they're in, hun?" She asked, grabbing a tablet from the counter and walking around to stand beside me.

"Wing?" I stuttered. "I'm sorry I don't, I don't know what you mean."

She nodded, taking a look at my ID before handing it back to me. "That's okay sweetie. What are they here getting treatment for? Do you know?"

I swallowed, uncomfortable at the idea of saying the words out loud. They tasted sour enough when I had to say them the first time. "A— , um, anorexia," I said. The word stung on my tongue, and fizzled out leaving silence between me and the nurse.

"Okay," She said, her voice noticeably softer than before. She started walking, not bothering to look back and see if I was following behind her. "Follow me, I'll walk you over to the right wing," She said.

I jogged to catch up, falling into step behind her.

"How old are you?" She asked as we walked down the hallway.

"I'm thirteen," I said.

I looked into the rooms as we passed by them. Trying to get a glimpse inside so I could get a feel for what to expect when I walked into Allie's room. There was a window with blinds, and the rooms were dull and grey if they were empty, but the rooms that patients stayed in were decorated. They had brought blankets and pillows from home, and had art and decorations hanging from the walls. They had decorated the rooms as if they had no idea how long they would be sleeping in it.

"That's quite young," She said. "How old is your friend?"

"Fourteen," I said.

She didn't say anything more, she just led me over to a different nurse's station with only one nurse sitting behind the counter.

"Hi, can you tell me where—" The nurse cut herself off, turning to me. "What's your friend's name?" She asked.

"Alaska Hughes," I said.

"Can you tell me where Alaska Hughes is?" The nurse asked, repeating my words.

"Oh, she just came in a couple of days ago. She's in room 509," The other nurse said pointing to the left. "Down the hall and to the right."

"Alrighty, thanks," She walked past me. "C'mon sweetie, let's go."

I jogged to catch up to her once again, and we walked the rest of the way down the hall in silence. I scanned the room numbers on the right side of the hallway, slowly coming to a stop as we approached room 509.

"Alrighty, here you are," The nurse said, turning to me. "Was there anything else I could help you with? Do you want me to stay with you?" She asked.

I shook my head.

"Okay, I'll be going then, sweetie."

I watched her as she walked away, before turning back to the door. I peeked in the window that opened into the hallway and saw Alaska sitting on the bed, her legs crossed and her face resting in her hands as she read a book. She had on a hoodie and a pair of leggings, and the room she was in had yet to have any life breathed into it. The only thing in the room that was hers was the clothes she had on her body and the book she had in her hand.

I took a deep breath and knocked on the door that was cracked open before pushing it open all of the way.

"Allie, hi," I said, taking a step into the room. "I brought you flowers."

Her posture stiffened and she scowled at me slamming the book shut. "Ita, what are you doing here?"

"I came to visit…" I said. "I just wanted to see how you were doing."

"Oh, don't act like you care about me, I know that you don't."

"What are you talking about?" I asked setting the flowers down on the bed next to her.

She scoffed and rolled her eyes. "I confided in you as a friend and you turned your back on me and told on me to my parents! Now look at me!" She said standing up. "I'm caged up in the hospital like some sort of crazy person!"

"Allie, I…" I paused. "I was just trying to help you. I was just worried. You didn't look good, Allie. I thought you were going to get sick, or faint again."

"But you had no right to tell my parents! If you were truly worried you would have stayed out of it! I told you that I was handling it," Alaska exclaimed. "I was working on getting better by myself!"

"But Allie…"

"No, I'm not doing this," She said walking around the bed. "I trusted you with my secret and you blabbed it.

I told you because I trusted you to keep your mouth shut!"
She grabbed my shoulders and started pushing me toward
the door. "Are you happy now? I'm a wreck and it's your
fault! Does that make you happy?" She cried.

"No of course it doesn't!" I exclaimed, turning and
grabbing her hands. "Listen if you just let me explain, I
can—"

"Go home!" She said, shoving me out of the door.
"Listen, we're not friends anymore. Whatever trust I
had for you is gone. I never want you to show your face
ever again. I want you to walk out of this building and
never come back." Her eyes were puffy, and she had tears
streaming down her face, and yet I couldn't do anything.
All I could do was stand there silently and take it. "I
thought you loved me."

"I do love you thoug—"

"If you loved me you wouldn't have done this,"
Allie said, shaking her head. "Just," her words came out of
her mouth between sobs. "Get away from me."

She grabbed the door handle, pulling it shut, leaving
me standing in the hallway.

I could feel the tears dripping down my neck and
soaking my shirt. I walked down the hall, past both nurses'
stations, and into the waiting room where my mom sat.

I walked into the waiting room and lost all of the
strength in my legs.

"Mom," I croaked. My knees buckled, and I fell as
my mom looked up at me.

"Ita," She said, running over to me. "What
happened, are you okay?" She asked, sitting in front of me
and wiping the tears from my face.

"She hates me," I sobbed, setting my head on her
shoulder. "I ruined everything."

My mom didn't say anything. She just pulled me
into a hug and ran her fingers through my hair, trying her

best to soothe me. I sat in the middle of the waiting room, the murmurs of the people in it putting my head underneath water. Their stares made my skin crawl, but I didn't have any fight left to give. I couldn't stand.

When I finally stopped crying, my mom picked me up in her arms and we took the elevator down to the ground floor. My mom walked me out of the doors and to the car, and I could see the spot in the flower beds where I had picked the ground clean of any flowers that had been planted there. I thought about the time it would take for the flowers to grow back and I thought about the time it would take for the flowers I had picked to die. I wondered if the time I had taken to pick them was time that I had wasted.

Mom opened the car door, and I sat down in the passenger seat.

My mom sat down on the driver's side, and we sat silently, her looking at me, and me looking out the window.

"Do you want to talk about it?" She asked.

I shook my head.

"Do you want to talk to dad?" She asked.

Again, I shook my head.

"Do you want to talk to anyone?"

I shook my head again and looked out the window squeezing my eyes shut as they began to water again. I tried to keep the tears in, knowing that if I started crying again, I would make my mom more worried than she already was.

"Is there anything at all that I can do?" She begged.

I shook my head and put a hand over my mouth, trying to keep the sobs from escaping my throat.

"Okay, let me know if there is," She said, starting the car.

As we drove, all I could think about was how badly I had messed up. I ruined my relationship with my best friend. I betrayed her, and now she never wants to talk to me again. And there was nothing I could do to change it.

December 27th, 2022

I came to this party with the cheer team. I hoped it meant I would be able to get closer to them. But it seems I had only been invited out of courtesy because as soon as we arrived they all went off to their own thing, leaving me alone in a house full of people I barely knew. After having wandered the house doing this and that for over an hour, a boy with red hair, who claimed to know my team, dumped a girl on me.

Of course, it would be me who would get stuck babysitting a drunk girl that I didn't know at a party that I didn't want to go to.

"Wait! Don't just leave me here!" I called.

Before I could protest anymore the boy, whose name I didn't even know, had already walked away, leaving me to take care of a girl who laid heavy against my shoulder.

"Hey," I said, shaking her. "What's your name?"

The girl didn't respond, she just wrapped her arms around my neck, putting all of her weight onto my shoulders while giggling.

"Oh, c'mon!" I exclaimed trying to break her grip from around me. "Are you being for real right now? I'm not a crutch! Stand up!" I pulled her arms away from me and hooked them around her waist pulling her up into a standing position while holding her tightly. "Now I'm hugging a stranger." I said to myself, rolling my eyes.

She put her face into my chest and inhaled against my skin, making me jump. "Hey!" I exclaimed. "What do you think you're doing?"

She pushed me away from her, squinting her eyes and looking me up and down before falling back into my arms laughing. "You smell familiar,"

I looked down at her, confused as to why she had any idea about what I smelled like. "You're weird," I said, pulling one of her arms over my shoulder.

I wrapped one hand around her waist and held her wrist with my other hand as I walked her out to my car. I managed to unlock my car by pressing the door button with my foot. After that I dropped the strange girl into the passenger seat and walked over to the driver's side, turning the car on and blasting the heat.

I sat and rubbed my hands together trying to get myself warmed up. I looked over as I breathed into my hands. She sat with her shoulders hunched forward, and her chin leaning into her chest. Her eyes were closed and she had a goofy smile on her face.

I leaned over and pushed her shoulders back so that she sat leaning against the seat. I grabbed the seatbelt, and pulled it over her, clicking it into place. When I looked back up, her eyes were wide open and she was staring at me. It was the first chance I had to get a good look at her. She had light brown hair, and it was pulled back into a messy bun with hair falling into her face, individual strands getting caught in the mascara on her eyelashes.

I reached out to brush her baby hairs back, noticing the mix of brown and blue speckled unevenly in her pupils.

"Heterochromia…" I mumbled to myself.

"A mix of celestine and smokey quartz," the girl mumbled, closing her eyes again. She pulled her legs up resting her cheek on her knee. "That's what my friend used to say it looked like. They're some weird crystals."

I froze, looking the girl up and down again. She closed her eyes, preventing me from getting another look at her eyes. It took me a bit to recognize her. Her hair was lighter than it was back then, her freckles were darker now than when we were in middle school, and she didn't have braces anymore.

"Allie?" I asked, grabbing her shoulder. "Hey, you are Allie right?"

She hummed in response, and I sat back in the driver's seat running my fingers through my hair. "Are you really just going to fall asleep like that?" I asked, looking at her.

I sighed and grabbed my winter coat from the backseat draping it over her. I'm glad I realized who she was because it meant that I definitely couldn't take her back to her house, that is if her parents are still the same as they were a few years ago.

I put my seatbelt on and started up my car, driving in silence back to my house in an attempt to not wake her up.

When we got to my house I scooped her up from the passenger side and carried her in the door and up the stairs to my room.

I placed her down on my bed and took her shoes off before covering her with a blanket.

I sat at the foot of the bed, with my knees pulled up to my chest and my hands on my neck. I couldn't take her home, but I have a feeling she isn't going to enjoy waking up to find me sleeping on the floor. There's no way she still doesn't hate me.

I watched light flood into my room from underneath the door as the hall light was turned on. Light footsteps had followed, and then there was a gentle knock on my bedroom door.

"Ita, are you home from the party?" My mom asked.

"Yeah, I'm home, you can come in," I sighed.

She opened the door slowly, her eyes widening at the sight of a random girl laying in my bed. She looked between me and the girl, trying to figure out what it was that she wanted to say.

Eventually she sighed, putting her hand on her hip and running her hand through her hair. "You brought a girl home,"

"It's Allie."

"... Allie doesn't look so good."

I nodded. "Allie had a little too much to drink."

My mom set the unopened water bottle she had been holding on the nightstand beside me. "Take care of her then alright?" I nodded. "Okay, I'm going to head to sleep now then. I love you, and don't do anything stupid."

"I love you too," I said watching as she shut the door behind herself.

I turned, resting my cheek against the mattress and looking up at her. It looked like she had gained weight, and I couldn't help but smile. I felt relieved to see her healthier. I hoped it meant that she was better now. It made me believe that I truly did do the right thing in telling her parents about what happened. She can hate me for it all she wants. I would hate myself too if I were her but I think I'm okay with that now. Cause at least I know that I made the right decision in the end. I closed my eyes and fell asleep leaning against the bed that my childhood friend was asleep in.

December 28th, 2022

I rubbed my eyes at the sound of someone whispering. The memories of yesterday came flooding back as I stood up opening my eyes. There was a frantic Allie talking on the phone in the bed beside me.

Allie sat on my bed with her hair falling over her shoulders in messy curls, and leftover makeup from last night smudged down her eyes. I sat down next to her, not daring to say a word until she willed me to be able to.

"Yes, I know, I'm sorry," She said into the phone. "I'll be home right away I promise, please don't be mad."

She said. I could hear muffled yelling from the phone as she swung her legs over the bed, almost hitting me in the face as she stood. "I'm sorry I didn't tell you, I'm coming home right now I promise." She paused. "Yes, my friend is going to drive me," She said looking at me.

I opened my mouth to object, but closed it as she glared at me shaking her head. She nodded, tucking her hair behind her ear.

"Yes, I love you too. I'll see you soon, bye," She said, hanging up and removing her hand from my mouth.

She crossed her legs, and set her phone down in her lap, staring at me while taking a couple deep breaths before running her hands over her face and groaning.

"I woke up in your bed."

I nodded.

"Did you do anything with me?"

"No! No!" I exclaimed, waving my hands around to hide my face. "I definitely didn't! I would never do anything to a sleeping person."

She sighed, rubbing the bridge of her nose between her index finger and her thumb. "You're driving me home."

"Okay," I responded, looking at my lap.

"And you're going to give me clothes so that I don't go home to my parents smelling of alcohol."

I nodded. "Okay."

"And as soon as you take me home, you'll leave me alone," She said, standing up and beginning to walk away.

I looked up at her. "Wait, so you know who I am, Allie?" I asked, grabbing her wrist before she could completely walk away from me. "You recognized me?"

She pulled her hand out of mine. "I wasn't sure if it was you, if I'm being honest. That photo of us on your dresser gave you away, though. I'm surprised that you still have it," She said, nodding to the framed photo I had on my dresser. She shook her head, as if trying to shake away her thoughts. "Now, seriously, give me some clothes." She said, pulling her shirt over her head.

"Oh, um, yeah, no problem!" I said, looking at the floor and turning my dresser. I pulled out a hoodie and some sweatpants and handed them to her, keeping my eyes on the ground as she changed.

"Remember," She said, opening my bedroom door. "You're going to take me home and then you're never going to talk to me again," She walked out the door.

I ran down the hall to catch up to her and put a hand on her shoulder stopping her in her tracks. "Wait! Allie, are you mad at me?" I asked. I held her shoulder firmly, once again afraid of her falling out of my grasp. "You don't hate me, do you?" I asked quietly.

She laughed a bit, turning to face me. "Hate you?" I looked up to see her glaring at me again. " I don't know. Maybe, I do. You really hurt me, you know," She asked.

"I'm sorry, I wasn't trying to hurt you when I told your parents," I said. "I was just worried about your health, and I didn't want you getting sick or anything. I'm sorr—"

"You seriously think this is still about that?" She scoffed.

I looked up at her just in time to feel her grab the collar of my shirt and yank me forward. "This isn't about that. It was never about that," She pleaded, shoving me away. "I don't care that you told my parents. I was able to get over that. In fact, I eventually became super grateful to you for it. But you left. You left without ever saying goodbye, and I had no idea where you went."

Her lips were pressed into a thin line, and her eyes were glossed over with tears. Between the two of us, Allie was always the brave one. Somehow though, she looked afraid.

"I couldn't find you anywhere. Do you realize how scary that was for me? And then come to find out

you moved to England? You ran away without a word…”
I stared at her as she angrily wiped tears from her face. “I
always get so stupidly emotional when I’m hungover,” She
mumbled to herself.

“Allie, I—” I tried to reach out to her, but she took a
step backward away from me.

“Just stop. Please, I don’t want to talk to you about
any of this. I don’t want to remember how badly it hurt to
lose you. Just take me home,” She pleaded. “Please.”

I ran my fingers through my hair and sighed. “Yeah,
okay,” I said. “Let’s go.” I walked past her and down the
stairs, trying not to cry.

I got into the car, slamming it behind me. “Do you
still live in the same place?” I asked as Allie got into the
passenger seat.

She nodded. “Yeah, I can put the address into the
GPS for you.”

“No need,” I said, starting the car. “I know how to
get there.”

She didn’t respond, and neither did I. I didn’t plug
my phone into the aux either. I let us sit in uncomfortable
silence for the thirteen-minute car ride to her house from
mine.

I pulled into her driveway, and parked the car,
waiting for her to get out and leave without saying a word.

Instead, she quietly asked, “Why did you leave?”

I let her question sit in the air for a moment. “My
mom got transferred there. I didn’t have a choice.” I said.

“Why didn’t you ever say goodbye?” She said, her
voice quiet and shaky. She sounded like she was on the
verge of tears. I didn’t blame her, I was too.

“I really did think you hated me,” I said. “You told
me to never talk to you again, so I figured you wouldn’t be
that mad if I just disappeared without a word.”

“Why would you ever think that?” She exclaimed,

grabbing my shoulders. "You were my best friend! You seriously believed me? And you just left…" She set her head against my shoulder and her breathing shaked.

I didn't move. I didn't know what to do or say to make it better. I didn't feel like I had any right to comfort her in an attempt to make her feel better. I felt like I was the last person she wanted any comfort from.

Despite that, I wrapped my arms around her, pulled her into a hug, and said, "I'm sorry."

For a moment, she didn't say anything, and she didn't move. She just leaned into me, letting me hold her silently.

"I really am sorry," I whispered.

She pushed me away and wiped her eyes. Her face was red, and her brows furrowed her entire face tense.

"Wait Allie," I said, opening my center console. I pulled out a travel pack of makeup wipes. "You have mascara all over your face, I know your parents will worry."

She sat, frozen before snatching the makeup wipe out of my hands. She unbuckled her seat belt and got out of the car, holding the door open before saying, "Stop saying sorry. It isn't going to make me feel better, so just leave me alone," slamming the door shut behind her.

I watched her run up the steps of her house, unlocking her door and shutting it behind her.

I sat in her driveway for a moment, tugging on the ends of my hair. She had bags under her eyes, and her undercut was grown out. Her hair was longer, and the blue streak she used to have in her hair was completely gone, as if it had never been there in the first place. I had a feeling that we might meet again, but I wasn't expecting such a sudden and bitter reunion.

January 5th, 2023

I was new to this team, and I felt like a wounded animal left to the vultures. They circled overhead, staring down at me as I struggled to move. They were waiting for me to die, to fail so that they could eat my remains. If I took too long to die, I had a feeling that they would resort to just eating me alive instead.

I was practicing with a group of my teammates, trying to do my best as a base, but it seemed that no matter how steady I stood, something would go wrong. None of our stunts were successful, and everytime something went wrong the girls would glare at me, using their eyes like daggers.

However, their gazes weren't the only ones that seemed to be stuck on me. Across the commons Allie was drilling holes into my back with her eyes, not diverting from me for even a second the entire practice. Between the vultures and Allie, I couldn't focus.

After practice was over Ana and Lyn approached me. Ana stood a few inches taller than Lyn, and she had long blonde hair that fell down her back like a river of sunlight, and Lyn, the other captain, who always found herself tied to Ana's hip, had shoulder length hair with purple highlights that peaked out from behind her ears.

"Hey, how was your first practice?" Ana said. She spoke softly, and had the smile of a mother. She was the one that I felt I could probably talk to if I needed.

"Did the others get to you?" Lyn asked. Lyn was far more blunt than Ana, and at times it felt like Ana was holding Lyn on a short leash, trying to keep her from saying the wrong thing and being unintentionally rude to others.

I shrugged. "It was okay. The others were nice, I'm glad to be on a team with you guys," I said, giving them a closed-lip smile. I looked down, trying to avoid their eyes as if they would pull the truth out of me through eye contact. So I kept eyes down, and circled my thumbs around each other.

"Alright…" Lyn said in a suspecting tone. "Well, did you have any questions for our coach?"

Ana nodded. "Or for us?"

I shook my head. "I'm all good, did you maybe have any thoughts for me?" I asked. "Please tell me if there's anything I can improve on. I want to know what I can do better, so that I'm on the same level as you guys."

"Oh, of course! I think—"

"You should smile more," Lyn said, cutting Ana off.

"Lyn!" Ana pulled on her cheek.

"What?" Lyn said, pulling away. "She asked!"

I tilted my head at them. "Do I not smile enough?" I asked.

Lyn and Ana looked between each other, and then to me.

"You can take care of it, Ana, I think you'll be able to word it better than I can," Lyn took a step backwards. "I have to talk to the coach about something anyways." Lyn turned on her heel, and jogged over to where their coach stood.

Ana sighed. "I swear I have no idea what I'm going to do with her." She turned to me. "I guess the others just think you're a bit stand-off-ish. You could stand to be a bit friendlier, so that they can connect to you, and you guys can get close, does that make sense?" Ana said.

I nodded, rocking back and forth on my feet. "Yeah, I got it, I'm sorry if I was making anyone uncomfortable."

"It's okay, they're just adjusting to you mostly, especially because you have more cheer experience and skills then a lot of the members on our team," Ana said. She put her hand on my shoulder. "I'm here if you need anything okay?"

"I will, no need to worry about me."

"Alright, you have my number, so just contact me,

and don't forget to have your hair dyed to a natural color by our first competition in a few weeks alright?" Ana said.

I nodded.

Ana turned around and waved Lyn over from where she stood watching. "Have a good night, alright?"

"Yeah, you too," I said as I watched Lyn run over to where they stood.

Ana and Lyn walked away, waving goodbye to me as they did.

I stood in the center of the commons, not being able to move my feet from where they were planted. Cheer was over, and so with the later hours starting to hit the commons was clear of most students. However out of the corner of my eye, I could still see Allie sitting at the table. With headphones on and her hair pulled back into a messy bun as she typed away at a computer. There was a notepad on her left and a camera sitting on the table to her right.

I walked over to her cautiously not wanting to spook her.

"Hey," I said. She looked up and glared at me, opening her mouth to say something before I cut her off, continuing to talk. "Listen, I know you told me to leave you alone, but it's really hard for me to do that when you're been staring at me for over an hour."

She looked away from me and shut her computer, standing up and packing her things. "I'm doing this because I have to," She said, putting her notebook in her bag. "I was watching you because I have to write something this week for cheer, and considering you're joining the team late you're the perfect thing to be a subtle focus of this week's article. I can emphasize how well you were able to just fall into place with the other members, getting along and laughing like you had known each other for years."

"Wait, but that's— that's not true—" I started.

She rolled her eyes and cut me off with a scoff.

"Obviously. I know that. You know that, anyone watching could have gathered that much. But I can't possibly write that now can I?" She said, "I'm supposed to build you guys up, so you can get the support of your classmates when you go to championships. It's not my job to be accurate. Plus I'll get my teacher in trouble if I write anything negative about anyone. He has done a lot for me, so I'm not going to let him down."

I put my hands behind my back and looked down, rocking back and forth on my heels.

"It's not like I want to be doing this either. The only reason why I'm here is that no one else was able to, and I have covered cheer in previous years, so I was the obvious pick," She said, throwing her bag over her shoulder. "I don't want to talk to you, but I really don't have a choice, now do I? And since I'm stuck doing this anyways, I'm going to make the most of it. So, just be prepared and try to be normal when I interview you next week."

"But I—" I started to talk but she cut me off.

"After everything that happened, the least you could do is give me a damn interview." She paused, grabbed her phone and began to type. " I'll see you after your next rehearsal, so make sure to stay behind. And don't try to get out of it either." She looked up. "Understand?"

I looked between her and the floor, before sighing. "Yeah, sure. I got it."

"Good, see you," Allie said, turning on her heel and walking away.

"See you," I murmured.

I stood frozen again, wondering if things will ever be the same between her and me, or at least, some form of normal. But, I didn't have very high hopes. Just unrealistic fantasies of her forgiving me and us being friends again.

January 3th, 2023

I held my notebook against my chest as I followed the librarian around. She showed me where all of the different books were located. She pointed out to me where the shelving carts were, and the locations of the charging stations for students who would come during free periods.

After she showed me around the library, she took me over to the circulation desk and sat me down in front of a computer before showing me how to check books out for students. She showed me how to do everything, she handed me a stack of books to shelve in order for me to become more familiar with the layout of the library and locations of their different books.

The library was big, and unlike my old school, students were allowed to eat in here, and they were less strict on keeping quiet. It was less of a place for silent study and more of a place for student collaboration.

I was over at the shelf with the graphic novels when I noticed a book open on a table that had a diagram of a meteorite open. I recognized it from my astronomy textbook from my sophomore year of school. At the table sat a boy with curly brown hair and a pair of glasses open on the table in front of him.

I looked at the worksheet he was working on, and couldn't help but notice his mistake, along with the name "Noah" scribbled on the corner of the page. I walked around the shelf I stood at and sat down the stack of books on the table beside him, causing him to look up at me from where he sat.

"This is wrong," I said, pointing to the question asking him to distinguish the temperature between meteors, meteoroids and meteorites. "You've got them mixed up." I flipped to the following page in the text book that had the diagram of a meteor.

"Really?" He raised an eyebrow at me. "What are

you, a meteor expert?"

I shook my head. "No, I just like space. When it passes through Earth's atmosphere, that's when we call it a meteor. Meteors get super hot because of ram pressure. But," I said, dragging my finger across the diagram. "When it hits Earth— which is when it becomes a meteorite— it's actually cold due to the moisture in the air as it falls to Earth."

"Oh…" He said.

I picked up the textbook and flipped forward and back a few pages trying to find the section on the Meteors. When I found the page, I set it back down on the table pointing to the paragraph where it talked through the temperatures.

"Be careful with this textbook. You can't rely on just the diagrams at the end of the chapter. The diagrams in this textbook sometimes miss information that is asked about in the curriculum."

"Oh," He said, pulling the textbook closer and scanning the page in front of him. "Wow, thanks for your help. I've been struggling all semester but I think this will really help me out."

I nodded. "No worries. I know a lot about this stuff and I'll be here all period, so just let me know if you need help with anything else."

"Titania!"

I looked up to see the librarian waving me over from their spot behind the circulation desk.

I picked up the books I had set down, as I watched the boy erase and rewrite his answer to the question on the worksheet.

"Bye," I smiled.

He smiled back at me, waving as I walked away over to where the librarian was.

"Try not to talk to the other students too much

alright? They're here to study, you're here to help us, remember?" The librarian said, setting a hand on my shoulder.

"Alright, I'm sorry. I didn't know," I said.

She shook her head as if trying to swat away my worries. "It's not a big deal, just be careful about it in the future. Get back to working on those books alright?"

I nodded, taking the stack of books back over to the shelf I had been working on.

The boy turned around, mouthing the words 'sorry,' to me.

I shook my head, trying to signal to him that it was fine and I didn't really mind.

Spending the rest of the period silently shelving books, I wondered if places like home would start to feel as natural as they seemed to feel here.

I still hadn't unpacked my books, and I hadn't even bothered to put up my telescope on the balcony.

I was scared, but I was excited to see what the stars would look like from my new home. Especially knowing there would be a taste of nostalgia in the way the stars lined up outside my window. Similar to the ways they would when I was little, sitting criss-cross on my back porch with Allie next to me as I pointed out the lines that connected them. Allie was never able to connect stars into constellations the way that I was able to. We both knew it, but neither of us pointed it out. Because at the time seeing the stars wasn't the part that mattered to me. It was who I was seeing them with. And I hadn't realized how much I had missed them, until the way the stars lined up in the sky reminded me of those sleepless summer nights from childhood.

January 7th, 2023

I always felt at peace at the library. The smell of

the books and the sound of the pages fluttering between peoples fingers worked in tandem to create a symphony of senses.

The local bookstore had a similar feeling. People were welcomed to come sit and read for however long they wanted, with the added bonus of being able to buy and keep a book if they so wished.

I honestly didn't think this old building would still be here. It was run down and the bricks were falling out of the wall. The gutter on top of the roof was rusted, with moss along the edges of it, and ivy following the path of the gutter down towards the ground. The windows were dirty like the history of the store was written in the dust on the panes.

But the bookstore still stood. The gutters had been replaced, and they were no longer rusted and covered with moss. The ivy still crawled up the wall of the brick and the gutter, and the windows were no longer covered in dust, but had a mosaic film over them, casting rainbows onto the sidewalk and into the puddles from last night's rain.

When I walked in, the kind old lady who used to sit behind the desk wasn't there. Instead there was a boy with eyes the same color as the ivy on the outside of the building. There was curly red hair peeking out from underneath a beanie as he leaned on the counter that he sat at. It took me a moment to realize, but he was the same boy who had dropped Allie on my shoulder at the party.

The beanie had cat ears, and along the cuff of it there was a rainbow button and a name tag with the 'Leo' written out in cursive and 'he/him' written in text below it.

He looked up at me when the familiar chime of the gold bell rang, shutting the book that he had laying in front of him.

"Welcome in," He said. "There's a coffee cart and vending machine for different brews by the back. Feel free to stay as long as you like and just let me know if you need anything.”

I nodded to him, looking left and right. I peeked over the desk as I approached it, stopping at the edge of it and making eye contact with the boy behind the counter.

“Um,” I started. “I did have a question, actually.”

“What’s up?” He said.

“I used to live around her a few years ago, back in 2019, and I was wondering where the old lady who was always working is?” I asked. “All those years I spent coming here and I never learned her name,” Looking at the floor and rocking back and forth on my heels I smiled at the idea of seeing her again.

“She passed away.”

I looked up, my stomach dropping. “Wait, what?”

He nodded. “Yeah, Gran died in 2020.”

The old lady was one of the sweetest people I had ever met. She was kind, gentle, and always gave me candy when I came in to look at books. I often heard her humming old nursery rhymes behind the counter. I would sit at the carpet in the back of the book store and listen as her husband read picture books. For some reason, it never crossed my mind that she might’ve died.

“You’re her grandson?” I asked, my voice quiet.

He shrugged, leaning back in his chair. “I guess you could say that.”

I stood in silence, watching the boy at the counter not being able to find the words.

“Did Allie cause you any trouble?” He asked. “Y’know the day of the party.”

I looked up. “I don’t know how to answer that really.”

“If I knew who you were I never would have let you take her,” He said rubbing the bridge of his nose. “So, sorry.”

"I know I hurt her."

"Yeah, you did. You really did."

"I thought that she didn't want to see me ever again," I said, choking on the words that I was trying to say.

"I know. She hurt you too," he said. "But you left her alone without anyone to lean on during a really hard time for her."

"I didn't mean—"

"Do you care about her?" He interrupted me with a loud sigh, almost as if he was tired of listening to my voice. I wouldn't blame him for how he felt, because I was also tired of hearing my own voice.

I nodded. "Of course I do. I mean she was my best friend."

"Was she?"

"Yes!" I exclaimed. "Why are you doubting how much I care about her? I love her so much it hurts me."

"I'm doubting you because you left," He said, standing up. "When I met her, she was broken and she was alone. She was so lost. She was confused and she was hurt because you left."

"I know," I said. "I left without saying anything. I changed my number, I dyed my hair green instead of pink for a couple of years. Hell, I moved halfway across the damn globe." I stopped. "But I thought that she didn't need me. She said she never wanted to see me again."

"And you believed her?" He asked. "Is that what you wanted? Did you also never want to see her again?"

"I—"

"In a relationship, decisions need to be made between both parties. Even if what you are deciding is whether or not to end it." He sighed. "I'm not saying Allie is in the right either. She pushed you away when all you wanted to do was help her. And she knows that. She knows she messed up. But of course, Allie is prideful."

I looked up at him.

"Neither of you did anything wrong or right, but you still hurt her. She deserves an apology because of that. Especially because it's because of you that it's so hard to gain her trust now."

"Both of you need to stop being stubborn and need to talk to each other," He stood up and walked around the corner. "But don't you dare walk back into her life if you plan on running away again at the first sight of danger. I won't let you hurt her again. Do you want her back in your life?"

I nodded.

"Then you need to prove it."

"How can I? How do I work on mending this relationship with her when she won't even talk to me?" I asked. "She refuses to talk about what happened with me."

"I don't know," He said, walking back around the corner and sitting down. "That's not my job. If you really want her back you'll find a way to get through to her because not only is that the only way she'll listen, it's the only way to gain her trust back. To show her that you really do regret leaving without a word."

"I will," I said. "Even if she doesn't want to be friends, I at least want to talk to her. I want to settle things and I want to apologize properly. I want to get through to her."

"Then, good luck," He said.

I stood, not knowing whether or not I should walk away or if I should stay and listen.

"I don't want you thinking that I'm on your side, because I'm not," He said. "But I watched them agonize over you leaving. And I saw how badly it hurt. They didn't know where you had gone or what had happened. And I think she would be really relieved if the two of you could be friends again."

"I think you're wrong."

"Then think I'm wrong," he said. "But, she looked for you, y'know? I helped her try and find you on social media."

"I deleted everything when I moved."

"Why?" He asked.

I shrugged. "I kind of wanted to start over, I guess. I didn't want to think about what had happened when I lived here. How I was hurt, or how I hurt others."

He ran his fingers through his hair, sighing. "She was left with so many questions. She wondered if you missed her. If you were happy. I think it would make a world of a difference if you explain completely. Even if she doesn't forgive you, I think she could use the closure."

I nodded silently, scratching at the palm of my hand as I stood there silently. I couldn't tell if the conversation was over, or if he had more to say.

So, like the coward I had always been, I left silently, without a word, letting history repeat itself in front of me.

January 9th, 2023

I sat at the high table of the cafeteria after rehearsal. Allie sat across from me with a camera and laptop laid out in front of her. She typed away at the keys silently, not saying anything after she had called me over to sit.

I was uncomfortable in the silence, but I didn't think I had any right to speak. I was waiting for her to say something, anything.

But as she continued to let the silence hang in the air, I felt like I had gotten my first good look at her since we met again.

Her hair was longer than it used to be, and it seemed to have lost some of its life, her once bouncy curly hair having thinned out and turned into large frizzy waves that fell just below her shoulder. The lenses of her glasses looked thicker, and the placement of her freckles was unfamiliar to me as they had seemed to change over the years.

I watched her type, seeing that she still carried the habit of biting her bottom lip whenever she was trying to focus, or ignore something.

I saw as her eyes moved, following the words she was typing across the screen. The specks of brown and blue in her eyes were still the same as they had been before. It was the one thing about her that was familiar, as even her hair color had gotten lighter.

Her eyes darted up, and we made eye contact. She stared at me, her hands having stopped on the keyboard beneath her fingers. I looked away, trying to pretend I wasn't looking at all.

"What?" She asked.

"Oh, uh," I started. "Nothing…"

"You sure?" She asked.

I nodded, not bothering to say anything else.

She looked at me, and I could see the gears turning as she tried to decide whether or not she wanted to believe what I was saying.

"Okay," She said, beginning to type again. "Well, I just need to finish up my notes from your rehearsal today and then we can start the interview, does that sound fine?"

"Yeah, I'm fine with whatever," I said quietly.

"Cool," She said, her eyes leaving mine as they went back to following the words that she typed.

I thought back to what Leo had said to me in the bookstore. I thought about how I found myself trying to fit into a place I had forgotten how to feel comfortable in.

I wasn't having fun cheering, and I felt uncomfortable and tense at Allie's side. I missed how it used to feel, where her body fit next to mine without fail, our arms looped around each other fitted perfectly to each other's shape.

I was scared of what it would be like to have a conversation with her again, but I wanted to maybe talk and clear up some stuff that had happened. I wanted to be honest, tell her the truth, and apologize. I wanted to hear an apology as well, but more than anything I wanted to take responsibility for the pain I had previously caused her.

"Okay," She said, pulling out her phone and setting it on the table, the voice recording app opened. She hit record and pulled out a pencil and a notebook from her back on the floor. "Let's get started, is that okay?" She asked. Her voice was void of any emotion.

I nodded. "Yeah that's fine," I said, crossing my legs and folding my arms in front of me.

"So, how have rehearsals here in America differed from how they were back in England?" Allie asked me.

I didn't make eye contact with her, just kept my eyes down and my voice as calm as it could be as I answered her questions. I didn't want to reveal how I was feeling to her, and I didn't want to interrupt her to talk to her about what had happened.

I was trying to wait it out, to put proper effort into my answers knowing what it meant to her.

As we did the interview, I was happy to know that at least that hadn't changed. She still put 110% effort into everything she did, whether or not she enjoyed it or not. She talked to me without malice, putting on a mask to ask me questions without any sort of hostility or anger in her voice. But because of this, she sounded numb.

After the interview was over, she didn't tell me whether or not I was good to leave or not. She just wrote in her notepad, erasing her words and rewriting over and over again.

"Allie?" I said.

She looked up from her paper, raising an eyebrow

as she tilted her head a bit. "... what?"

"Can we talk?" I asked.

Her expression turned dark, and she shut her laptop getting up out of her chair. "I don't want to," She said quietly.

I stood up and grabbed her wrist, stopping her from continuing to pack up her things. "Please, don't leave."

She stared at me, her eyes sad and her body shaking as I held onto her wrist. "What do you want to talk about?"

"Us," I said. "I want to tell you about everything that's happened." I paused. "And I want to apologize again. Or, more so, I want to hear your side of things. I want to understand. Please, let me try."

Allie stood, unmoving as I could see her go back and forth trying to make a decision on whether to leave or to stay. She sighed, and the tension in her arm relaxed as she stopped actively trying to pull away from me. "Fine, we can talk, but I'm not promising anything."

I nodded. "That's okay."

She sat back down in her chair, closing her notebook and setting it on top of her laptop. "So... talk."

I took a deep breath and folded my hands in front of me on the table. "I don't really know where to start if I'm being honest." I said. "I mean, I should probably start from the beginning, but I don't want to start there. I want to start with how I hurt you. I want to understand how I did that."

She didn't respond, and I could tell she was stubbornly sticking to the idea of me talking, and her just listening in silence.

"When you told me about your eating disorder, I didn't plan on telling your parents," I said. "I really didn't, because you said you had it under control and that you were working on getting better. But then I saw you as time went on. You seemed to be getting worse rather than better. I was worried about you. Your methods didn't seem to be working and you were looking sicker by the day. I thought you were going to faint whenever I saw you. I thought your bones would snap when I tried to give you a hug.

"I didn't do it because I wanted to betray your trust," I said.

She pulled at the ends of her hair. It seemed she hadn't lost that habit. "I know that. I didn't know that then but I know that now." She said, "You don't have to tell me."

I nodded. "Then I won't. But I will say that I'm sorry," My voice cracked, and blinked a few times to try to keep the tears from rolling down my cheeks. "I'm sorry I didn't say goodbye. I know I ghosted you, and that wasn't very fair of me. I thought that you didn't want anything to do with me ever again. That you would be better off, and happier if I left without a word."

Allie looked away, and I could see the tears forming along the edge of her eyes as she tried to keep her face neutral.

"I wanted to ask, what was it like for you…" I went quiet as I saw the expression on her face change, wiping away the tears before they could fall down her cheeks as she turned to look at me.

"I was so hurt," She said, choking on her words. "But I felt so bad. I knew that I had to have been at least part of the reason as to why you left without saying goodbye. I mean I said such mean things to you. I yelled, and I cursed, and I pushed you away. Both physically and figuratively. I didn't want to admit that I had no one else to blame but myself for losing you."

I sat silently, the tears rolling down my cheeks and down my neck. I didn't know what to say, because I knew there were probably no words that would make either of us feel better in this situation.

We both had jumped to conclusions, and we both

had done things that hurt the other. We acted without thinking, and acted like there was nothing that could be done to save our dying friendship. We both fought each other's feelings, in the interest of trying to preserve our own.

And now we are together again.

Sitting across from each other at the table in the cafeteria of the high school that we both go to. Tears shared between the two of us, as we wondered how it turned out like this. Sitting in silence, both angry and hurt, there were no more words. Because again, we were at a stand still, neither one of us knowing or being able to accept the other's apology.

Messy Beginnings

Alaska

<u>Messy Beginnings (Alaska)</u>

May 2nd, 2018

The girl next door was someone I never had to hide my heart from.

She had stupid pink hair and a stupid telescope on her back deck. She had stupid fairy lights tied around the railing of her deck, and stupid glow-in-the-dark stars stuck to her balcony door. She was so stupid, and she left without saying goodbye.

The 'For Sale' sign in the front yard mocked me as I walked up her driveway. I had heard from my mom that they had moved out without a word, but I had a delusional fantasy of maybe seeing her family inside, sitting around the living room, with smiles on their faces and laughter ringing through the air.

The grass was brown, and the previously flower-filled front porch was empty. The porch swing was gone, and you could see a faint outline on the pavement where the flower beds used to sit. All of the lights were off, and I couldn't see inside the house from where I stood. I knocked on the door, but was met with silence. Blinds covered the window, but there was a small area where the inside of the house could be seen between two broken blinds. I turned on my phone's flashlight and held it up to the window, squinting my eyes to get a peek inside.

There was no furniture, and there were tarps down over the carpet, the walls all in varying stages of being painted. The kitchen was empty and clean. It was as if every ounce of personality that was in that house had been sucked dry. What once was a lively living room, now sat empty with no story to tell. I cupped my hands above my eyes as I pressed my face against the glass, trying to get a closer and clearer look of the inside. I was looking for something that showed proof of her family's existence. Something to show that these people weren't just something I made up in my head. That she was real. That her family was real. And that they lived in the house next to mine.

I heard the sound of a car door slam shut, and I turned to see an older man in a business suit walk up from the driveway and over to where I stood on the porch.

"What are you doing here?" He asked me. His pants were too short, and there was a stain on the pocket of the suit. I looked him up and down, before turning back to the house.

"What happened to the previous owners?" I asked, turning back to the window.

"I don't know. It's not my job to know about the previous owners, it's just to find new ones." He sighed. "Just go back to wherever you came from so I can get back to work." He walked past me and unlocked the front door. "Go." He opened the door.

I stretched my head to look around him as he walked inside, trying to get a peek of the inside. "Wait-" I began, walking closer to the door.

He turned, and shut the door in my face, ignoring

me.

I stood there for a few minutes, looking at the familiar red door of my neighbor's house for a moment more. I turned on my heel and walked down the driveway and back over to my own.

I opened the car door and pulled my pillow and blanket out of it, before walking up my porch into the house.

I grabbed my suitcase from the living room, walked past where my parents stood in the kitchen, and made my way up the stairs to my room.

"Alaska!" My mom called. "Come eat!"

"Not hungry!" I yelled as I walked to the end of the hall where my bedroom was.

I could hear my mom yelling from downstairs, but I ignored her.

My bedroom door was open and I had found it was almost exactly the way I had left it. The lock on my bathroom door was gone, and so was the scale that was next to the tub. I had clothes folded neatly on my bed, and a couple of my dresser drawers were open.

I jumped at the light knocking on my door. I turned and saw my twin brother leaning against the door frame.

I stood looking at him, waiting for him to say something.

He stared, waiting for me to say something.

"Allie," He said.

"Kota."

We stood in silence for another moment, waiting for the other to add to the conversation.

"So…" He started. "You're back."

I nodded. "I'm back." The silence hung in the air, and I waited for his response, expecting to be met with some sort of cocky retort.

But, all he did was smile. "Welcome home, Allie."

He said, before walking away.

I stared at the place where he stood for a few more moments, before turning my attention back to my clothes.

I started unpacking my clothes from my suitcase. The smell of my own room felt unfamiliar, and that was when I fully comprehended how long it had been since I stepped foot inside of it.

Cicadas were chirping outside my window in the summer humidity, but I still had my stocking from Christmas hung up, along with the tinsel that I had strung across the headboard of my bed.

I set down the clothes I was holding, and ripped the tinsel from my headboard, shoving it into the trash can beside my desk. I stuffed the stocking into my closet, and tore down the calendar that still read 'December'.

I sat down on my bed, looking at the room that no longer felt like it belonged to me. It smelled different, and the walls didn't look like they were the same color as when I had left. My bed didn't have any blankets or pillows and there was no evidence that anyone had lived there for months. I saw my phone sitting on my nightstand.

I picked it up, the weight feeling both heavy and unfamiliar in my hands.

I hit the power button and watched my phone start-up, as the notifications began to pour into the screen. Four months' worth of missed events and text messages.

I opened my contacts and found Ita's contact page. Her contact photo was one of her and me that my mother took of us from third grade.

We went to a petting zoo for our third-grade field trip, and the photo had a picture of Ita with dark brown hair and purple streaks, and I rocked a bowl-cut as a goat ate grains from our hands. It was the first time I remember ever fighting with Ita. She wanted to go feed the bunnies lettuce, but I was too stubborn to be willing to go do that first before feeding the goats. In the time that we spent fighting about it, we probably had the time to feed both the bunnies and the goats, but we were both too stubborn to go do what the other wanted first. In the end, Ita agreed to feed the goats with me, and at that point, we had run out of time and never got the chance to feed the bunnies. Ever since Ita's favorite animal has always been goats, and mine has always been rabbits.

I hit the call button and held the phone up to my ear.

The ringing seemed to bounce around impatiently in my head, only for a moment before the ringing was cut to the sound of an automated voice.

"*The number you have dialed is no longer in service,*" The voice said.

I hung up and set the phone back down on my nightstand. I sat on the floor next to my bed and pulled my knees to my chest.

Ita left. She really left. She left without warning. Without any form of goodbye. And I had no idea where she went.

December 25th, 2022

I had woken up early to do last minute Christmas present wrapping with my brother. It was almost eight, and we sat in our room with the door locked, knowing that our younger siblings would come get us before our dad when they woke up.

"Do you think we'll finish in time?" Kota asked, gliding his scissors through the wrapping paper.

I nodded. "We only have a couple left, we'll make it."

"Leave it to mom to dump this on us before she leaves for her 48 hour shift," He mumbled.

"Hey," I said. "There's nothing we can do about it now. I'm annoyed too but this isn't about mom, this about

Aria and Atlas."

He nodded, annoyed. It sucked but we didn't have the time to be annoyed by our mother's last minute gift shopping. We were stressed enough trying to complete the last minute gift wrapping that she decided we were the ones responsible for doing.

Our doorknob jiggled, and Kota and I stopped in our tracks, making panicked eye contact with each other.

I could hear the chatter on the other side of the door as Aria and Atlas banged against it.

"What do we do?" Kota whispered.

I stood up, throwing my blanket over the half wrapped presents. "I'll take care of the kids, you finish wrapping."

Kota nodded as I went over to the door, unlocking in and quickly slipping through the crack I had made into the hallway where Aria and Atlas stood, still in their pajamas.

"Morning, Allie!" Aria said, hooking on to my leg. "Is Kota asleep still?"

I nodded. "He's a little tired, so let's let him sleep for a bit more, okay?" I said putting my finger over my mouth to get them to be quieter. "And Dad is still asleep too so we gotta be quiet."

They mimicked me, nodding while they put their fingers over their mouths as well.

"Good, you guys come with me, and we'll make breakfast for everyone together," I said, putting my hands on their backs and guiding them down the hallway.

The twins were quiet as we walked down the hall and into the kitchen, their innocence rang clear through the house as I saw them jump in excitement at the empty plate and half drunk glass of milk that sat on the dining room table.

They didn't know that Santa wasn't real, and they

had yet to learn that most people didn't drink milk by itself, which had been made apparent when I went down in the middle of the night to pour half of it down the sink.

I pulled the stool out of the pantry and unfolded it at the stove.

"You guys can talk now, but we still need to be quiet since dad's room is on this floor," I said, pulling the box of pancake mix out of the cabinet.

"Santa came!" Aria whisper screamed while jumping up and down.

I nodded. "He did, but remember we need to wait till dad wakes up and casts the magic smell that breaks the barrier on the presents. In the meantime, go get the bacon from the fridge in the garage for me."

Aria nodded, running through the living room and towards the laundry room.

"Atlas, can you get the biscuits from the fridge?"

"Mhm!" Atlas hummed excitedly, grabbing the dough from the fridge and walking back over to where I stood.

"Thank you," I said as Atlas handed me the roll of dough. I cracked it open, starting to peel the biscuits apart and place them on the baking tray I had set out last night.

"Allie?" Atlas asked.

"What's up?"

"Mom left last night, right?"

I looked over to where Atlas stood, playing with the edge of his sleeve.

I sighed and bent down to his level, ruffling his hair with a smile on my face. "She did, she has to work. Someone needs to be at the hospital in case anything happens."

He nodded, looking down at his feet and frowning. I could see him trying to hold his tears in, while simultaneously trying not to hide his emotions like I had told him to.

"You need to cry?" I asked.

He nodded.

"You don't want to?"

He pointed over to where our dad's room is, as he squeezed his eyes shut.

"You don't want to wake up dad," I said.

He nodded again, and I pulled him into a hug, holding him against my chest.

"If you cry into my chest, it'll muffle the noise and you won't wake him up, alright?" I said, running my fingers through his hair.

He cried into my chest, gripping the sides of my shirt tightly.

When Aria got back from the garage, she looked between Atlas and I, and for a moment she seemed confused as to why he was crying, and didn't know what to do. She eventually came over and put her hand on Atlas's back, rubbing it gently while she looked at me to see what it was that had made him cry.

When Atlas stopped crying, we went back to making breakfast, but unfortunately I couldn't do anything to make Atlas smile and feel better. His mom wouldn't be home for Christmas, and unlike his sister he seemed to be a bit more sensitive about it.

Once breakfast was ready, I had the twins set the table, Kota coming downstairs and setting the last minute gifts down in the living room before coming into the kitchen.

"Did you guys make breakfast?" He asked scooping up both of the twins and holding them in a tight hug.

They giggled, fighting against him to try and get him to put them back down. "Yes! We made breakfast while you slept in like a baby!" Aria laughed.

He set down the twins, giving them one last hug

before walking over to me. "How about you guys go wake up Dad, while I talk to Allie?"

"Okay!" They exclaimed in unison.

Kota and I watched them disappear around the corner, before he turned to me, sighing.

"They woke up early," He said, rubbing the bridge of his nose.

I nodded, my eyes wide. "I know, it scared me."

"How have they been?" He asked.

"Aria has been bouncing off the walls like usual," I said. "And Atlas must have heard mom leave for her double shift last night, because he woke up asking where mom was."

He nodded. "I mean, this is the third year in a row she hasn't been home for Christmas. If I was as smart as him at my age, I would've gotten suspicious too."

I set my head on Kota's shoulder, and he rubbed my back as I caught my breath for the first time that morning.

"Tired?"

I nodded against his shoulder as I heard the giggling of the little ones get closer, followed by my dad's heavy footsteps.

I lifted my head and smiled, sitting down at the table as the twins and Dad came into the kitchen.

We ate breakfast together, and I did my best to make conversation and jokes to cheer Atlas up. He would laugh for a moment, but then he would get sad again. I knew there wasn't anything I could do to make him feel better, but still, I tried. Because I wasn't going to let Christmas become a bad memory for him. At least, not without a fight.

December 27th, 2022

I thought that maybe I had seen a ghost.

Her hair was different. It was shorter now, but it seemed that she had stuck with the same dusty pink color she had had since fifth grade. I watched her sit on the couch with Ana and Lyn from the cheer team. She had a few more piercings that she did when I had last seen her. She had taken out her snake bites, and replaced it with a single piercing down the middle of her bottom lip. She was better at eyeliner now; she was better at makeup in general. She was so pretty.

"Allie?"

I snapped my focus back to Sonali who sat across from me at the bar. Her head was tilted in confusion, and she had her chin in her hands as she swirled the straw of her drink.

I looked away from Sonali, back to where I had seen Ita. Or rather, to where I thought I had seen her.

When I looked back over, Lyn sat in Ana's lap, and they laughed while they held each other tightly, whispering things in each other's ears.

"Allie, did you see something?" Sonali asked.

I shook my head. "No, I thought I did, but…" I looked around the living room, seeing not a trace of her in it. It seemed like the alcohol had been messing with my head. "It was my imagination." I took another shot, hoping the alcohol would mess with me further. I hoped it would impair my judgment, and I could be a little stupid, and make bad decisions for the first time in a while.

"Sonali, can I ask you something?" I said.

She nodded. "Go ahead."

"Have you ever liked a girl before?"

She sat up straight, and blinked a few times as her face got redder. "Well, I mean," She started. "Not personally…"

"It sucks." I set my head down on the counter, grumbling into my elbow. "Especially the first one…"

"The first one?"

"Yeah!" I said sitting up. I grabbed the nearest open

bottle, not bothering to read what was written on the label before drinking a large swig of it. "You'll never be able to forget her. That shit fucks with your head. I mean, here I am, having hallucinations of my middle school crush and best friend."

Sonali stared for a moment, before she started to feel around the counter near me. "I think you've had enough to drink, Allie."

I pulled the bottle from the counter and wrapped my arms around it, hugging it to my chest. "No! Let me have fun for once!" I whined.

"Allie, c'mon let's go get some air, okay?" Sonali said, grabbing my arm. "Ah, that's where it is," She grabbed the bottle out of my lap and held it in the air above my head where I couldn't reach it.

"I don't wanna," I whined. "I don't want to get air. I *want* to do something stupid.".

"Like what?" Sonali asked, rolling her eyes.

"I want—"

"Sonali, there you are!" Monty said coming over to where she and I were. "I was looking for you, y'know."

"Oh, hi Monty." Sonali smiled, and I took the opportunity to get them out of my hair.

"Monty! You should take Sonali out to the bonfire, I think she'll like it!"

"But Allie—" Sonali.

"I'll be fine!" I said putting a hand on each of their shoulders. "Go go!"

Once I had gotten rid of them through forcefully pushing them out the door, I went downstairs to Leo's basement, looking for something to distract myself with.

I found another bottle, and I drank a bit of it, unable to actually read any of the print written on it. I couldn't stop thinking about what I had seen.

She seemed to real to have been a hallucination, but

I couldn't fathom as to why she would be anything else but that.

I sat down on the floor and leaned against the wall by the backyard door. I reached out my hand, and I thought about how close she was. I wondered if I would have been able to touch her if I had gotten close enough.

She looked like she had changed lots, but also not at all. She was still petite and curvy, and I could see doodles across her arms the same as they were when I was little.

I turned onto my side, to see Noah jogging across Leo's yard to the bonfire where Sonali and Monty sat. He looked panicked, and his face was red when he sat down beside them.

The last I had seen Noah was with Leo, so I wondered if it was him that caused Noah to get that look on his face.

I stood up and wandered back upstairs, knowing for sure that it was probably Leo who caused that look on Noah's face.

I looked through the living room, hoping I wouldn't see the girl again, despite knowing I was probably delusional looking for a hallucination. When I didn't find her, but found Leo, I went over to him, hoping to ask about what he had done.

Again, I was looking for someone else to blame. I didn't want to admit that what I had seen was true. So I blamed the alcohol and looked for entertainment and comfort in someone else's relationship problems.

December 28th, 2022

It wasn't a hallucination. It wasn't the alcohol. I had woken up in the bed of someone I hadn't seen in years. Her room looked like it had just been moved into, the only thing resembling any sort of story being the photo that sat on the dresser. One of her and I from middle school.

After a panicked call from my parents, I got her to take me home, unable to accept the fact that she somehow miraculously showed up in my life again.

I opened my front door slamming it shut behind me, my legs giving out below me and making me fall to my knees in the entryway.

"Where have you been?" My dad yelled from the kitchen as he stormed into the living room. I sat on the floor, feeling my heartbeat all throughout my body with a ringing in my ears. My dad looked me up and down before saying, "Whose clothes are you wearing?"

I rolled my eyes, and put my hands on the side table using it to push myself to my feet to find the strength in my legs again. "Wouldn't you like to know," I mumbled.

"What was that?" He asked.

"Nothing! Okay?" I exclaimed. "I was safe and I'm home now so why does it even matter?"

"Why does it even— Of course it matters! You have a curfew for a reason, Allie. Your siblings were confused and worried about where you were too."

I went to walk past him and go to my room, but he blocked my path. "I didn't mean to worry either you or them."

"I never said you did mean to, but it's your responsibility to take care of them when your mom and I are working," He softened his tone, and I could tell his anger was turning into sympathy, his actual feelings being revealed after he had a moment to calm down.

I stood there silently, waiting to hear what he really had to say.

"We knew you would be at a friend's, but you never told us when you would be back, and when you didn't answer our texts we were worried, okay?"

I sighed, running my hands through my hair. "I

know, I'm sorry,".

"You're usually more responsible than that. What happened?" He said putting a hand on my shoulder.

I thought about what I wanted to tell him. Whether I wanted to tell him the truth about what happened.

"I ran into an old friend, so I forgot to answer my phone," I said. I settled on telling him part of the truth, not being fond of the idea of telling him I was drinking. "I'm sorry, I promise I didn't do it on purpose."

"Who did you run into?" He asked.

I sighed and took a step forward before leaning into him, putting my head on his chest. "Ita,"

"Ita?" He repeated.

I sighed. "Y'know? Ita? Titania? Has had the same pink hair since fifth grade? Was our neighbor for like, forever?"

"Really?" He asked.

I nodded. "I didn't really know what to do."

"Wow, that's really far," He said. I could feel him look down on me, and he put his hand on the top of my head running it over my hair. "I'm sorry I got mad, I shouldn't have yelled at you."

I shrugged. "It's alright."

"Go up to your room and get some rest, okay?" He said, grabbing my shoulders and gently pushing me towards the stairs.

I nodded silently and walked up the stairs. I could hear my brother talking from down the hall and when I walked into our room I could see him sitting at his desk. I flopped onto my bed and stared at my brother who had headphones on while he played games.

He took his headphones off pausing his game before turning to me. "Rough night?" He asked.

I rolled over and grabbed my pillow, pressing it over my face and groaning. "You have no idea."

"Mom and dad were worried," He said. "Atlas and Aria too."

"I'm sure they were," I said sitting up. "Where are they?"

"Atlas and Aria are hanging out at the neighbors house. What happened last night?" He asked. "It was your turn to put them to sleep, not mine."

I rolled my eyes and threw a pillow at him. "Y'know it would be nice if people would stop asking me so many questions."

He tossed the pillow back to me, putting his hands up in the air in the surrender. "Okay, okay. I'll stop badgering you. But I was genuinely worried, y'know? Are you okay?"

I nodded. "As okay as I can be."

I fell over onto my side, curling my legs up towards my chest and hiding my face in my knees. I remembered the way she recoiled into herself, and the pained look in her eyes during the one time she had come to visit me when I had been hospitalized. How I said some really hurtful things, and how she never came to visit me ever again.

January 3rd, 2023

I walked into my Journalism class and sat down at my usual seat by the window in front of the teacher's desk. Mr. Swiler sat at his desk typing on his computer as my classmates filed in before the bell rang. I folded my arms in front of me on the desk and set my head down, closing my eyes.

Since I saw Ita, I haven't been able to stop thinking about her, and the more I thought about her the more hurt I felt. Just the thought of her brought up so many bad memories for me. So seeing her put me in such a bad place mentally.

The bell rang and Mr. Swiler stood up tapping my

desk. "Alright, heads up everyone," He started. "We're going to go over the expectations for the new quarter, and about what we're going to be doing throughout the next nine weeks regarding the magazine so get into your groups and I'll walk around and give you guys your assignments."

I stood up from my desk and walked over to the back table by the lightbox. I sat down next to my classmates, Daniela and Luna, as well as Leo, setting my laptop down on the table and starting it up.

"How was your break, Alaska?" Daniela asked.

I shrugged. "It was okay, just spent time with friends and family. Y'know just what most people do over winter break."

"Oh how cute!" She said, "I went to London to visit my grandparents. Have you ever been to London?"

I shook my head. I didn't respond, just kept my eyes on the loading screen of my laptop and wondered if Ita ever went to London while she lived overseas.

Mr. Swiler walked over and pulled out a chair sitting next to me as he set a couple of folders on the table. "How are you guys doing? I hope you guys had a good break."

"Mhm!" Daniela piped up. "I know I did."

"Glad to hear that," He said with a heavy sigh. "Okay, so with almost all of the fall sports having ended, I'm gonna assign most of you guys to spring sports." He sorted through the folders and picked one up, handing it to Daniela. "Daniela, can you start covering soccer?"

Daniela groaned, before reluctantly saying, "Fine."

Mr. Swiler nodded. "Luna, can you handle lacrosse and field hockey? Your sister is on the team right?"

Luna took the folder he held out to them, and nodded. "Yeah, she's on the JV team, but I'm sure she can find out some stuff from varsity for me."

"Sounds good, thank you, Luna," Mr. Swiler handed

me my folder of reference material, and before I could open it he said, "Alaska since the football season is officially over, that means you're no longer performing with the marching band right?" He asked.

"I still have Jazz Band, but the marching band season is over, yes," I said.

"Great, I'm putting you in charge of covering our competition cheer team," He said. "Since the football season is over it means that they're turning their attention to competitions. You've been in my class for two years already, and you've covered them in years prior, are you still good to keep that up?"

I nodded and opened the folder flipping through the reference pages he had given me, which were mostly my previous articles written last year and the year before. "That shouldn't be a probl—" I paused when I saw the list of members written on the very last page in the folder. Third from the top the name Titania Cirillo was written. I couldn't help but stop and stare.

"Is everything alright?" Mr. Swiler asked.

I cleared my throat and closed the folder. "Yep! Everything is fine. I can definitely cover the cheer team, especially considering I already have a pretty good understanding of their schedule,"

"Awesome," He said standing up. "I'm going to go talk to the other groups, so you guys can go ahead and get started on what you're gonna work on and when. Call me over if you need anything or have any questions, okay?"

"Alrighty!" Daniela exclaimed.

I nodded, along with Luna.

"Oh and Leo?" He said.

"Yeah?" Leo said, sitting up.

"Go back and sit with your group."

Leo groaned, rolling his eyes as he stood up. "Fine." He walked around the table to where I was, leaning down towards my ear. "Call me later about what happened after the party, okay?"

"I will," I mumbled as he walked away and sat at his assigned table.

I opened the folder back up and looked over the list of names one more time, hoping that maybe I had imagined it. But, I hadn't. Still sitting third from the top, was the name, Titania Cirillo.

And after I told her never to speak to me again, here we are. Hopefully, I'll be able to avoid having a conversation with her specifically. However, I don't exactly have a good feeling about this whole thing. Something in my gut told me that things were about to go very wrong for the both of us.

January 5th, 2023

I walked into Cafeteria B, finding the cheer team already beginning to gather. They clumped together at a table by the courtyard doors, all sitting in various places around the table. Some sat on it, others in the chairs around it. Two girls sat on the floor for whatever reason, and the captains were standing.

I walked over to Ana, one of the captains that I had met back in my freshman year. "Hey Anna, where's your coach?"

Ana shrugged. "She's gonna be late I think. Are you covering us again for the newspaper?"

I nodded. "You'll get a small feature every week on the sports page, same as last year and the year before, no change."

Anna groaned, and I couldn't help but chuckle as the other captain Lyn walked over, draping her arm around Anna's shoulder.

"Hey, the newspaper covering us again?" Lyn asked.

I nodded.

"Cool, are you gonna write about all of the petty drama that's already started?"

Anna elbowed Lyn in the side, shushing her.

"Hey!" Lyn exclaimed. "I was asking a genuine question!"

I shook my head. "You guys know I can't. Mr. Swiler said no last year. There's no way he's going to let me do it this year. Besides, it would get him in trouble with admin anyways, and that's the last thing I want to do."

Anna nodded understandingly, and Lyn just groaned.

"I miss the captains from our sophomore year, things were chill then. Now everyone's at each other's throats and we haven't even gone to our first competition yet." Ana sighed. "And it's even worse now since Lyn and I have to deal with it."

I nodded. "What does most of it have to do with this time?" I asked, crossing my arms.

"Our new member who joined late," Ana said. "Everyone is pissy because they think it's unfair that she got in without an audition, even though it's completely reasonable considering her team won championships where she lived."

"Oh?" I said.

"Where did she live?" I asked, a sneaking suspicion climbing up my throat.

"Crouton?" Lyn said.

Anna laughed. "No, Croughton, y'know in England. Not like the salad."

"Oh, Titania right?" I asked.

"Yeah, how did you know?" Ana said.

I hesitated before saying, "I used to know her."

"Really!?" Lyn exclaimed, grabbing my shoulders. "Tell us everything you know about her 'cause I swear this girl has no personality."

"Lyn!" Ana said, pulling her away from me. "Shut up!" She whispered.

I looked past them, spotting their coach walking into the cafeteria.

"I'll talk to you guys later, your coach is here so it seems like you should go ahead and get started," I said. "I'm going to go sit."

"Talk to you later Allie!" Lyn yelled while waving to me as I went to sit down.

I waved back and watched as Ana grabbed her cheeks, pulling on them while telling her to stop yelling.

I couldn't help but be jealous of them, as they fought like an old married couple. They were the perfect example of what I wanted. I wanted someone I could find comfort in, the way Ana and Lyn found comfort in each other.

I walked backward to the table, watching as the cheer team gathered around their coach, the air in the cafeteria going from filled with chatter to complete silence, everyone waiting for instruction.

Someone slammed into my side. I fell to the ground nearly dropping my laptop and knocking my pencil case onto the floor.

"I'm so sorry! I should have watched where I was going,"

I sat up to see Ita on her knees picking up my pencils and putting them in my pencil case. "Are you ok— Allie? What are you doing here?" She asked.

Before I had time to respond, the cheer coach called, "Ita! Get over here!"

"Oh, uh," Ita looked from side to side before handing me my pencil case. "I have to go, Allie, bye!" She stood up and started running over to where her teammates were. "Coming!"

I grabbed my pencil case and stood up, watching her as I walked over to my usual table to watch the practice.

I watched them give instructions, ask each other for help, and work individually. Despite all the drama that happened with the team last year, and what has happened so far this year, it never ceased to amaze me how quickly they could put aside their disagreements to work together and create a performance.

They never looked at each other with malice, and any tensions between teammates were invisible to anyone outside of their bubble. It was an environment I could never understand and I thought that all of them were amazing for it.

However, despite how amazed I was with all of them, and despite my reason for being there, I couldn't help but keep my eyes glued to Ita the entire time I watched them.

Despite how loud she used to be, it seemed like there was a bubble around her as she practiced. She only spoke when spoken to, and when she did speak it was quiet. I questioned the difference between the Ita from a few years ago, and the one I was watching now.

She was expressionless, and her entire body seemed tense and robotic as she moved. She was incapable of expressing any emotions at all.

And I realized for the first time that our time apart didn't only happen to change me, but it changed her too. And she had become someone I no longer recognized.

I watched the sun lower in the sky as I drove home. I parked in the driveway and walked up the front porch hearing yelling through the door. I opened the door quietly and snuck past my screaming mom and up the stairs.

When I walked into my brother's room, I saw him sitting on his bed, with one younger sibling tucked under each arm. They were wearing headphones. Both had blankets wrapped around them, and a stuffed animal held tightly in their arms.

The door shut behind me and I turned on the white noise machine that I had sitting against the door frame and sat down quietly on the bed next to my brother.

"Thank god you're here," He said. "They've been asking for you for a while."

I pressed their headphones against their ears. "How long have mom and dad been fighting?"

Kota shrugged. "I don't know, they were fighting when I got home from swim club twenty minutes ago," He said, scooting closer. "I can comfort them, but I can't stop Mom and Dad from fighting the way you can," He said, nodding his head towards the door. "They only ever want you since you can get Mom and Dad to be quiet for once."

I sighed. "It's because I'm good at distracting mom and dad from whatever it is they think they're right about," I said, running my fingers over the kids' hair. "Thanks for taking care of them, Kota."

"I did what I could," He said.

"How was that cheer thing?" Kota asked. I glared at him, and he held his hands in the air. "Okay, got it, you don't want to talk about it."

"Did they even eat dinner?" I asked, looking at the clock.

"What do you think, Allie?" Kota sighed.

"Just, give Mom and Dad another ten minutes, and then I'll go get them to stop fighting," I said, taking my hair out of the bun I had it in. "They'll feel bad about fighting, so I can probably coax them into giving us money to get an apology pizza before mom heads out for her night shift. Hopefully, it'll help the kids feel better."

"Anything you want me to do?" Kota asked.

"When the pizza is ordered can you take the car to go get it?" I asked, looking at the door. "And then I can take care of them and help them calm down while you're out."

"Sounds like a plan," He paused, looking between me and the clock. "It hasn't been ten minutes, but you're going to go get them to stop fighting now, aren't you?"

I nodded, gently nudging Atlas and Aria. They looked at me, and I just held my finger up to my mouth, smiling. "Time to keep playing the quiet game, can you do that?"

They both nodded.

I put my hands on their heads before standing up and walking out of our room and down the stairs, the wood creaking beneath my feet. I walked into the kitchen where my mom and dad stood on opposite sides of the island.

"When are you going to get it through your thick skull, I want to be able to have a life outside of this family?" My mom yelled.

"And why can't you see that it's too much?" My dad said, rubbing the back of his neck. "You're never home, and the kids miss you. You get off of work before they get out of school, but you're never here when they get home. You're always either staying late at work or out doing who knows what who knows where with whomever you want."

"And what about you?" My mom screamed. "When are you ever home to spend time with the kids? You work just as much as I do!"

"And yet I still get home at a reasonable time to make them dinner. And the one time I'm home late, I come to find out that instead of coming straight home as I asked you to, you left two seven-year-olds alone for three hours." My dad added.

"Why should I have to come home to take care of them, when Kota and Allie get out of school an hour earlier?!"

"For the third time, stop yelling. You're going to

upset Atlas and Aria," He sighed. "And it's not Kota or Allie's responsibility to take care of their siblings, they should be able to have a life outside of that."

"So Allie and Kota can have a life outside this house but I can't?"

"Because they're kids too; they're not mothers with mouths to feed."

I tapped the ground with my foot, clearing my throat. "I'm home," I said looking at the ground. "What are you guys talking about?"

My dad shook his head. "Nothing you should have to worry about sweetheart," He said glaring at my mom. "When did you get home?" He came and wrapped his arm around my shoulder, pulling me into an awkward side hug and kissing the top of my head.

"Just now. I went and set my stuff down, and Kota was hugging the twins to keep them from crying. You need to stop fighting like this. If you need to fight, go somewhere else, do it quietly, or don't do it when they're home. It scares them," I wiggled out of my dad's arm and looked between the two of them.

"Don't talk to me like that!" My mom yelled, placing her hands on her hips. "You think you know everything? Acting like you know better than us? We're the adults here, not you."

I rolled my eyes. "I am eighteen you know."

"Why—"

"You're right sweetie, and I'm sorry, we'll try to be more aware," My dad said, cutting off my mom's words. "But don't get it wrong we weren't fighting or anything," He said. "Just having a discussion is all; so there's no need to worry."

I didn't respond, wondering if he really thought that I would ever believe what he was saying. It seemed he thought I was far more gullible than I actually am. "Right…

well the kids haven't eaten, do you maybe have money
that Kota and I could use to order pizza for us?" I asked. "I
want to make sure that they eat properly, and you and mom
haven't been grocery shopping in a bit, so there's not a lot
to eat in the house."

"Yeah yeah, of course," My dad said softly, pulling
his card out of his wallet and handing it to me. "Here,
use this. And I'll buy groceries tomorrow, just send me a
shopping list of what you guys need."

I took the card and put it in my pocket smiling.
"Thanks, I'll give it to Kota since he said he would go pick
it up."

I turned towards the stairs and grabbed the railing,
leaning back and pushing my weight into my heels. "And,
don't fight again tonight, please. If you do, they aren't
going to be able to sleep by themselves, and they can't keep
sleeping in Kota and I's room, they won't grow up like
that."

My dad nodded, my mom scoffed, and I just smiled.
Strings connected us; they were pulled tight and at risk of
fraying apart.. An island dividing them, and a kid hanging
from the railing on the stairs, waiting to see if they had any
last words or final grievances before I shut them down for
the rest of the night.

My dad was considerate, but he wasn't without
flaws. My mom was inconsiderate and lacked any ability
to feel empathy for those around her. She stopped taking
care of us when I had gotten hospitalized, so it feels right
for them to always find themselves fighting in the kitchen.
Because not only can an eating disorder ruin your own
life, but it can also ruin the lives of those around you. And
people will stop thinking that you're worth taking care of.

I waved to my parents, as they continued to stare,
waiting for me to leave. And I swung around the railing
back up the stairs. I could hear footsteps behind me, and

it was pretty easy to tell by the heavy steps that it was probably my mom. When I heard a door slam so hard that it shook the house, from the opposite side of the hall, I knew for sure that it definitely was my mom who had followed my example and come upstairs.

I walked back into Kota and I's room and found him sitting with our siblings. He was playing his switch, my siblings sat draped over his knees still wearing their headphones. They still were clinging to him, but they seemed less stressed than they were before, completely enamored in whatever stupid game he was playing.

"Hey," I said, tossing my brother our dad's card. "Here's the card, I don't think they'll be fighting more tonight," I said. "But I'm going to give Aria and Atlas the gummies with the pizza."

My brother took my dad's card from where I had tossed it beside him and stood up ,handing my siblings his switch. "Okay, I might have a few of them myself," He said. "Should I just get what we usually get?"

I nodded, sitting down beside my siblings. "Yeah, love you, and be safe."

"Yep, see you," My brother said, shutting the door behind him.

Aria played on my brother's switch and Atlas stared at the screen, the game displayed having him hooked.

They weren't even out of elementary school yet, and already they were starting to show symptoms of severe anxiety. And since I was just me, there was nothing I could do to help them. All I had the power to do was hold them through the yelling, messing with their hair, and playing rock paper scissors with them to keep them as distracted as possible.

I had already ripped a hole in multiple of my relationships with my hospitalization. I'm lucky enough that Aria and Atlas don't remember it too well.

Ita popped into my head like a virus. I wondered if I could blame my hospitalization on our ruined relationship as well. Despite my attempts to keep away from her, not only did it seem that was going to be something that would be very hard to do, but I also couldn't keep her out of my thoughts either no matter how hard it was that I tried. She was there always, in the back of my head, mocking me for ever thinking that she cared enough about me to say goodbye. For thinking that she would be there for me when I got out of the hospital. Mocking me for what I had said to her. Knowing that maybe if I hadn't said something so hurtful, none of this would have happened. But I felt too much pride to admit that I was the only one at fault. Because she still hurt me at the end of the day, regardless of if I had caused my own downfall or not.

And with all of these thoughts, there was the thought of talking to her again. Leaning on her shoulder for support, and telling her about all of the things that had happened to me over the past few years. I wanted to tell her everything and nothing or both at the same time. Every time I thought of saying something to her this past week or so, there was a looming memory that would make my blood run cold.

Remembering how she had left without a word. How I stayed in bed for days, scouring the internet for where she might have gone. I looked for social media under her full name and her nickname, only to find that she had deleted everything when she moved. Leo even tried to find her, but came up empty. Every single time I thought of her, I thought of being her best friend again, but I also thought about how I never wanted her to show her face to me again for all of the pain and heartache she put me through.

These two thoughts existed simultaneously, and different parts of myself got pulled every which way trying to make a decision about what to do with the sudden reappearance of my childhood friend. I wanted both of those things at once, but like two sides of the same coin, you couldn't have both heads and tails. You could only pick one. I had to make a choice for myself as well. And so of course, I picked the side that got me hurt the least. I was so tired of being hurt by her, and I couldn't be hurt if there was nothing to hurt me in the first place.

I leaned back against my pillow and wrapped an arm around Aria, giving her a quick squeeze into my side.

She giggled, wriggling out of my arms. "What was that for?"

I shrugged, smirking at her. "I don't know, I just felt like it."

"That's not fair, I want a hug too!" Atlas wset down the switch and crawled across the bed to me.

"Oh, of course you do," I pulled him into a tight hug and squeezed my eyes shut.

I pulled Aria into the hug as well, and I didn't let go of them. I held them close to my heart and wanted to keep them there forever.

"I can't breathe," Aria squeaked.

"Allie is having a moment again," Atlas said.

I snapped my eyes open and loosened my arms from around them. "I'm sorry."

Atlas shrugged, flopping down to my right, as Aria huddled into my left side. "It's okay," Atlas said.

Aria nodded. "Mhm, you just want to protect us."

I laughed at how perceptive they were, my arms falling beside them.

They were right. I wanted to protect them from anything and everything that could ever possibly hurt them. I wanted to be the person I needed then. I wanted to make sure that they got to keep their childhood close to them. I was going to look out for them the way I had needed someone to.

January 7th, 2023

I sat at the desk in my room, the fans of my computer whirring. I was editing the photos that I took at the last cheer practice, flipping through them mindlessly with my cheek in my hand. I flipped to one that I had taken of Ita, watching the other cheerleaders go over their routine, while the coach stood next to them and told them about where they would fit into the routine. Her eyes were focused and she had her hands on the back of her neck, and her bottom lip between her teeth.

There was a knock on my door frame, and before I had the chance to close the window on my laptop, there was a gasp from my doorway.

"Woah!" Kota said, looking over my shoulder. "Is that Ita?"

I turned around to look at him. "Wait, you recognize her?" I asked.

He nodded. "Of course I do, you don't?"

I turned back around and shrank in my seat. I shrugged. "I didn't when I first saw her."

"What's up with you?" He asked.

I sighed and closed the tab on my computer before shutting it down and turning around to look at Kota. "Ita came back last month." I pulled my knees up to my chest, shrugging. "She was in England."

"But she's here now?" He asked. "Wow, that's crazy!" I stared at him, and he immediately dropped his shoulders. "Are you not happy that she's back?"

I shrugged again.

"Hey, stop it with all your shrugging. You want to talk right? So, talk. Tell me what's up."

"I mean, she's back but I also didn't even know she had left. I mean, you saw how torn up I was. She fell off of the grid completely. She abandoned me without a word." I said.

"And, so you're upset" He asked.

I nodded.

Kota didn't say anything, he just sat in silence, watching me. He was waiting for me to speak, but I wasn't sure I had anything much more to say. One day she was here, and the next she was gone and I was completely unaware of it when it happened. There isn't much more to the story than that.

"But Allie," He started. "Weren't you the one who pushed her away?"

"No, I—"

"Allie, I distinctly remember hearing you yell down the hospital hallway, telling her that you never wanted to see her ever again," Kota said. "I get it. You were mad that she told mom and dad about your eating disorder. I would be too. But you can't blame her for doing what you told her to do. Especially after your reaction when she did what you told her not to do. I think she was trying not to cause any more harm to you than she already had."

"But she—"

"Allie!" Kota exclaimed, interrupting me. "Listen, you were sick, and you were hurting. I get it. But that doesn't make you blameless. You think that you didn't hurt her when you yelled about how much you hated her? Just because you were sick doesn't mean it made you incapable of hurting the people around you."

He sighed and ran his fingers through his hair. "Allie, I love you, but you need to grow up. You can't keep seeing everything as being either right or wrong. You aren't wrong, but is she wrong because of that? I mean, didn't you miss her?"

It was a question I never expected to be asked. A question I never bothered to consider the answer to until that moment. Everything that I had been feeling hit me all at once, and I couldn't hold the tears in anymore.

I let out a sob, and covered my mouth before another one could escape.

"Oh, Allie," Kota stood up and walked over to where I was. "Come here," he said, grabbing my arm.

He pulled me towards him, and I fell out of the desk chair and into his chest, wrapping my arms around him and grabbing onto his shirt tightly.

I didn't hear anything else he said after that. Emotions I had been refusing to acknowledge up until that point pulled at my heart. It kept nipping at my skin, tearing away little parts of myself until there was nothing. I didn't move, I just sat on the floor in his arms, crying until my eyes went dry and no more sound would come out. My mind went from racing, to completely silent. The entire time, Kota didn't let me go. He didn't say anything either. He just held me until I stopped crying and I think that meant more to me than anything he had said earlier in the night. There was a hole in my stomach from the loneliness I wasn't used to feeling. And even though this loneliness was unlike anything I had felt before, I could only focus on the way Kota hugged me.

I wondered, when was the last time I was held while crying. Even after racking my brain over and over, I couldn't remember.

January 9th, 2023

"I didn't want to admit that I had no one else to blame but myself for losing you."

She sat across from me, her cheeks flushed in a way similar to how they did when we were kids. Her brows furrowed, and I watched her try to hide the tears that were falling down her cheeks. I didn't know what else I could say, and she stayed quiet, waiting for me to speak.

So instead we sat quietly, not being able to find any

more words I wanted to say.

"I really did think you hated me," Ita choked.

I closed my eyes and shook my head. "I didn't. I never did," I grabbed her hands and held them tightly. "I was hurt, trust me, but I couldn't bring myself to admit that you did what you thought was best for me. It was easier to just believe that you hurt me. Then it was to believe that what you did saved me."

She looked up, her eyes red and her eyelids puffy. "I saved you?"

I pulled my hands out of hers, and looked away. "I mean, yeah. I was sick. Really sick. I thought that I could do everything on my own. That I didn't need anyone."

I looked up over at her and smiled, my breath catching in my throat as I prepared myself to be honest for the first time in a while. "I'm sorry. I was angry, embarrassed, and hurt. So, I said stuff I didn't mean. Ita I don't hate you. I don't think I ever did. I was just…" I paused, swallowing as I tried to catch my breath. "I was so scared."

She sniffled, and tilted her head down as she sobbed, wiping the tears from her face.

I wrapped my arms around her, and pulled her into a hug, crying into her shoulder.

"I can't promise I won't push you away again. But I want to at least try. I mean, what are the chances that I got to see you again? I've been given a second chance with you, and I don't want to let that go."

I grabbed her hands and held them against my face, bringing her gaze up to meet mine.

"So, please," I choked. "This time, don't leave without saying goodbye. This time, stay with me!"

She nodded, squeezing her eyes shut as she rested her forehead against mine.

We stayed like this for a while. Just leaning on

each other as we took each other in. I couldn't let go of her hand. I was afraid that if I did she would leave again. And I would have to grieve losing my first love for a second time. That was a pain I never wanted to experience again.

January 23rd, 2023

I sat at the cafe table with Leo and Ita. Leo looked at me suspiciously, and Ita looked down at her soup, not eating it but stirring her spoon across the surface.

"So, y'all are good now?" He asked. "Just like that?"

I shook my head. "Not just like that. Things are still awkward and we've already experienced it being hard but," I turned to look at Ita, and she looked up from her soup to smile at me. "I'm trying."

Leo looked to Ita. "And you?" He asked. "What about you?"

Ita looked at Leo. "I'm gonna stay by her side this time."

Leo sighed and sat back in his seat as he sipped his coffee. "Well, then I guess there's nothing I can do. Should we introduce Ita to the others?"

I nodded. "I actually invited them here. They'll be here soon. We've grown up, and things have changed, so I want to mend our relationship and introduce her to the people who have held me up all these years she's been gone."

He nodded. We both snapped our heads at the sound of arguing. Outside the window there was a man and woman standing by a car. The sound of fighting made my stomach twist inside my body.

"Allie?" Leo asked, bringing my attention back to the conversation. "You alright?"

"Yeah, I just…" I swirled my straw in its cup, the

strawberries moving with the ice. "Just thinking about my parents."

"Oh… they're getting a divorce right?"

I nodded. "Finally. I think they were trying too hard for too long to make it work."

"How do you think the twins will take it?" Ita asked.

I shrugged. "Atlas probably won't take it too well, and I don't think Aria will understand completely until she's older."

I took a sip of my drink.

"Things are messy, and I don't know how anything is going to turn out." I said. "But I hope that things will turn out okay in the end."

I looked between the two of them, my eyes falling onto Ita. She sat smiling at me. So many things about her had changed, and I was a little scared of what about her had changed. But I knew I would find comfort in the parts of her that have stayed the same. Like the way her nose would scrunch up when she smiled, or how she would rub her ear when thinking.

Finally, I thought, things were starting to fall back into place. They didn't quite fit together perfectly, but they were starting to take shape in ways I couldn't fathom possible.

I heard the door to the cafe chime, and Noah, Monty, and Sonali all waved and said hi as they made their way over to the table, cramming ourselves in to fit into the tiny booth.

Some of these people I had only met recently, others I'd known for years. One, I had been reunited with after having needed to struggle on my own. I was excited to experience this messy beginning with the people I was closest to, as our last summer slowly approached us in the distance.

Epilogue

Roughly Two and a Half Years Post Graduation

<u>Monty</u>

I sat at the table in the back room of the flower shop, wiping off the surface of the table, trying to get rid of as many yellow specks as I could before taking a shot of the DayQuil that had a permanent home on the back room shelf. I blew my nose a couple of times, the skin underneath the tip of my nose dry and cracked due to the constant rubbing of tissues.

I opened the backroom door, going back outside to the chaos of the post-easter flower sale.

"Hey," Lyn walked up beside me and rested a hand on my shoulder as I went back to trimming the stems on the batch of morning glories that sat on the back counter. "Feeling any better?" She asked.

"Ask me after the DayQuil kicks in," I mumbled.

Lyn nodded, giving me a sympathetic pat on the shoulder before walking away.

I went back to cutting, looking at the blend of colors on the flowers. I picked up one of them, white petals with a bloom of purple on the inside, like an explosion of life against a dull background.

I snipped off the end of it, placing it in the basket inside the sink.

"Excuse me?"

I turned around at the familiar voice, seeing an all too familiar cane tap against the front counter. She had cut her hair shorter, and it fell in loose curls over the edge of her shoulders instead of straight hair that melted down her back.

I looked her up and down, before my eyes found hers again. She didn't have a rainbow trail following close behind her, and she didn't glow in the chromatic way she did when we were kids. She was just human.

"Excuse me?" She said again. Her voice came out softer that time and she reached out her hand to find the edge of the counter. "This is the register right?"

"Oh, yes!" I said setting down the sheers and flowers I was holding.

Her eyes fluttered for a moment, and she squinted them at me as if she was trying to make out the features of my face. I could see the gears turning in her head, but I couldn't even begin to figure out what it was that she was thinking.

"Monty?" She asked, a light smile spreading across her face.

I laughed awkwardly, having not seen her in person since the party Leo hosted at the end of our freshman year of college.

"Yeah?" I said.

"It's really great to see you," She held her cane straight up and down, opening her arms out to me for a hug.

I put my arms around her shoulders, giving her a quick hug before pulling away.

"It's really good to see you, Sonali," I said. "How have you been?"

"Good, I've been good. And you? Are you painting again?"

I shook my head, a bittersweet feeling creeping into the back of my throat. "No, not yet. I still don't think I can."

She nodded, humming quietly.

"What are you here for?" I said going to the computer and opening the order sheet. "Do you need catering? A custom bouquet? Or do you want one of our pre-made ones?"

"Uh, I don't think I need catering, but I am looking for a bouquet," She said, taking a step closer to the counter.

"What's the occasion?" I started filling out the information on the order form, surprised I could still remember her birthday.

"I'm meeting my girlfriend's parents and I wanted to bring them flowers."

I stood silently for a moment, a mix of emotions trying to fight their way out of me, as I tried to figure out how exactly it was that statement made me feel. Eventually, the uncertainty settled and I smiled.

"Are you happy?" I asked.

She tensed and looked at me wide-eyed, like I had asked the weirdest possible thing I could have asked. Her shoulders dropped, and she broke out into a smile, her cheeks turning a shade brighter.

"I am!" She exclaimed.

"I'm glad," I said. "If it's for her parents, then brighter colors would be better. Yellow, orange, and pink would work well. And I'd say tulips would be your best type of flower."

"Okay, let's go with tulips then. Girlfriend?" She asked, raising an eyebrow with a devious smirk spreading across her face.

"No girlfriend," I said. "Or boyfriend."

She stayed silent for a moment before tilting her head at me. "You want one?"

I shook my head. "I don't. Turns out I'm aromantic."

"Oh," She said. "You live alone then?" She asked.

"Nope, I have a roommate and a cat, her name is Picasso, and the three of us live together in a tiny two bedroom apartment down the street."

"Monty," I looked up from the computer screen to see Sonali smiling at me softly. "Are you happy?"

I stared at her for a moment, before smiling. "I am."

"Good, I'm glad."

We didn't talk much after that. I filled out her order form for a custom bouquet, and then Lyn started putting it together at the back counter while I checked people out and set them on their way. As I did I watched Sonali wandering the store, her hands guiding her as she brushed her fingertips over the petals and leaves of the different greenery around the shop.

"Monty," Lyn said gently, moving me away from the register. "I got this, go say goodbye to your friend, alright?" She said, handing me the bouquet.

I nodded, taking the bouquet from her and heading over to the table that Sonali stood at.

"Sonali," I said.

She looked up towards the sound of my voice, her hands falling away from the flowers and folding respectfully in front of her. There was a bit of scarring on her upper arm. Bruising accompanied by black stitching. I wasn't sure what they were or if I should ask or mention them.

"Are they done?" She asked.

"Yep," I said, holding them out. "I have them right here in front of you,"

She reached out and grabbed the bouquet from me, staring at it momentarily before smelling it and humming happily.

"They smell beautiful," She said. "How much do I owe you?"

I shook my head at her, a bubbly feeling forming in my chest. "It's my treat."

"No I couldn't—"

"Sonali," I interrupted. "Don't worry about it. It's a gift."

"Are you sure?"

"Positive."

"Thank you, Monty."

I watched her for a moment, trying to find something in her eyes. Back in high school, she would often hold things up to the light and try to make out the shape of them using lights and shadows. However, it seemed like there was a lack of focus on her face. She was looking at me, but it didn't feel like she was making eye contact, almost as if she was seeing through me.

"Sonali?" I started.

"Yeah?"

"Are you—" I started. "I mean how are your— y'know— how is your vision?"

Her expression changed, her smile falling ever so slightly and her gaze traveling down to the floor. I decided not to mention seeing the scars.

"Gone."

I looked back up to her. "What?"

"It's almost completely gone. I can barely see anything now." She said bitterly. "It's been hard adjusting, but I'm handling it pretty well. I'm actually getting a guide dog pretty soon. Exciting, right?"

"I'm so sorry, Sonali," I said.

She shook her head smiling. "Don't be. Don't look at me with that pitying look I know you're giving me. I said I'm happy, didn't I?"

Her tone of voice was soft, but she smiled genuinely, her eyes crinkling up as she did so.

"You did." I said. "It was nice seeing you again."

She nodded. "It was nice seeing you too."

"Good luck meeting your girlfriend's parents, I hope everything goes well," I said.

"Thank you, Monty."

We hugged goodbye, and I watched her walk down the sidewalk past our store, the bouquet in one hand and her cane in the other.

I walked back over to the counter where Lyn stood saying goodbye to the last person that was in line.

She looked at me and smiled, crossing her arms over her chest and tilting her head to one side. "That was

Sonali? From high school?"

I nodded. "Did you want to talk to her?"

Lyn shook her head, turning around to the back counter and picking up the sheers. "Nah, I didn't ever know her very well, I wouldn't have anything to say to her."

I stood next to Lyn, and pulled the leaves off the morning glories as she started sniping at the end of the stems, dropping them into the basket in the sink.

"The closing shift comes in soon, right?" She asked.

I nodded. "Yeah, and we have to stop by the store on our way back to the apartment. Picasso is almost out of cat food," I said.

"You'll have to go by yourself, sorry!" She exclaimed. "I have a date with Ana tonight actually."

I rolled my eyes at her, laughing. "Listen if you aren't going to put it on the calendar in the living room the least you could do is text me or something."

"I know, I know, I'm sorry!"

"I'm not mad," I said, nudging her with my elbow.

Lyn went quiet for a moment, before turning to me. "I'm actually proposing tonight," She laughed awkwardly while rubbing the back of her neck. "I'm way more nervous than I thought I would be."

I took the sheers that she held so dangerously open out of her hands, closing them and setting them on the counter.

"You've talked about getting married for the past year and a half. I'm sure it'll be fine," I said. "You've been together forever, she'll say yes."

Lyn nodded, letting out a relieved breath. "You know that means I'll probably move out soon right?"

I nodded. "Don't worry about me, I'll be fine. I'll have Picasso."

She laughed at me, shaking her head before saying, "That's just like you."

The shop was filled with sunlight, bouncing off of the suncatchers in the windows and casting rainbows across the walls and the floor. I ran my hands through my hair, the smell of flowers both relaxing my mind and irritating my nose at the same time.

I heard the bell that hung above the door chime, and I made eye contact with Lyn, both of us smiling before going to greet the customer that had walked in.

I never thought for a second I would ever give up painting. When I was younger I imagined myself doing it until I was old and my skin was wrinkled. I thought that painting was one of the few things that would ever make me happy. But here I was, having not touched a paint brush in over two years, and somehow I was happier than I had ever been holding one. I managed to create a life that I could live in; one without painting, and one without a muse.

<u>Sonali</u>

I sat across from Dr. Regardo, the usual exam room appointment being replaced with an office meeting. The cushioned chair was much more comfortable than the exam table, and rather than hearing the anxious leg bouncing from my mom, Panya, my girlfriend, held my hand, her thumb rubbing circles into the back of mine. Her hand was colder than mine, and she had callouses where her fingers met her palm, formed after years of sewing. Sat in front of me was a dog that I was told had brown and white fur. Her fur was soft, and its touch brought me a feeling of calm.

I could hear the whirring of the AC, and then there was a very dim barely noticeable glow to the left of me. Despite the AC, the air was hot, but that might've just been me.

I heard the shuffling of papers, and a sigh accompanied by the sound of tapping.

"Sonali,"

I flinched at the sudden words, Panya squeezing my hand in response.

"You have maybe another year or so before you have no vision left," Dr. Regardo said.

I nodded, crossing my legs and folding my arms over my lap.

"Have you been doing alright?" She asked. "How are things going with Xena?"

"It's been a bit of a struggle getting used to having her in my dorm room, and I worry about if I'm taking good enough care of her sometimes."

"You're doing great for someone who has never had a dog before," Panya said from beside me.

"Thank you," I said, squeezing her hand.

"And how are your injuries healing?" Dr. Regardo asked.

I shrugged, running my hand over my arm, feeling

the stitches and raised line of skin. "They've been okay. I will get my stitches out soon, and hopefully I will get concussion cleared next week when I go in for my follow up appointment."

She hummed from across the desk, before I heard the sound of wheels rolling across the wood floor, and felt the shift in my hand as Panya stood up.

I stood as well, Xena standing up as I grabbed the handle on her harness.

"I'm glad things with Xena are working out," Dr. Regardo said. "I know it was a hard decision to make—getting her, I mean."

I nodded. "I was worried about whether the financial burden would be worth it, and it definitely is." I smiled.

"It was good to see you again," Dr. Regardo said. "You guys are good to head out."

"Bye Dr. Regardo," I said.

"It was nice meeting you," Panya said as we walked towards the door.

We exited his office, and I walked with one hand on Panya's elbow, and the other holding onto the handle of Xena's harness.

We walked in silence to the car, the air a little chillier than when we had left campus early that morning. It felt less like home, and more like memories, the smell of wood and trees filled the air, rather than the smell of salt and the breeze coming in from the coast.

"Are you okay, Sonali?" Panya asked, tapping my elbow with her finger to signal that we had made it to the car.

"Xena, door," I said, letting go of Panya's elbow. I felt the slight pull on the harness, and followed it till Xena settled into a heel beside me.

I ran my fingers along the car door, finding the

handle to the back door, and opening it to let Xena hop
inside. Once she was inside, I slid my hand to the right,
finding the handle to the passenger seat and getting in
beside Panya.

"Sonali?"

I turned to Panya. "Hm?"

"I said are you okay?"

"Oh," I said. I shrugged, trying to make out her
figure, but not being able to distinguish her from everything
else that must have been around. "I'm okay, it's just weird.
I just forget sometimes that being blind isn't normal for
most people."

Xena nudged my elbow from the backseat, setting
her chin on the armrest and whimpering.

"Xena seems to think otherwise," Panya said.

I pet Xena, smiling at how hard it had become
to hide my uneasiness since I had gotten her. "I don't
know. I'm just… I think I'm still afraid." For a moment,
I remember the sound of my cane snapping against the
concrete, before quickly shaking away the memory. "I feel
safer with Xena, but it's still hard."

Panya put her hand on my shoulder, and I put
my hand over hers, before pulling it off my shoulder and
kissing the back of it.

"Romantic, are you?" She chuckled.

I laughed with her, happy to be sitting beside
someone that made me feel grateful to no longer be alone.

"Let's go get food, yeah?" She said, starting the car.

I nodded. "I'm in the mood to try something new, so
just drive around a bit till we find something?"

"Yeah that works," I felt the shift of gears as Panya
pulled out of the parking spot.

I connected my phone to the car, playing and
singing to the music that came through the speakers with
Panya as she drove.

"Let's make sure to buy something for my mom too," I said.

Panya hummed in response, and I noticed that after she had stopped singing along to the music with me.

"Nervous?" I asked. She let out a loud sigh, and I took that as a yes. "That's okay, I understand. My mom can be one scary woman, I won't lie. But you've said hi to her on calls before, and she always asks about you whenever we talk. She's wanted to meet you for a while."

"I know, but I don't want to say anything that will offend her."

"You won't, I promise. Just take your shoes off when you walk in the house and you'll be fine."

She took a deep breath, and I heard her hit the steering wheel a couple of times. "Okay okay okay. I can do this."

"Yes, you most definitely can," I said, holding out my hand.

She grabbed it and held it against her face. Her cheeks were warm, and a couple of curls fell over the back of my hand. I brushed them out of her face, before setting my hand back down on her thigh.

"Find a place to eat, yet?" I asked.

"I did, it's just a chicken place though," She said.

"That's alright, my mom and I both like chicken, so it'll work." I rubbed my thumb against her thigh, humming to the music as she pulled through the drive thru of whatever place she had decided to take us to.

I listened to her voice as she ordered, a feeling of contentment bubbling up from my chest. I used to think that I wasn't mature enough for love. And I was right, I wasn't. I really didn't understand it. I don't think I wanted to understand what love was, I just wanted to be a person who received it. Love was something that I had never previously considered to be something within my reach. I didn't think it was something that I would ever receive. Though, all of that changed when I met Monty. I learned what it meant for someone to love deeply, and what it meant for someone's love to only go skin deep. It was hard.

I had grown so much after going to university. I realized I was more dependent on the people around me than I had previously thought, and I had to relearn going about my day to day life. But with relearning came new discoverings and new people, those who taught me so much about what it means to feel the world around you.

I took a deep breath, the smell of chicken filling the car as we exited the drive thru. The seat I sat in was uncomfortable, but as were most car seats. I could hear panting from Xena in the back seat, and Panya had gone back to singing along with the music.

I had been surrounded by love, but I couldn't accept it until I had been able to be the person giving out the same amount of effort.

When we had arrived back at my house, I listened to the way Panya's voice shook ever so slightly as she and my mom talked at the dining room table. The sound of silverware clattering against plates. Having not been home in over six months, I had forgotten what my own house smelt like, and I was happy to be able to smell it consciously, even if just for a moment before the smell of rice was overpowered by the takeout food strewn about on the dining table.

"So, how is your vision, Sonali?" Ma asked, her voice a bit unsteady.

"Barely there," I said, ripping up the chicken tenders I had on my plate.

There was a bit of silence, before my mom asked me, "Are you sad?"

I shook my head and smiled. "I'm not."

"Then I'll try not to be either," She said. "I should

be hearing back from the lawyer in a few days about the case. So, just hang tight."

I nodded. "I don't really care much about them getting jail time or whatever," I said between bites of food. "But the medical bills are expensive."

"Yeah, and we have college too," Panya added.

"How is college?" Ma asked. She must have been nervous, because she was bouncing around topics quickly in the same way she had always done when anxious.

"It's good, I'm working with my advisor about getting my credits transferred since I had to change my major."

"What are you majoring in again, Panya?" Ma asked.

"Oh, my focus is in glass work, so I make sculptures and vases and stuff from glass," Panya said. "It's nice because the ceramics studio and glass studio are near each other, so Sonali and I get to see each other often."

I nodded. "And my professors have been super accommodating this year too, unlike last year."

"Good good," Ma said.

I zoned out of the conversation as Panya jumped in to tell my mom more about her glass work. I listened to Ma and Panya talk back and forth like they had known each other for forever. The shakiness in their voices slowly subsided and was replaced with the sound of laughter echoing through our house.

I was grateful to be here with these people, and I was grateful when I remembered the people I had previously spent my time with. I ate my chicken, knowing that today would become another day that I would look back on fondly. Knowing that Monty had come into my life to teach me about love, so that I would be able to give love to the people I have in my life now. I will never forget him, and his painting will stay with me till I'm old and grey. Even if we weren't exactly meant to be, I know that we were meant to find each other. He will remain an important part of my story, as I break through the cracks in the concrete.

<u>Leo</u>

On the other side of the counter were two boys. They fidgeted nervously, and their feelings for each other were obvious in the way their cheeks flushed. I had gotten used to seeing couples over the years, but very rarely did I seem to come across a pair of people who had yet to realize their feelings.

One of the boys had blonde hair to his shoulders, layers pulled back into a half up half down ponytail, and the other had short hair that barely fell over the edge of his ears. The blonde boy fidgeted with his hands, and the other kept them in his pockets, but he couldn't seem to make eye contact.

They glanced over at me a few times, whispering between each other. They seemed young, maybe fifteen or sixteen. They walked over to the counter, pretending to look at the display of books beside it, as their eyes kept finding their way back over to where I sat on the other side of it.

When they got closer, I saw two patches sewn into the short haired boy's messenger bag. One was the trans flag, and the other was the gay flag.

I watched them, wondering what it was they were saying that had to be discussed in hushed whispers.

They slowly came over to me, stuttering over their words as they tried to speak to me.

"Can I help you find anything?" I interrupted.

"Oh, no, but we wanted to ask you if you're a model?" The blonde boy murmured.

I smiled, the reason for the two boys staring and whispering becoming apparent. "I am. I just did a feature in a queer fashion magazine."

The two nodded, and the boy with black hair pulled out the magazine I had mentioned out of his messenger bag.

"Would you be willing to sign this?" He asked.

"Of course," I grabbed a pen from the cup on the counter, and took the magazine from him. "Where do you want me to sign?"

"Uh," He leaned over, flipping through the magazine to the page that had my photos and interview spread across it. "Can you sign here please?"

"Sure, and what's your name?"

"I'm Rowan, and then this is Everett," The boy with short dark hair told me.

"Are you two friends?" I asked while I started to sign the magazine.

"Yes, we are," Rowan said.

"Right now anyways," Everett added.

Rowan elbowed Everett in the side, his embarrassment finding its way into his cheeks as they turned red. "Ever— stop saying unnecessary things!"

I chuckled, closing the magazine and sliding back across the counter.

Rowan put the magazine back into his messenger back before turning back to me. "Is it true that you're married?"

I nodded. "I am, I wouldn't have said it in the interview if I wasn't."

"Oh, uh, right." Rowan said.

"Is it hard?" Everett asked.

I got a bitter taste in my mouth, and I looked down at my hands folding them in front of me. These two boys were young, and I wonder what of the worlds horrors they have and have yet to see. I sighed, looking up at them and trying my best to smile. "It is. It's so much harder than you probably know."

"Is it worth it?" Rowan pleaded

Noah popped into my head, his smiling face making me do the same. I thought for a moment about the ways it hurt, but then thought of all the ways it didn't. "Definitely."

Rowan and Everett looked at each other, smiles spreading across their faces as they looked at each other.

I grabbed my phone out of the drawer and walked around to the otherside of the counter where the two stood. I opened my phone and started flipping through my photos. "Here, let me show you something," I said, holding my phone out to them. "This is my husband, Noah." I swiped a couple more photos. "This is when he proposed."

I hit my home button and swiped to the side, trying to get the app icons out of the way. "It's a little hard to see, but this is when we got married."

I turned off my phone and tapped the screen, making my lock screen appear. "And then this is us, our dog Casper, and my little brother Felix."

The two boys smiled at me, and the photos I showed them. I told them about Noah and I, and about me. I walked them through what people hope being queer is like, and the unfortunate reality. How great it feels to love, but also the unfortunate bitter taste that you get in your mouth when people stare, or even worse speak.

"What do you think?" I asked. "Do you think it would be worth it?"

Rowan and Everett looked between each other, their eyebrows furrowing as they thought for a moment before turning back and smiling at me.

"Yes," Everett said, glancing at Rowan, who nodded silently. "It has to be."

I nodded. "Good answer."

I heard the bell to the bookshop chime, and looked back to see Noah walking in through the door.

"Speak of the devil and he shall appear," I said to the boys.

Noah walked over to where I stood. I wrapped an arm around his shoulder and pulled him close to me, kissing his cheek.

"So I'm the devil now?" He chuckled.

I shook my head. "Nah, you're definitely an angel."

Noah stared at me. He was smirking, but the red on the tips of his ears gave him away. He pushed my face away from his, chuckling a little. "Oh hush."

"Who are these two?" Noah asked.

"Some customers; they had seen my new magazine feature." I said.

"I admire you two a lot," Rowan said. "You make me feel less afraid."

Noah looked at me, an eyebrow raised. "Just what have you been saying?"

I shook my head. "Nothing much honestly, I was just bragging a little bit."

Noah rolled his eyes and put his hands on my shoulders, pushing me back behind the counter. "Clock out already so we can go pick up Casper from the vet and head to your parents."

"Yeah, yeah," I said.

Ana came out of the backroom, walking up behind me. "Yo, heading out?"

I nodded. "I gotta get my dog and go home. I'm watching my younger brother tonight so my parents can celebrate their anniversary." I explained.

Ana hummed while watching me as I turned my pockets inside out and showed her the inside of my wallet. "Okay, your bag checks all done, be safe on your way home." She said.

I clocked out, and walked back around to the other side of the corner, my hand instinctively finding its way into Noah's, without even needing to look.

Rowan and Everett smiled at Noah and I.

"Thank you," Everett said.

"I'm happy," Rowan said. "That there's proof,

y'know?"

I nodded. "It was nice meeting you two. Cherish each other, okay?"

They nodded, looking between me and each other. "Bye!" They said in unison as I pulled Noah out the door.

I waved goodbye to the young boys. We left the bookstore and started walking down the street to the vet clinic.

"What were you talking about with those two?" Noah asked. "Proof of what?"

I shook my head, swinging our arms as we walked. "That there's happiness to be found in the people around you," I said, nudging him.

He smiled at me, before turning his head back and looking in front of him as we walked. "Of course there is. I think that it just takes a little time to find."

"I agree."

We walked the rest of the way to the vet in silence, the sun setting behind the buildings around us, and the slight breeze in the air keeping Noah and I's hands from getting clammy despite the hand holding.

I pushed the button for the crossing light, listening to it's quiet beeping and waiting for the loud ding of the bell accompanied by the white fluorescent light on the other side of the street to signal to us that we could cross.

We walked into the vet office, and I leaned on Noah's shoulder as he talked to the receptionist about Casper's behavior while getting her nails clipped.

"I'll have the vet bring her out for you," The receptionist said. "You guys can take a seat in the waiting area if you'd like."

"Okay, thank you so much," Noah said.

He pushed me off of his shoulder gently, pulling me over to the chairs that are lined up beneath the window.

"Look at the way the sun is hitting us," Noah said,

opening the camera on his phone as we sat down.

"We look like we're on fire," I laughed.

"Let's take a picture," He said, holding his phone up.

I smiled as he took the photo, the light from the setting sun casting an orange glow over us both. "I feel like you take way more photos than you did when we were younger."

Noah shook his head. "The amount of photos I take are the same. I think the difference is that I prefer to take them with both of us, rather than taking photos of only you behind your back."

"You did do that a lot in high school, huh," I said, standing up as I heard the sound of barking getting closer.

One of the doors opened, and the vet came out with Casper at his side, walking over to us and letting go of Casper's leash once he got closer.

"How was she?" Noah asked while putting on her normal collar and leash.

"As loud as she always is," The vet said. "If y'all don't have any other questions you're all set to go, just wanted to let you know to maybe bring her to get them clipped a little more frequently before the quick of her nail gets too long."

Noah nodded, while I petted Casper as she barked excitedly at us, her tail wagging so hard her whole body was shaking.

"We will, thank you," I said, grabbing Noah's hand. "Have a good night."

"See you guys in another month or so," The vet said, waving as he walked away and back through the door he had come through.

We left the vet office and headed over to where Noah had parked the car. He got in the driver's side and started the car while I buckled Casper's leash into the back seat.

We made small talk as we drove. Asking about what we would have for dinner, or if we wanted to play a game or watch a movie with Felix when we go back to my parents house. His hand was on my knee, and my hand was on top of his as I leaned on the door, rolling down the window to feel the breeze from the outside.

When we got to my parents house, Noah went to let Casper into the backyard, as I grabbed our things from the car.

I unlocked the front door, hearing the sound of laughter from my family echoing down the hallway and into the air around me. Noah quickly jogged around the house from the back gate, over to where I stood on the porch smiling as he slipped his hand into mine.

I smiled, grateful to be able to feel the warmth and comfort of home in his hand. A hand that I had forgotten how lucky I was to be able to hold.

<u>Noah</u>

I did not think I would be the one proposing. In my head, when I thought about it, it would always be him. Even when he and I had discussed it, we both agreed it would be him. We also had agreed that we would take our time with it. We would go out to dinner. Something fancy that I would ultimately end up deciding tasted disgusting. He would be his usual snarky self with a side of extra fidgeting. We would go for a walk somewhere nice, like the park or a garden. He would start talking about simple nothing's. We would talk about high school and then he would start on his speech. He'd lead me somewhere with a view and while I looked out at the sky he would sneak onto one knee. I would turn around and see him, holding a ring box. And then he would…

But none of that mattered. How I thought it would happen, didn't matter. Because here I was, in a ring shop with my mom. Thirty minutes before we were supposed to meet back up with Leo to take her to the airport to go back overseas.

My mom chatted happily with the employee assisting us, asking about a necklace in a display case on the other side of the store while she had assigned me the job of looking at the rings.

I looked through the cases, trying to find something that would fit him. All of the rings seemed both extravagant and expensive. Neither of which I wanted and neither of which would fit Leo. He preferred more simple jewelry, that way he would be able to leave it on whenever he modeled.

The employee came over to me, leaning on top of the glass countertop. "Do you know her ring size?"

"I do, but it's not for a girl," I said, realizing at the same time that all the rings I was looking at were definitely for women.

"Oh, okay!" She said her facial expression was unchanging. "That's my bad for assuming. If you want to follow me, I can show you the men's rings at the other counter." She said, walking over to the counter on the other side of the jewelry store.

I followed her, looking at the rings in the case.

"Are you looking for a ring in gold or silver? There's also white gold as an option or even platinum," She said. I had no idea what any of that meant, only really understanding the difference between silver and gold.

My mom came up behind me, placing her hands on my shoulders. "Don't worry about the price, honey."

"But Mom, if I'm proposing I want it to be on my own money. My own effort," I said, turning around. "But, I don't know what my savings could buy."

"Then what if you pay for it with what you have in savings, and then I'll pay for the difference. And you can pay me back later." I thought about it for a moment, before nodding. "I don't want you to think about the price, I want you to think about what would make Leo happy."

I nodded, turning back to the case. "Do you have anything with blue gems?"

I asked.

The employee nodded, unlocking the glass on her side of the case and pointing to a rack of rings a few steps to my right. "These are our rings with colored gems."

I looked through them, my eyes falling on a simple ring. It shined the same way that silver did, and it was a simple band with one diamond shaped blue gem, and then white diamond like gems on either side of it.

"Do you have this in a size eight?" I asked, pointing to the ring.

She grabbed the ring, and looked at the tag attached, and I turned my head in an attempt to not think about the price as my mom had told me to. "Let me check real fast,"

She said.

I turned to my mom, looking over her shoulder at her phone. "How much time do we have?"

"Relax, we still have a bit of time so long as he isn't early." My mom said,

"He won't be early, he'll be late," I said, bouncing on my toes. "He's always late."

The employee came back to the counter, setting down and opening a ring box, the same ring that I had pointed out inside. "This one is a size eight."

I turned to my mom, who gave me a smile, and then turned back to the employee. "Can I take that one please then?"

The employee nodded. "Of course, if you follow me, I'll get you all checked out."

After we left the store, the only thing I could think of was the ring that I had in my pocket. The box weighed down the jacket, and despite my mom saying it didn't, I worried it was noticeable from the outside.

I was in a daze. I barely remembered meeting up with Leo, just that he was late, as expected. The drive to the airport went by quickly, and I sat in the backseat of the car, with my jacket set carefully in the seat beside me. I said goodbye to my mom, before getting back into the passenger seat of the car, leaving my jacket in the backseat in hopes of the ring being undiscovered.

I don't remember when I fell asleep. All I know is that it happened. And that when I woke up, my jacket which had previously been in the backseat was draped over me.

"Noah?"

I hummed, not wanting to turn my head to face the driver's side.

"We're home, it's time to go inside," Leo said.

I felt my jacket shift, and when I did I turned my

head to Leo, the ring box falling out of the jacket pocket as Leo pulled it off of me.

"What's thi—" Leo started to bend down to pick it up, and without thinking, I panicked.

"Don't look!" I exclaimed. I covered his with one hand and used the other to snatch the box off the floor.

"Gah!" He reached up to pull my hand away from his eyes, but being weaker than me he was unsuccessful.

I let go him and pulled the jacket out of his hands. I put the ring in the pocket of it, folding the jacket over itself in a way where the ring couldn't fall out again.

"Noah what was—"

"Nope! It was nothing!" I said, opening the car door. "Let's just go up to our apartment!"

I got out of the car and sped over to the staircase, the cold hitting against my face as I climbed it to the second floor. I could hear Leo close behind me, but I didn't care, because all I knew was that if he saw my face it would give away what was in the box.

When I got to our door, I started to punch in the code to the apartment, doing it incorrectly twice, which gave Leo the time to catch up to me.

"Noah," He said, softly putting his hand over mine and pulling it away from the keypad. "Take a breath," He punched in the code to our apartment, holding the door open for me to go inside.

I walked past him into the apartment, hearing it shut and lock behind me as I tried to rush past the living room and into our room.

I may have always been stronger than Leo, but he was always faster than me. And with only a few feet between us, he quickly made it to me, grabbing my wrist and stopping me in my tracks.

"That was a ring right?" He asked. "It was a ring, wasn't it?"

I froze. I couldn't move and I didn't know what to say either. I had only just gotten the ring. I hadn't made any plans of when I was going to give it to him, or what I was going to say when I did. I had already been caught. I hadn't even had it for half a day yet and already I had been caught.

His hand slipped down from my wrist and into my hand, pulling me to face him, as he rubbed my wrist with the thumb of his other hand.

"Sorry, did I grab you too hard?" He said.

I looked up at him, seeing the worry he had about me written in the way he pulled my wrist close to his face to see if he had left any marks.

"I'm okay," I murmured.

He looked up at me, and smiled. "I'm glad."

He pulled the hand he was holding closer to himself, pulling me into a tight hug, squishing the jacket between him and me.

I heard him laugh a bit. "It is a ring, isn't it? I can feel the box poking against my stomach." I tried to pull out of the hug, but he only held me tighter. "Nope, no getting out of this."

I sighed, and nodded. "Can you please let me go?"

He let go instantly, his hands rubbing my arms comfortingly. "You don't have to tell me if you don't want to yet."

I sighed, knowing that even if I didn't want to tell him about it right now, I would spend more time thinking about what he was thinking about it, rather than actually planning the proposal.

I swallowed, my voice coming out quieter than usual. "I only just got it today… I haven't planned anything yet… like when or how I'd give it to you, or what I'd say."

"Wait here," Leo leaned in and kissed my cheek, before leaving in the hallway and going into our bedroom.

I heard the sound of boxes moving, and he came out

of our room with his hands behind his back, and a smirk on his face. I thought, *I doubt it.* But however unlikely I thought it to be, when he pulled his hands out from behind his back, he held a small box in them.

"I've had it for a while, I just haven't found the right time to do it," He said. "It was your Pa who told me to get it actually. It was when he was in the hospital last year. He said I would know when the time was right, and that I should be prepared for when that time came."

I looked between him and the box, before my knees buckled and I fell to the floor, relief washing over my body.

"I seriously thought I messed everything up," I sighed and covered my face with my hands, trying to regain my composure.

Leo chuckled and bent down to sit on the floor with me, cupping my face in his hands, and tilting my head up to look at him.

"I was so nervous about it," He said, resting his head against mine.

"Me too, especially because I decided to do it on such a whim," I said, wrapping my arms around his neck.

We sat in comfortable silence, as my heart rate finally began to slow.

"You mad that I beat you to it?" I asked.

"Hey, you didn't beat me to it. I bought my ring months ago. Technically I beat you to it. I just saw your ring before you saw mine."

I rolled my eyes, pulling my face out of his hands and leaning against his chest.

The back of his neck was warm, and I could tell from his heartbeat that he was just as nervous about this situation as I was.

"So…" I started my voice trailing off.

"Don't you dare," He chuckled.

"Do you want to marry me?"

He pushed me away from him, and smacked me on the arm. "I was going to do it!"

I shrugged. "If you were going to beat me to the ring, I was going to beat you to the proposal."

Neither of us bothered to look at the actual rings for who knows how long. We just laughed together, sitting on the floor in the dark of our tiny one bedroom apartment. I didn't need to see the ring he got me because I didn't care what it looked like, I just cared that it came from him. He seemed to feel the same.

I didn't have to see the ring to know that I was exactly where I needed to be. And that I had made the right decision, all those years ago. I took a leap of faith, and instead of falling, I flew. And I couldn't wait to build a new life with him. Him, who kept his feelings for me a secret for three years. And sitting here with him, I hoped that I made those three years worth the wait.

<u>Ita</u>

I rubbed my eyes, trying to get them to open. I could feel my eyelids getting heavier each time I blinked, and the warmth from the summer air certainly didn't help me feel any less tired.

I looked back through the telescope, marking my observations down on the sheet of paper in front of me. The star chart I had was of the sky that I should be able to see from where I was in the United States. Whenever I found a star on the chart using the telescope, I marked it with a red pen.

"Titania?"

I turned my head towards the voice.

"You snuck in here again?" Professor Bandello said, flipping on the light switch. "You know only upperclassmen have access to the observatory past ten."

"But no one else is even in here!" I said, gesturing around me.

Professor Bandello shook his head. "It doesn't matter. C'mon, pack up your things and head back to your dorm, alright?"

"But I—"

"Titania."

I sighed and started to roll up my star charts and put away my notes. The unique smell of the observatory being an indescribable mix of the smell of a museum and the smell of old books.

"If I hadn't taken a gap year I would be an upperclassman," I mumbled, putting all of my things in my backpack.

The professor chuckled, walking over to where I sat on the telescope platform. "Well, then maybe you shouldn't have taken that gap year."

I shook my head. "No, I definitely needed it. But still."

I finished talking with the professor and left the observatory, looking at the outside of the building for a moment, before starting to head back to the dorms.

I could hear the sound of cicadas, and the street lights prevented me from being able to see the sky. Despite going to a university in the mountains, there still managed to be light pollution.

I hummed to myself, kicking my feet while I walked back to the dorm hall.

My phone buzzed, and I saw a message from my roommate, not bothering to read it, knowing that it probably had to do with my absence in our room.

When I got to our dorm room, I walked down the hall, noticing the light leaking out through a crack in the door to my room.

I approached it cautiously, peeking inside to see Luna sitting at their desk with their computer open to a random RPG game and a bowl of ramen in front of them. they pulled their headphones down from their ears, setting them around their neck and turning to me.

"You forgot your key," They said, nodding to the hooks by the door, petting the chinchilla in their lap.

I shut the door behind me, locking it and kicking off my flip flops.

"Sorry," I said.

"You know I hate leaving the door open. It means Nibble has to be leashed," they said, unhooking the harness from their chinchilla.

"I know, I know," I whined climbing my loft bed and flopping down onto my pile of pillows. I hung my head over the edge of my bed, noticing the suitcase beside Luna's desk as they gamed. "Are you going home for spring break?"

They nodded. "Are you?"

I nodded. "I'm not going back for a few more days

though. The observatory will be less crowded and I will be able to use it more.”

“You and your stars,” Luna said, rolling their eyes.

“You say that as if you aren’t also studying astronomy.”

“I’m minoring in it. You are majoring in it. There is a difference.” Luna said, throwing their plushie at me.

I laughed and threw it back to them, rolling over onto my back and looking at the star stickers I had put on the ceiling above my bed.

I looked up, the light green plastic stars stuck on the ceiling panels in the pattern of constellations. Allie had helped me measure them out when moving in, so that they would be as accurate as possible to how they actually appear in the sky.

I sat up and went over to the end of my bed that sat against the window. Looking outside it, I could see Orion’s belt to my right, the stars dim compared to other stars around it. The sky was dark, and the stars were sprinkled across it.

I opened my notebook next to my bed, doodling the constellations I could see fully, and filling in the stars within the constellations that were only partly visible.

My phone rang, lighting up with Allie’s name at the top of the screen.

I answered the phone, putting it to my ear.

“Hi Allie,” I said.

“Morning ma amour,” Her throat sounded a little dry, and I could tell by the way her ‘m’ sounds stretched out that she was just waking up.

“What time is it over there?” I asked, thinking for a moment. “It’s probably like, around five in the morning?”

“Mhm,” She said. “Pourrais-je avoir un Earl Grey s’il vous plait ? Pas de lait,” She said. Hearing her speak French always took me by surprise, but her voice always sounded so pretty when she did. It probably had something to do with it being one of the romance languages.

"You on your way to class?" I asked.

"Yeah, I'm getting there early to work on my group presentation for my fashion history class," A pause. "Merci beaucoup. "

I heard the chime of a bell and the sound of a dog barking on the other side of the phone.

"You at your dorm?" She asked.

"Yep, I'm gonna go to bed soon probably, since I got kicked out of the observatory by Professor Bandello."

"Again?" She laughed.

I smiled. "Again."

"Is Luna there?"

"Yep, Luna's here," I said, sitting up and looking down over my bed.

Luna turned in their chair looking up at me.

"Is that Allie?" They asked.

I nodded. "Did you want to say hi?"

"I did yeah," Allie said.

I put the phone on speaker. "You're on speaker."

"Hi, Luna!" Allie said.

"Hi, Allie," Luna said.

I took the phone off of speaker. "I think I should let you go, yeah?"

"Yeah, I should go," She said.

"Okay," I laid back down in bed, finding my eyes drifting to the sky again. "Text me okay? I'll talk to you later, Allie. I love you."

"I love you too, goodnight ma amour. Sleep well."

I heard the click of the phone hanging up, and set my phone down on its charging port beside my pillow.

"Simp," Luna said from below me.

"Shut up," I said, sitting against the wall and pulling my blanket over my legs. "You're just as much of a simp as

I am."

Luna nodded. "True."

I yawned, and took my hair out of the ponytail I had it in, my hair falling over my ears. "Night, Luna."

"Night."

I leaned my head against the wall, looking outside, seeing the observatory in the distance. I still hadn't gotten used to the dry heat of the southwest. The sky was almost always clear, and the air didn't stick to my skin or make my hair frizz up the way it would on the east coast.

I looked at the moon and opened my journal, flipping back to the beginning of the book. I flipped through the pages and looked between the doodle of the moon I had drawn and the way the moon looked in the sky in front of me.

The moon was in the same phase when I had left for the UK as it was when Allie left for the UK. The moon was a sliver in the sky when she had asked me to date her, and it was full when we had our first kiss.

I thought about how I would be able to see her in a few days, noticing how it seemed the moon would be in the opposite phase that it was on that night of the party.

I thought about all of my important moments with her. When we talked about what had happened, and about us. I thought of when I had met her parents, and when she had met mine. I didn't notice it until recently, but she used to always make sure I was able to see the sky during the important moments. Whether it be through a window, or by leading me to the back porch of her house.

I think she knew that it was always the sky that had made me feel the most at ease. The dark blanket that covered the earth when the sunset always made me feel safer than anything else ever had.

I no longer look to the sky to feel safe with her. Because I would find the constellations in her freckles.

I didn't need to see the sky to feel safe when with her anymore. Because now all I had to see was her blue and brown speckled eyes, and Orion's belt underneath her eye. And I knew that I was right where I needed to be.

<u>Allie</u>

I pulled into the park, trying to find parking by the river. Ita sat in the passenger seat of my car, her chin in her hands as she looked out of the window, the reflection of her smile in the glass.

Luna sat in the back seat, holding onto the lawn chairs to keep them from falling over.

"There's a spot over there," Ita said pointing to my left.

"Oh thanks ma amour," I said, turning the wheel to get to the parking spot. I parked my car and checked my mirrors before taking off my seatbelt. I turned my head, seeing the familiar van that Leo had been driving since our junior year.

"Do we know where everyone got set up?" I asked.

"I know this park really well," Luna said, getting out of the car and putting the lawn chairs over their shoulders. "I know where we need to go."

"Awesome," Ita said.

We got out of the car and opened the trunk, trying to figure out how to balance and carry the chairs and the food as well as our other things.

I carried the pizza and the tote bag that had the fireworks and the chips inside. Ita had the cooler, and Luna carried the lawn chairs.

I waved over to Leo and Noah, who had parked opposite of us and were carrying their own cooler and lawn chairs. We waited for a moment, but they waved to us, motioning for us to go ahead without him.

We started walking over to the curb where the park started, the tall trees creating shade away from the bright summer sun.

As we walked, Luna leading us, I heard Leo's laughing from behind us, and the sound of their footsteps as they tried to catch up with us.

"There they are," Luna said pointing.

I turned to where Luna pointed, seeing a large picnic table that was covered in food and other things. Sonali sat with her girlfriend, Panya, across from Monty, Ana, and Lyn. Xena lying beneath the picnic table.

I hadn't seen any of them in over a year, the only people I really kept in touch with regularly being Ita and Leo. I was worried that it would be awkward when I saw them. That I wouldn't know how to talk to them anymore. Like our friendship was only as good as how good we were at keeping in touch with each other.

But when Monty looked up and we made eye contact, it was like no time had passed at all. He tapped the table, and I saw him say something, making Sonali turn around and look in my direction, waving over to where we were.

Leo ran past me, running over to the table and carelessly dropping what he was carrying on the ground. Noah caught up to me and the others, looking at Leo with a smile on his face as we made our way over to everyone.

"Hi, guys!" I said, setting my stuff down on the bench. I walked over to where Sonali stood, tapping her lightly on the shoulder to get her attention before pulling her into a tight hug. "Ah, Sonali!"

Sonali chuckled a bit as I let go.

"Hi!" She exclaimed.

I looked over to see a girl with dark skin sitting on the bench and smiling up at Sonali.

"It's so nice to meet you in person, stand up so I can give you a hug!" I exclaimed, jumping on my heels.

Panya laughed, standing up and walking around the end of the bench to give me a hug. I squeezed her tightly, before letting go.

There was a tap on my shoulder. "Allie," I turned to see Monty standing behind me with a gentle smile and open arms. His hair clipped back with the same clip that I had noticed Sonali had in her hair.

I hugged him, being a bit more gentle knowing that he wasn't the biggest fan of tight hugs.

I turned to see Noah standing and talking with Ita, his back to me. I made eye contact with Ita, and held a finger up to my mouth, to signal to her to not say that I was behind him. I walked over slowly, making sure to be quiet so he wouldn't notice me walking behind him.

When I got close enough, I jumped on his back, causing him to yelp and stumble a bit in an attempt to grab onto me.

"Allie!" He exclaimed.

After scaring him, and walking over to hug Lyn and Ana, everyone started to settle down, us gathering around the picnic table to eat all of the food that laid across it.

"You're married now," Ita said across the table to Leo and Noah. "Show us the rings!"

Leo rolled his eyes smirking, and I could see red spreading across Noah's cheeks as he looked away. Leo held out his hand dramatically, and Noah barely put his hand over the table for us to see.

"And you're at university on the other side of the country, right Ita?" Sonali asked.

Ita nodded. "Yep! You said you changed your major to ceramics right? Can I see any of your pieces?"

"Yeah sure! I don't take any of the pictures, so Panya has them," She said, turning to Panya.

"I can pull them up!" She said, grabbing her phone from off the table.

"How's your body handling the time change?" Monty asked, pulling my attention away from Sonali and Ita.

"Not great," I chuckled. "I'm so tired, and my body hurts so bad. How's Picasso?"

Monty handed me his phone showing me his lock screen. "Big. The vet said he might be a maincoon."

"Oh wow! He really did get huge!"

Monty nodded.

"Wait, I wanna see the cat," Luna said from across the table.

"Yeah sure," Monty passed his phone down to where Luna sat.

I got lost in the noise for a moment, before Leo stood up holding his hands out. "Wait! Everyone stop!"

The table went silent and everyone turned to him, wondering what nonsense he planned on saying as he climbed up to stand on the bench. He gestured to Lyn and Ana, who glanced at each other wide eyed.

"They're engaged! We gotta make a toast!"

Everyone broke out into laughter, holding our drinks into the air.

Leo moved a few things, and stepped up onto the table.

"Hey! Get down, that's dangerous!" Noah laughed, grabbing onto his legs.

"Hey!" He said kicking off Noah's hands. "Let me just make the toast real fast!" He started talking quicker, in an attempt to finish the toast so he would be able to get down from off of the table. "Congrats Ana and Lyn on your engagement! Cheers!" He exclaimed before stepping down and sitting back down on the bench.

Ana and Lyn laughed while we all whooped and hollered for them.

The laughter was infectious and my cheeks were hurting from how much I was smiling.

We ate, and we drank, the wind making the hot weather just cool enough to be comfortable, and the sun breaking through the trees was casting fun shadows across everyone's faces.

It had been a while since I had come home, and I had somehow forgotten what it was like to be somewhere with people you could relate to. I had friends in France, and I loved them just as much as I love the people I am sitting with now.

It was something about having known these people since high school that made me feel so much more at ease. I learned, and I grew, and I cried beside them. I graduated on the same stage as them. We tossed our caps in the air, together in the senior parking lot as the sun set casting an orange glow on everyone.

I was scared that after we graduated, we would never see or speak to each other the way we did before.

We all had plans, and things we wanted to do. We had more growing to do. And even though I had grown alongside them, it had become time for all of us to grow as individuals.

I thought that when we all graduated, and separated from each other, that that would be it. For a little while there, I was sure I was going to end up alone again. But after a bit of time had passed, and everyone had gone their separate ways, I still found myself keeping up with them.

It wasn't often, maybe every few months or so, but someone would always reach out and we would spend a day together, just catching up and talking. Whether it would be over the phone or getting together in person.

Ita and I had found our way back to each other.

Even after I decided that I needed to leave, I still didn't feel like I had left them behind me, in my past. Because I always found my way back to them.

I got to see them smile, and laugh. When we wore our caps and gowns, we cried as if it would be the end of us. That our senior year, and the people who were a part of it would be left behind in our memories.

And unfortunately some people did. We left a lot

behind at the school. People, ambitions, relationships. Some of us even had to say goodbye to the family we held closest to us.

But even as the world changed around us, and we changed too, I was sure now. I didn't have a doubt in my mind.

These were the people I would never let go of, no matter how far away from each other our paths strayed. I knew that we would find each other again, one way or another.

<u>About The Author</u>

Kitti Pierce is a young author born and raised in Northern Virginia. They graduated from Colgan High School with a CFPA Certificate in Creative Writing. They have multiple pieces published in Colgan's student run literary magazines Siren and The Megalodon. During their time at Colgan their nonfiction memoir Driving With the Windows Down received a superior rating in the 2021-2022 VHSL Creative Writing submission packet. They plan to go to university for Creative Writing with the goal of one day opening a book cafe.

Instagram: kitti.pierce
Tiktok: kittipierce
Email: kitti.pierce.18@gmail.com

www.ingramcontent.com/pod-product-compliance
Lightning Source LLC
Chambersburg PA
CBHW061533210726
48287CB00006B/1936